FREE LOVE

By
Tony Garnett

Strategic Book Publishing and Rights Co.

Book Design/Layout by Kalpart. Visit www.kalpart.com

Strategic Book Publishing and Rights Co.
12620 FM 1960, Suite A4-507
Houston TX 77065
www.sbpra.com

ISBN: 978-1-62212-280-6

You know who you are.

Chapter 1

"**N**o, Charles, I am not on the Cote d'Azur for the sun, the sea, the sand, or even the sex. I am here to escape the temptations and fleshpots of London, which you are no doubt enjoying, in order to write my life.... Yes. As we speak, I am cloistered like a medieval monk, in a study overflowing with papers. This is the evidence of a long life, Charles; you must bear with me.... Yes, good progress, much of the material is organised and the writing marches steadily forward. But Charles, I think we both underestimated the scale of the task, certainly based on your miserly advance .... No, I won't give you a precise date; I don't want to break my word.... Charles, I promise you a draft as soon as .... I'm working every day, seven days a week, like a bloody—I won't complete that phrase, I know how politically correct you are—just joking, Charles. Yes, good to talk to you .... No, of course I don't mind you checking up on me. Take care. Bye."

Fuck.

Roger was indeed standing in a room surrounded by boxes and bags full of material. It would become the concrete evidence of his working life, if only he could organise it. He put down the phone and looked round, sipping his Scotch. What he saw was detritus. He did not have the energy or the will to transform it. Not one word had been written. He knew that a book of his life, a memoir of exculpation, was his only chance of redemption. It would put him on the front foot, answer the character assassins, and maybe lead to a revival of interest in his other writings.

But he knew he had been deluding himself. If it were to be written, it would not be by him. In the end, he just could not be arsed.

So, who could he persuade to do it? Who would care to? For nothing—the advance had been spent. Who could be trusted? His mind was a blank behind the haze of alcohol. Finally, he decided a good lunch was merited.

He put on his Panama against the strong sun, and set off down the hill to Marius. He would sit on the square and rely on the benign effects of the bouillabaisse with lots of aïoli to restore his well-being.

**

He was contentedly winding down his lunch with the triple C—cognac, coffee, and cigar—looking forward to his afternoon nap, when an idea jabbed him sharply alert.

Clive. Of course. Why didn't I think of him before? Perfect. Bloody perfect. Will he still be too pissed off with me? Haven't seen him for... If I could just get him down here, I bet I could persuade him. Genius. Do I have his number? Somewhere....

He paid the bill and hurried home.

**

Celia, in her faux self-deprecating way, would claim that she was imprisoned in a tangle of clichés. Ealing was itself a cliché, answering to the accusation of "leafy suburb" with an apologetic, smug smile. Her living room, Conran set in aspic, was now just a pathetic seventies signifier. She looked up from the Guardian, and watched Clive, who was pouring tea and arranging twee madeleines au miel in his pernickety way. He had baked them with plodding obedience to the recipe, and now he was about to offer her one as an act of contrition for a misdemeanour he could

6

not remember committing. He, she thought, was the ultimate cliché.

Locked in a semi with a retired academic bore. Life is just a scratched record. Roll on, Alzheimer's. That might be interesting, the machinery going berserk. Make a change.

At that moment, the phone rang. Celia looked at it crossly: the sound was uninvited and intrusive. Clive put down the teapot, walked over, picked up the receiver, and said, "Hello?... Yes, this is Clive...Who is this? I'm afraid...Oh, my God...What a surprise, I don't believe it; I thought you'd forgotten all about us...Well, yes, we were rather hurt, I admit, but...Well, anyhow, how are you? There's nothing wrong, I hope...So, that's where you ended up?"

Clive stood and listened, nodding occasionally, his eyes widening in surprise, like a mime artist. Celia stared at him, her anger rising. She already suspected the caller's identity.

"Well... I see... Of course, if you need me, yes, of course... I suppose... Well, but can't you tell me what the problem is, what I can do to help?... I see, well, it's all a mystery but yes, well, why not give me your number and I'll call you... Tomorrow... Yes... Well, I would need to organise... Yes, you too, Roger... My goodness, yes, it has been a long time...Too long, Roger, I agree... Yes, of course. Bye."

He put down the phone and stared at Celia.

She glared back. "Roger fucking Burton. So that shit's back from the dead."

"Yes, how extraordinary. Typical, I suppose. Casts us off, nothing for years and then he calls out of the blue, cool as a cucumber, as though he'd only been round for dinner last week. That's Roger all over." Clive smiled and shook his head.

"Well, whatever he wants, you should tell him to take a running jump. But by the sound of it... What did he want?"

"He says he needs to see me. He needs my help. Only I will do. I asked if he was in some sort of trouble, but he said he has a proposal to put to me. Face to face. Most intriguing. He's in the south of France, Provence, he says. Living there now. Lucky chap. Oh, he said to give you his love, hoped you were well."

"Well, he knows where he can stick that. Clive, you're not to go running to him whenever he whistles. I don't care what he wants. Be a man. Tell him to go fuck himself."

Clive wilted. He had learned, over the years, that the way to deal with Celia was to avoid confrontation. Her firepower was too accurate and fierce. When faced with it, he tended to back off out of range and create a diversion until it was spent.

"Most peculiar. He's probably drunk. I'll call him back tomorrow and he'll have forgotten the whole thing. You know what he's like."

Celia knew exactly what he was like. Roger's unexpected intrusion had put her in a blacker mood. She looked forward to six o'clock, the earliest she could allow herself a gin and tonic. She would sip it while Clive finished preparing the dinner.

***

The next morning, Clive waited for Celia to go off to the British Library before Googling the airline. He booked a flight to Toulon, which Roger had told him was near Hyères. He hovered over the date for his return. He decided on a week—the visit was a mystery, so any date would be arbitrary. If he hurried, he would just be in time for the morning flight. He then wrote a note to Celia, telling her what he was doing. He knew this was cowardly and underhanded. But he had made up his mind to answer Roger's call for help. It would be easier to face Celia afterwards— at least then she would be unable to influence his decision.

Chapter 2

The plane dipped a wing as it turned into its approach and Clive saw the sunlight flicker on the Mediterranean waves. After this obeisance to the beauty of the Provençale coast, the plane straightened out for the serious business of landing at Toulon.

He's up to something. He has some scheme he wants to entwine me in. How on earth could I be useful to him, now? Is he in some further trouble? I wonder if it's something to do with the Anna Chisholm business. It all died down, mysteriously. He sort of vanished... Oh, well, I'll soon know. If he needs me, I'll be there for him. We are all getting old. Life is too short to bear slights. I was hurt to be dropped, Celia even more so, I remember. It was as though he had outgrown our usefulness, and we were ignored. The famous Roger moved on to a more important milieu, with the glamorous Anna on his arm. But that's Roger. We had been best friends. I wonder how he's coped with his fall from grace.

The prospect of seeing him again, of staying in the Cote d'Azur—what a delicious mouthful of a phrase—and getting away from the tensions of home, all combined to lift Clive's spirits. He felt younger. He had extravagantly bought some new clothes at the airport, and he felt pleased with the dark blue deck shoes, the light cotton trousers, and the sports shirt with the little crocodile motif. The windcheater jacket asserted a nautical utility. Not that he expected to go sailing, but it was chic and he did not want to look like a tourist. He felt like a naughty schoolboy. The adventure had begun. A Panama would wait 'til Hyères. It was an option if the sun proved too fierce.

It hit him as he stepped out of the cool, clean marble terminal. The heat stole his energy, but it felt good, like an embrace. He followed Roger's instructions and asked a taxi driver to take him to the Old Town.

At one of the tables outside the Excelsior cafe sat Roger, looking majestic, as though he owned the place. He was a regal figure, if now rather overcooked. Imposingly tall, with broad shoulders, Clive noted that he was rather less impressive than in his youth, because fat now overlaid his once muscular physique. His manly chest was turning into plump breasts, and his stomach threatened to burst its bounds—he was not even trying to hold it in. It was flaccid and content, asserting its place in the world. His complexion was florid. His luxuriant hair had retreated, revealing a large circle of bald scalp.

Roger had a glass of beer and a cigarette, and languidly waved. Clive walked over to him, his wheelie case trundling behind. They embraced, grinned and exchanged, "Good to see you." and "How long? God, the years," and sat down.

Roger ordered coffees, and a slight young woman with short hair served them. Clive struggled for a word to describe her look. It was his idea of typically French, yet confusingly he had first seen it many years ago on an American, Jean Seberg.

Still, it was in a film about France, so that's what counts. Gamine, yes, that's the word.

The girl was brisk, moving efficiently from table to table. Her father was working the coffee machine and presiding over the bar inside.

"This is Marie, Clive." She smiled indulgently. "She is the

reason I patronise this establishment. The town, as you will observe, has more coffee shops than it has people, all serving similar coffees. But only this one has Marie. We are to be married, of course. She finds me irresistible. Told your father yet? Votre père?"

"Mon père?" She smiled at him fondly.

It was clear to Clive that she had not understood anything. Probably for the better, he thought. Roger took her hand and gazed at her. "Isn't she delicious? Like a fem teenage boy. Neat. Brings out the gay side, clearly."

She playfully smacked his hand. Having chided him, she went about her business. Clive had little doubt this flirtatious gavotte was a daily dance. He made no comment. It would not have surprised him if Roger had really thought sex with her was an option. He was fifty years her senior, grandfather-aged, obese, and balding. She was an attractive, respectable, no doubt chaste Catholic girl who knew that two plus two did not make five. Roger was on another planet. Did he think he was still twenty, slim, and handsome, or could be a credible lover for such a girl? Had he looked in the mirror? Had he made no adjustment now that he was an old man? Was he truly deluded, or was he sending himself up?

"Well, here it is, Clive. My domain. Wait 'til I show you the Old Town. It's so beautiful it'll make you cry. Buildings age so much more gracefully than humans, unfortunately."

Roger's voice was a fruity baritone. His accent was educated Lancashire. He had never been sure how much accent he should retain. His public persona demanded that he should sound like an honest proletarian toiler, uncontaminated by bourgeois pretension, but he feared that the effort to retain it made him sound not only like a fussy Lytham librarian, but one who is still in the closet. It was not important now, but in his youth, when everyone played lefter-than-thou politics, these nuances could win women as well as arguments.

Roger took out a small cigar, and as he struggled to light it, Clive studied him.

Well, that baritone voice hasn't changed. It would always resonate inside you; make you think he really was playing you like a violin. But my, he's gone to seed physically. I mean, he always was a big, heavily built chap, but he was never fat, rather slim hips, actually. Now he's twice the size he was. That can't be healthy. I bet his vanity hates that. How could he let himself go like this? He was like a young god. I wanted to be him. Not so sure now.

"Clive, my old friend, you are about the only person I know I can trust. You are an exceptional man. Honest, discreet, loyal. No," his arm batted away Clive's faux modest protest, "That's all true. Your problem was your modesty, always hid your light under the bloody bush—or whatever the saying was. So, this is what's going to happen. I'm shortly going to take you to lunch at a local restaurant that you will salivate over. I will show you this gem of a town—on the promise you won't spread the news, I don't want it full of English riff raff—and then, in due course, I will put a proposition to you."

He smoked ostentatiously, as though he was Orson Welles in a cigar commercial, and smiled broadly. Clive knew better than to interrogate him. He would go with the flow. It was Roger's show.

They went into the Old Town, walking up the narrow hill of shops. It was crowded, but people seemed to part as Roger sailed through, waving his *bonjours*. There were fishmongers at the bottom, then greengrocers and a cheese shop at the top. There were Arab shops full of nuts and sweet meats and exotic fruits. There was even a shop specialising in tapenade, with large baskets of different olives out front. The entranced Clive wanted to investigate all of them.

They emerged into a square, dominated by the Tower of the Templars, where a handful of restaurants filled the space with their tables. Roger chose one, and signalled for Clive to sit down. He was tired and out of breath. Christophe brought a bottle of Bandol immediately, and they ordered.

It was a large lunch and so delicious that Clive felt almost guilty. He was not used to lunch. Even now, retired, he would do some cheese on toast and make a cup of tea, eating a proper dinner in the evening. By the middle of the afternoon, after an industrial strength espresso, plus a cognac, he was overfull and pissed. He could not refuse the cognac because Christophe had just poured it.

"On the house, Clive, you'll cause a rift in Anglo-French relations if you turn it down."

"How did you find such a lovely place?"

"I had a little fling with a French woman at a conference and she told me. I'd been going on at how awful the Cote d'Azur was, you know, a rip off, too many Brits, the Med like a sewer, my usual happy riff, and she put me right. It was short and very sweet with her, but what she said stuck, so I motored down and found she was right. Hill's a bit steep, they need one of those watchamacallit funicular thingumies, but the Old Town's lovely. And not many Brits shouting the odds."

He grinned and lifted his glass.

Eventually they tottered further up the hill to Roger's little house. It was exquisite, although too small for his bulk. Clive was glad when Roger announced a 'postprandial nap for the purpose of recuperation,' and disappeared. A nap was by now essential. This was frustrating; his curiosity was intense. Roger had a proposition for which Clive was uniquely qualified. Very flattering. What on earth could it be?

***

Clive gradually swam into consciousness and looked at his watch. Six-thirty. He had a headache and a dry mouth. He rummaged in his luggage, retrieved the tea bags he had thoughtfully brought, and went downstairs to the kitchen. The sink was full of dirty dishes.

Clearly not much of a housewife, but I didn't expect him to be. He never was.

There was no milk, but after a cup of black tea, he felt better, and started to explore. The rooms were tiny, the walls thick and the floors stone. It was immensely old but had been sensitively modernised. Clive thought he had been flown to heaven that morning. He was going to love this trip, whatever Roger's mysterious proposal turned out to be. He did not want it to end.

At just after seven Roger appeared, looking ghastly, but regained his jauntiness after a stiff whisky. Clive declined. They took a taxi to another restaurant. Its large windows were on the sea. The long evening light danced on the calm water. Tiny white patches of sails dotted the horizon, the little boats struggling for traction in the breeze.

Roger watched the seduction. Clive had never tasted fish so fresh, so perfectly cooked, so simply presented with local olive oil and herbs. The goat cheese was clean and fresh, without a hint of the farmyard. The assertive lemon sorbet refreshed. Clive looked up with a dreamy smile and Roger knew he was hooked. It was time to reel him in.

***

Roger settled in his living room with a cognac and a cigar. Clive sipped a mineral water.

"Clive, what do you know of my recent history?"

Clive did not quite know what to say. "Well, I do take the Guardian, Roger."

"I guessed you probably still did. The Pravda of the public sector worker. Where would the Lefties in education get their gossip if the Guardian shut up shop, eh Clive? So, you no doubt read Anna's demolition job of me, as a man, and as an intellectual, under the guise of a review of my last book. Also the letters from all the other dungarees who crashed out of the woodwork to join in the fun. Assassination is not too grand a word. I'd given them all the time of their lives, at one point or another, and they couldn't forgive me. It's called the battle of the sexes. Well, the book flopped, got lost under all that feminist derision and I crawled away, ending up here. I've now done enough licking of wounds and feeling sorry for myself. I intend to hit back and I need your help."

He sipped his cognac and leaned forward, fixing Clive with a stare.

"In that room," he pointed dramatically, "is my life. Boxes and boxes of stuff I collected, or rather dumped, over the decades. Speeches, diaries, press cuttings. You are already familiar with the

14

books. Letters, all sorts of detritus from the University, politics, my personal life. It is worth nothing, lying there. It is waste paper. But organised, written up, it will be ammunition. It will blast me back into view, and restore my reputation. Otherwise the dungarees will have won."

"Well, Roger, if you want a hand organising the stuff, you know, putting it into chronological order, that sort of thing, I'd be happy to give help, of course."

"No, Clive, I want more than that. I want you to be my biographer. I want to give you access to all my papers, access to all my private thoughts, and I want you to write my life. Put the record straight. You see, a memoir, an autobiography, would not carry the weight. It would be seen as self-serving, the case for the defence. But a book by you would be seen as outside the fray, as more objective, definitive even. And I can trust you. I can be frank with you, knowing you will not betray me. It will be seen as a responsible book, a contribution. I'm relying on you, Clive."

Clive was stunned. This was the last thing he expected. He was flattered but uneasy in a way he could not fathom. "Roger, it sounds like a large commitment. Could I sleep on it? I need to think it through. I hope you don't mind."

"Of course. Let's talk some more in the morning. It's great to see you anyway. It's been too long."

***

Clive lay in the dark trying to order the torrent of thoughts and feelings ricocheting in his head. He knew that he must consider each on its merits. Since childhood, he had been taught to value tidiness as a virtue. Like cleanliness, it was next to godliness. His possessions were stored and labelled, his academic work was always neatly filed away, and his clothes were folded. This virtue was derided after he left home. At University he was labelled *anal retentive* and *uptight* and told to, "let it all hang out." He had no idea how to do this and thought he would rather not try. He noted that although he was the subject of pity, his notes and preparation saved Roger's ass. He had watched Roger play instead of work and then borrow his diligently made notes at the last minute. With them Roger squeezed a first, a rather better one than Clive's.

Roger might have been brilliant, but he still needed Clive's ordered mind. It looked rather like that now. Clive did not buy Roger's story. His guess was that Roger, faced with the drudgery of organising boxes of material, would do an hour or so, get bored, and prefer the bar, followed by a good lunch, after which he would be too frazzled to function. Solution? Send for Clive.

You're flattered. Admit it. Discount it. It's irrelevant. You must think about this rationally. Do you want to commit a year—maybe two—on this? Forget what Roger wants, what do you want? That's the question.

There was a manipulative streak in Roger. Clive knew that the intention was to use him. Clive resented this, but he was also intensely curious. He wanted to dig deeper, to answer the why questions. This would be his opportunity. He just needed to be wary, to keep some independence. He would put his own proposition to Roger.

The next day, Clive woke early and despite the hangover, the price of sharing Roger's company, he could not wait to explore the town. The sun was up, and the sky was blue. The streets were newly washed, the shops were opening, and he marvelled at the brilliance of these people, creating such a perfect place. He knew that he was sentimentalising a little, as a visitor, but he did not care. That was a visitor's privilege. He lingered in the pâtisserie, finally choosing treats to take back. He could not wait to get his own kitchen, where he would try to cook Provençal dishes with all this wonderful produce.

Roger appeared about eleven and they went to the café. After a black coffee and a cognac, he was again in charge of the day. "Well, have you slept on it productively, Clive?"

"Yes. This is what I am prepared to do. I will spend some time ordering your material and making it useful. I will question you extensively and make detailed notes. At the end of which, we will decide whether I should actually write your biography or whether a memoir would be preferable. If the latter, you will have my notes and all the material there in chronological order, ready for use. My only demand is that you devote a sober couple of hours most days to talk to me and that you talk honestly and fully. You know how discreet I am. But no censoring. Also, I will find somewhere to live. Your house will be where I come to work. Mornings only."

Roger looked at him. This was Clive the Head of Department speaking. No matter. He thought he could live with it. As for complete honesty, well, honesty is a tricky word. Clive could be managed. "Sounds very fair, Clive."

He held out his hand and they shook.

"When do you start?"

"I'll start now, by looking at what you've got."

It truly was a disordered mess. A jigsaw puzzle was not a problem for someone with Clive's personality. It was the careless nature of it all, the stuffed shopping bags, the suitcases, and black sacks. The chaos was what offended him. He had always respected evidence and felt reverence for old documents. Each scrap of paper was a contribution to our history, a connection between generations. Roger's ego had stopped him from destroying anything about himself. But what was the use of it in this state? It was the difference between a library and a slagheap. "How on earth did you get it all down here?"

"I drove it down in that old Saab. Then I sold it. No desire to drive any more. When I think of all the money that I wasted on silly cars… Well, it'd be caviar all the way now… So, sorry about the state of it. Needs an ordered mind, Clive. I'll leave you to it."

There was a dining table at one end of the room. Clive cleared it and decided to begin by making piles divided into roughly five years or so. He would then be able to manage it more sensibly. He wanted the chronology because only then would he be able to construct a narrative, if indeed there was one. It would also throw up questions for Roger.

Shall I talk to him sober or drunk? I'll try both. See how it goes. Drunk might be less trustworthy, but if he has it in mind to manipulate me, then his guard might be down after a few. In vino veritas, and all that.

17

It all seemed daunting at first, but after a few days, the beginnings of order showed their quiet authority. The material started to behave under his discipline and the mess magically transformed into usable information. The temptation to get absorbed in a particular document delayed progress. Clive knew it would cause delay without reaping any benefit, but sometimes he could not resist. It was *his* life being evoked, too. Each document marked a moment in Roger's life and sparked a memory in him. His younger self emerged from deep in the shadows of lost memory. But he was strict with his time. He worked from nineish 'til almost one, and then shut the door. Outside were the delights of Hyères. His first task was to find somewhere to live.

Chapter 3

The Saturday morning market hit his senses, making him reel with its profligacy. In addition to the little shops, the whole of the main square, overflowing into the surrounding streets, was filled with stalls, selling a dazzling variety of foods, clothes, household goods, pottery, and bright yellow cloth full of flowers. He stood back, breathed it all in and marvelled. He was not unsophisticated. He and Celia had been abroad, of course, on holidays. They would go to Brittany, occasionally to Scandinavia. When younger, they had gone walking in the Italian Alps. He had been to Paris and visited the Louvre, of course, and hated it. Everyone seemed so rude, so superior, and so dismissive. Did London feel like that to foreigners? He hoped not, but feared that it did. He thought it might be the curse of capital cities. But here, everyone was so friendly, so courteous, saying, "Pardon," even if only casually brushing against you.

He strolled slowly from stall to stall. The range and quantity almost offended his minimalist temperament. A bewildering assortment of fish glistened on a slab, as though having just tumbled out of the sea, rigid with surprise. A fillet of plaice from Waitrose would not be the same again. The vegetables and fruit, much of it local, were more familiar, but the ripeness was not. Stalls overflowed with olives and anchovies and spices, and others with dried sausages and cheeses from the mountains. Some were overseen by old women with leathery faces and headscarves. He guessed they were from North Africa.

After he had been standing for a while before an olive stall, entranced and indecisive, a man stood by him, smiled and spoke quietly. "You look confused. Would you like some help? You are English, I am sure."

"Oh, yes. How could you tell?"

The man raised his eyebrows theatrically.

"I mean, I had not spoken."

The man grinned broadly, which made Clive grin, too. They stood looking at each other's faces and Clive felt amused and relaxed. He was drawn to this stranger, whose easy friendliness seemed infectious. Being here in the warm sunshine, enjoying the sensuality of the busy market, dissolved his uptight, defensive English reserve. He felt greedy and self-indulged. A knot untied and he expanded. He had always stiffly thought that to call someone Latin was to accuse them of emotional incontinence and poor self-discipline. But the word now seemed seductive.

"We speak not only with the spoken word, do you not agree, Monsieur? I hope you have no problem. I intrude, but I wish to practise my English. It is... rusty?"

Clive nodded, confirming his use of the word. "But your English is excellent. You should hear my French."

"I would like to hear your French. French spoken by an Englishman is.... The accent is very attractive."

"Not mine, I assure you. I am ashamed of my French."

"Well, I will practise English, and you can practise French. No? My name is Alain."

Clive smiled at him, rather at a loss faced with this unself-conscious friendliness. "Clive." He formally offered his hand, which Alain shook.

"I will help you. You are choosing olives?"

They slowly perambulated round the market. Clive's confidence grew, though not sufficiently for him to try his French. "The names in French sound so enticing. Artichauts, cebettes, fraises, betterave, blette, epinards, poireaux. Why is that?" Clive noticed Alain smiling at his pronunciation, but with pleasure. Clive did not feel put down. He felt encouraged.

He told Alain that it all looked exotic, not only because of the rich colours, but the sizes—the spring onions, for example, were on steroids. He did not wish to appear cynical, but the cautious realist guessed it was all commercially grown in the same hydroponic, chemical way as elsewhere. He was just too ready to believe that the tanned faces behind the stalls were peasants from the surrounding fields, bringing their traditional crops to market, as they had done for centuries. Alain told him that the produce marked "bio" was organic. It was local and good. So that was what Clive bought.

A van with an open side was selling meat. Clive looked closely. It said, "Boucherie Chevaline."

"C'est bon," Alain said, off Clive's scandalised reaction, which he had been too slow to conceal. "You do not like horse, Clive?"

Clive stared back, not wanting to offend, yet reluctant to lie. He had always been bad at lying. "I have heard of it, but…"

"You have never eaten horse?"

"No".

"Ah. It is good to eat. I will cook. Horse steak, eh? You would like to try?" He smiled encouragingly.

"Oh yes. Thank you very much, Alain."

He would eat barbecued cat rather than offend his new best friend.

They found an outside table at the crowded Excelsior, ordered coffees, and watched the people in the market. Everyone seemed relaxed yet purposeful, greeting each other and catching up on gossip as they shopped. It was reserved yet tactile. Even the men hugged and kissed each other's faces. There were many yapping, rather silly dogs. Thin, haughty teenage girls stood in groups, smoking aggressively. When they caught him staring, he looked away, scared of them.

How do they manage to look so stylish, so haute couture, in jeans and casual top? Confidence? Is it in the genes?

Alain was in a good mood, obviously enjoying speaking English with his new friend. His broad smile revealed bright white teeth in his sunburned face. Clive, comparing them with his own, suspected cosmetic dentistry, or at least teeth whitening, which he had seen advertised. In fact, Alain, although dressed casually, even carelessly, was so effortlessly and individually stylish, he made Clive feel awkward and shabby. He saw it as an example of French glamour. They did not even have to try.

Alain rose, picking up his shopping, and said goodbye. "Perhaps you will come one evening and allow me to cook dinner, Clive? Yes?"

"I would like that very much, Alain, you are very kind."

"That is good. Au revoir." He disappeared up the hill.

No arrangement had been made to see each other again.

Is that how it works? You assume you'll bump into people. What a nice man. I hope he meant it.

Clive looked down at all the food he had bought, on impulse. He determined to make finding somewhere of his own to live a priority. He needed his own kitchen. He could not wait to start cooking this lovely produce.

Chapter 4

By nine fifteen on Monday, Clive was back at the coalface, mining documents, scanning dates and putting them in piles. He was in an enjoyable rhythm until he picked up a student newspaper and saw the headline. "Women's Champion. Sensational Intervention Silences Rowdy Meeting."

He was instantly and magically teleported to another time and place. 1968. London School of Economics. Lecture theatre. Early evening. Witnessing a very different Roger face down a full meeting, shake it up and change many lives, particularly Roger's own. How had that Roger been transformed into the Roger he saw now in Hyères? That process, Clive thought, should be the book. But Roger would never write it, or permit it to be written. It probably was not the book that his publisher had paid an advance for.

Like most of the men there, Clive had attended the meeting out of curiosity. He had never thought about equality for women. They had the vote, hadn't they? A movement for women seemed weird. There were more than enough politics to be going on with. Anti-Vietnam marches, the violent clashes in Paris, the fighting in the Universities, even right here at the LSE. Everybody seemed to be joining some Marxist sect or other, and beating each other over the head. Everybody he knew, anyway. He had been affected by this climate of engagement, but his caution had held him back from aggressive involvement. Now the women seemed to want to get in on it. What was their gripe? He saw the stickers and decided to go along to find out.

He pictured himself going to the meeting. The lecture theatre is surprisingly full, with quite a few men inspecting the women with that automatic flick of the eye, from chest to face to legs, and back again. The women are mainly students, with a few staff members and others who seem to be outsiders. The men are good-natured, but rowdy—trying to chat the women up, or ribbing them. For them, it is clearly entertainment. As Clive looks round, he senses something else running below the surface. It feels like fear or anger—something that makes him uneasy.

A young woman, who he assumes is an undergraduate, walks to the front clutching a page of notes. She is unwisely wearing a short skirt. Her legs are long, and receive loud appreciation. She looks terrified and is shaking. She begins to speak. Her voice is light, does not carry, and is hindered by her nervous, fast delivery. She speaks, looking down at her notes, as though she wants to get this ordeal over with. Clive feels sorry for her, thinking she wants to be anywhere but here. The barracking, posing as appreciation, gets louder. The men are being cruel now, but have persuaded themselves that it is just witty banter. Some of the women chastise the men, but in telling them to behave, they add to the turmoil. The speaker is merely trying to introduce the main guest, an older woman, who has come from "Columbia." Clive guesses that this is the university in New York, not the country. It is all starting to turn ugly.

Then Clive sees a figure make his way to the front and whisper into the young woman's ear. She nods, steps back, and Roger faces the crowd. He looks coldly round the lecture theatre, his eyes daring anyone to challenge him. He reminds Clive of a maths teacher at school, Mr. Warden, who by sheer presence could quell even 4-c without opening his mouth. Roger is tall and heavily built, dressed in jeans, a T-shirt and a denim bomber jacket, looking more like a football hooligan than a teacher.

He begins to speak, clearly, but quietly. The crowd's curiosity has silenced them, and now they lean forward to hear him. "This is what's going to happen. My comrade…" As he turns to the young woman who had given way to him, there is a snigger at the word and he turns ferociously to glare at the source of the infraction. "My comrade has allowed me a few minutes to tell you pathetic idiots a few truths. So wrench your silly schoolboy minds away from the objectification of the women here, and listen. I'm then going to hand this meeting back…" and here he pauses for emphasis, "To my comrade, who will introduce the guest speaker. She has come all the way from New York to educate you, and fuck, do you need it. So you will listen and learn. Any man who misbehaves, I will personally throw out."

He glares round. It is silent. This is high drama and everyone is enjoying it. No one wants to take him on.

He continues, "I am a feminist and a socialist. You can't be one without also being the other. To be a socialist and not a feminist is to ignore the exploitation of half of humanity. To be a feminist and not a socialist is to believe that you can be free under capitalism, which exploits most of the population, male and female alike. So all the men here who think they are political had better grow up, and join their sisters in the struggle. By that I do not mean telling them to make the tea and lick envelopes, but equally in the struggle."

"In order to move things forward, and in the light of the pathetic inadequacy of the LSE's curriculum, I will be starting an evening lecture course on the condition of women and their struggles over the last century, focussing on the UK and America. You are all welcome. Bring your minds. I shall be exercising them. Details will be up tomorrow." He turns. "Thank you for allowing me to speak."

He then walks to the side of the theatre and stares back at the platform.

There is silence. Then a round of applause and an excited rumble of comment. The first speaker begins and the theatre falls silent. Clive could not remember anything more of what was said. But he knew a star had been born and thought he might sign up for the new course.

Sitting in that cluttered study on the Cote d'Azur, Clive thought, that moment was the turning point for Roger—that and the course itself. Clive had never heard of the women that Roger celebrated in his lectures. He had talked about American's like Winifred Harper Cooley and her Utopian ideas of a better world, not only for women, but for everyone. He talked movingly of the hard lives of English women, such as the factory worker Ada Nield Chew, who railed against women's working conditions for a "lingering dying wage." He placed their struggles in the historical journey of women over the generations.

In his memory, Clive relived the first lecture. The hall is packed, standing room only. It is mainly women, most of them undergraduates, but with a few who are older, whom Clive had not seen before. They are enthralled, as Roger puts their own half-formed ideas into a historical context; reminding them that the pain and anger they dare not feel are legitimate, have precedents. Above all, they are not alone in the fight. It has been going on for a long time and will go on for a long time. There are a few men. Clive assumes that they are curious, like him, or are possibly there because they know it will be full of women.

Roger does not play to the gallery. He cleverly gives no hint that he is there really to seduce the pretty ones. No one can detect that he has any other motive than to educate and show solidarity with the struggle. Clive realises that this makes him even more desirable to impressionable undergraduates. Roger seems to them to be principled, wise and unreachable—flattering them and making them more than willing to fall into his arms when he chooses them. He begins by giving an overview, trailing the meat of the future lectures, making them seem de rigueur.

The names and events mentioned in the lecture are unfamiliar to Clive, and as he looked round at the rapt but blank faces, to everyone else. The unifying link through it all is the progression of socialist and feminist ideas and the absolute necessity, in his view, for them to be in harness. This stark marriage of an idea familiar to Clive and an idea he had never given much thought to, stimulates him. He looks around. Some swots are making notes, others are just soaking it all in. Even the men there are nodding and thoughtful. Whatever the reason for their attendance, Roger has their attention now.

Clive expected Roger to finish with a rhetorical sweep, but he ended quietly and modestly. "Men and women are not enemies. I welcome the presence of the men here this evening and notice their improved behaviour."

There is a ripple of amusement and a few of the men smile and nod their heads in acknowledgement.

"These women are your sisters. And these men are your brothers. If we can remember that, then we can work together to make this world a better place. I thank you. I shall be here next week and hope to see you, too."

He then picks up his notes and walks out of the lecture theatre. Everyone rises and applauds. It dies gradually as he disappears, leaving an excited murmur as people turn to their neighbours, knowing that something important has happened in their lives. Roger had finally connected the dots.

Clive went back home that evening, to think it through. Everything was starting to make sense, for the first time. He felt excited. He also felt uncomfortable; even a little scared—the world looked different.

The lecture series transformed Roger from a promising academic to a leader, a media star, and a writer of big selling paperbacks. Within a year, he was a guru, celebrated, controversial, in demand. He was the centre of attraction and he milked it like a pro. His lecture series attracted Penguin and he turned it into a popular book. He was invited on radio and television, becoming a rent-a-quote voice, his telephone number was on every researcher's list. He spoke round the country.

***

Clive gradually returned to the present, the nostalgia for a lost world fading in a slow dissolve. He knew that he must talk to Roger about that event, but he had lived in enough history for the time being. That night he was due at Alain's, so he had arranged to drop in on Roger for a nightcap after dinner. He had been thrilled by Alain's shy invitation. They had bumped into each other in the Avenue General de Gaulle as Clive was buying his Guardian. The charming prospect of dinner with his new friend was clouded by a task he had been postponing. Knowing that it would continue to nag at him, he steadied himself and made the call to Celia. He dreaded her scornful interrogation, so he chose a time when he thought she would be at the British Library.

Her crisp voice on the answering machine, followed by the beep, was his cue. "Oh, hi Celia," he began brightly, "Just checking in, as it were. Sunny and warm here in Provence, as one would expect. Going to stay a while, to help Roger with his archive. Don't know how long. Will keep you informed." He thought that was enough. She had his mobile number, should she need to speak to him. He doubted she would.

So, having sloughed off this burden, he was free to think about the evening. He dressed carefully, but with little confidence. He had few clothes. He was thin and tall, with a long narrow face not enhanced by heavy spectacles. He would wear a clean and pressed shirt, some jeans and, daringly he thought, his new trainers. He was almost ashamed to be worrying about his appearance.

He did not know why he was nervous. Maybe it was the honour of eating his first French meal on his first visit to a French home. He did not want to do anything that exposed his lack of sophistication. At first, he agonised over whether he should take a bottle of wine or some dessert from the pâtisserie. But which wine? He might be considered an oenophile among the Tesco Best Buy crowd at home, but not here. The wines of this region were unfamiliar to him, and if he took a wine from Bordeaux, it might be considered a snub. He knew that French people often, as guests, took a shop-made cake for dessert, but what if Alain had made one?

In the end, he went to the chocolatier and bought a box of dark chocolates tied up in a pretty pink ribbon.

He presented himself at seven thirty. Alain graciously accepted the chocolates and sat Clive down with a kir. Clive looked around.

It seemed to be everything in one, kitchen, dining, and sitting room. He watched Alain, who was unselfconscious, totally absorbed in his cooking, his short compact frame moving gracefully from pan to pan, tasting and adjusting the heat. He looked different now. In the market he had worn a hat, tilted forward, its brim over his eyes. It had made him look like a film noir private eye. Clive remembered his father wearing a similar brown felt hat, a trilby, raising it to passing lady acquaintances. Possibly this association made him always think it old-fashioned, a relic of a previous generation. But on Alain, set at an angle, it had looked chic.

Still, he is bloody French. Not something that you could accuse my dad of being. He wouldn't have regarded it as a compliment if you had. Surprising the difference a hat can make. He looks like a different man, except for the smile and the eyes, which are bright blue and frank. Trustworthy. His face has an innocence, a kindness. He looks like a young boy.

Alain was serious about his cooking, yet relaxed, as though working well within his capacity. There was no tension or drama, none of the anxiety that poured out of Clive when he cooked. He knew there had never been another man he had liked so much. He felt lucky to know Alain, relaxed in his company.

Goodness knows what he sees in me. I'm not much. But I am someone he can practise his English on.

One of the interesting things about Alain was his unself-conscious interest in stuff which Clive had been brought up to believe were strictly feminine matters. This relieved Clive, just as the sight of his son-in-law pushing the pram and doing the weekend shopping had made him feel less like a freak. The younger generation, at least, were not stifled in the straitjacket of gender roles.

But Alain was of Clive's own generation. He had watched him carefully pick over vegetables and fruit in the market, conversing knowledgeably with the stallholder and buying judiciously. He knew about cuts of meat. More than the shopping and cooking, the man was soft and warm. There was no aggression or hard edge. He even smelled pleasant, yet not perfumed or feminine. He was a man. He did not mince and was not camp. Roger was clearly wrong—he was not gay. He was at ease with who he was, not caring whether some of it was feminine or masculine. For years, Clive had worried about it all. Not that he felt himself to be in the closet, most definitely not. But gender roles had always puzzled him. For instance, he did not enjoy housework. It was tedious. Celia felt the same. But he liked making good and enjoyed a neat and tidy environment. Why should it be a feminine obligation to ensure that? He had always enjoyed shopping and cooking. In the days of his youth, that was enough in itself to mark you as a sissy. If women now revolted against these jobs, yet were not attracted to men who liked them, then how would they get done? In his youth, if you were paid to cook, you were a chef, and that was masculine. If you did it at home, it aroused suspicion, being women's work. He hoped it was a generational thing and that the world was growing up.

Alain was shyly charming, warm, and self-deprecating. They laughed over each other's Franglais, although Alain's English was embarrassingly superior to Clive's French. For the first time in his life, Clive did not feel put down. Alain was encouraging and full of praise, correcting him in a way that did not discourage. He was grateful when Clive corrected him, saying how difficult English was.

He served some lovely wine and explained it, telling him about the vineyard and the grapes. Clive was very interested about the word terroir, which he had hitherto only vaguely understood. It had so intimidated him that he had wryly decided it was well named. Alain suggested a visit, it being only a few miles away.

The meal was amazing to Clive. First were some anchovy-crispy-starter things that made him hungrier, followed by a rabbit stew—although he called it civet de lapin, which sounded better. It was accompanied by a puree of sweet potatoes. Then a green salad, before the cheese. It ended with a simple baked apple. All this came to the table effortlessly, as though it had prepared itself. No panic, no interruption to their conversation. After this feast, Clive had no feeling of having overeaten or of indulgence. He just felt satisfied.

Alain said, "We had only moved to Hyères a few months before. We knew few people. We both had longed to settle in the South and had now managed it. I was a schoolteacher in Lyons. It was home, but we were both drawn to Provence. Then mon ami died. He had liver cancer. We had one year together here. A difficult year, watching him die. I was exhausted and bereft. Only now am I starting to embrace life again. Life must go on. Being here helps. The sun gives life."

This frankness emboldened Clive and he talked about his unsatisfactory life with Celia. About how lucky he had felt when she accepted him and about how inadequate he had felt ever since. "I don't think I've ever been relaxed in her company. It's been more difficult since our daughter, Emma left home. I think I'm afraid of Celia, of her disapproval. Which I assume I deserve— I don't know why. I respect her, Alain, but she is intimidating. To be frank, I'm rather glad to be here on my own. Is that weak of me?"

Alain smiled sympathetically. "No. You have the right to be yourself. To discover who that man is. Not to pretend to be whoever you think someone else wants you to be. What is the point of that?"

As he left, amid multiple thanks, Alain embraced him with a warm hug. Clive knew this was very French, but he felt an odd mixture of pleasure and embarrassment and daring. He walked down the hill in the warm night feeling deeply happy. He realised that already he was very fond of Alain. What was more; unaccountably Alain seemed fond of him.

***

Clive felt a little like the combination of the barrister facing a witness and a therapist with a client. Roger was looking at him warily.

"What have you got there?" Roger asked.

"I've spent the week trying to put some order into all that mess, but this morning I came across what I think is the key moment, the turning point. I want you to tell me what you remember."

He handed over the student newspaper. It had a photo of Roger on the front page, looking ruggedly handsome and movingly young. A fresh-faced boy compared to the ravaged man sitting opposite. Roger looked up and smiled grimly. "Cute little fucker, wasn't I?"

"Had you planned it?"

"In a way. I'd hoped to speak, but I hadn't expected all that childish hostility. It pissed me off. Not surprising the separatists and the dungaree dykes came in later, is it, faced with men like that? Assholes."

"What I mean is; how on earth did you just come out with all that?"

"You've forgotten something. My doctoral thesis was on the American Civil War and Lancashire's relationship with the South. Cotton and trade. I'm from Rochdale; remember. How can you be a slave in a mill, and be on the side of American slave owners? Easy. More interestingly, how can you be on the side of the slaves and risk losing the cotton and your livelihood? Anyway, I spent time in America, in the South, in DC, in New York. But it wasn't all in libraries. The women there were years ahead. It wasn't just Vietnam or even Black Power, it was the birth of the women's movement, and I really started to grow up. I had an affair with Marsha Simmons."

"You had an affair with Marsha Simmons? Good God. You had an affair with Marsha Simmons? I mean, I only saw her on TV. She was the most beautiful and terrifying ball-breaker I could ever imagine."

"Well, for your information, Clive, she was not a ball-breaker. She was a great woman. She taught me, and loved me, and I buggered it up."

"How?"

"Never mind how. Well, you could probably guess, knowing me. But the point is, by the time I got back home, I was light years ahead. So my appearance at that meeting—my attitude and what I said—wasn't a stretch."

Clive nodded. The book would need an American chapter.

"I'd always been angrily on the left, like the rest of us. It was de rigueur for students in the sixties, wasn't it? I was careering round, going on demos, half-joining the IS and then backing off, reading bits of Marx—well, mainly Marxist writers. But I hadn't considered the woman question, didn't know there was one. In New York, I couldn't avoid it. No argument against it held any water. So I put the two together under Marsha's cool gaze, the socialist class stuff, and the feminism. They fitted like a glove. I was armed and dangerous. The rest is history. Well, it would be, if you'd write it." He grinned at Clive.

Clive smiled back and went to bed. Roger had his cognac for company.

***

Roger sat allowing his mind to roam, listening to the inner conversation, rather than speaking it.

Marsha. What a great bird. Wonder what she's up to now? Probably looks like an old bag. Overweight. They all end up looking like their mothers. Christ, she was amazing. I was potty about her. So why did you fuck it all up? That other bird, can't even remember her name. I can see her now, but what was she called? Anyway, stupid. Marsha, no second chances with Marsha. Said she would have shared me, but couldn't have a liar as a lover. Out on my arse. I don't believe she would have shared me. All that 'we are sisters' talk. They fight over men; they don't share them.

He topped up his glass and sipped.

What if she had been serious, though? Imagine that. Never occurred to me. Not something that you think possible. Anyway. A long time ago. Probably wouldn't have lasted. But what a bird. Communist Party parents. What they went through. The red baiting, ruined careers, I couldn't believe it. Marsha was a chip off the old block, the genuine article. I was a fraud compared to her. But she taught me the whole handbook. It was like another Ph. D., going round with her. I've lived off her ever since, really. Funny, never thought of it like that. Don't suppose she'd mind, though. I'd get a slap now if she saw me. Puritan bitch. Good health, Marsha.

He lifted his glass, knowing he was getting maudlin, but too pissed to care.

Funny, I can remember the first moment I laid eyes on her, can see her now, but I can't remember the place. Someone's living room. Can't remember the district even, up two flights. Packed. Cigarette smoke. Couldn't keep my eyes off her. The long frazzled hair. No makeup. Long dress, looked like curtain material. Asked to give a talk. Decided to go with my strengths. "Delivering Labour to Capital. The Objective Role of Trade Union Leadership."

It worked. She singled me out, took me home. We talked for hours. I'd never come across any girl so direct. Took my breath away. She said, "I liked you, but I assumed you were just another soft shit with no politics, just passing through. You're not. You've looked behind the propaganda, seen how it really works." She'd been on a journey herself, moving away from her Stalinist upbringing. She stood up and extended her arm, as though to a child. "Good. We can go to bed now." Just like that. Fuck me. Then she got undressed and looked at me like, what are you waiting for? In-fucking-credible. I could hardly get it up, I was so shocked. Oh God, what I would give to have her now. Not the way she must be now, but like she was then. In-fucking-credible."

Chapter 5

L ife relaxed into a satisfactory rhythm. Roger liked Clive's effortless English company. He did not actually mind the French. He just did not know any, except superficially. He was happy to greet them on his daily perambulations, but a proper, intimate conversation was beyond him. It was exhausting and disappointing. One could never speak French well enough to satisfy them. Speaking to them in English—as though to a deaf child—was too much effort. His reputation had not travelled to Hyères, so he could not bask in the fame he thought was his due, although he was referred to as *le professeur*. At least with Clive, he had a common hinterland. The references needed no explanation. Chatting to him was like putting on an old glove.

Just as boring, mind you, but that's solid, reliable Clive. He'll do a meticulous job. He wants to write it, despite playing hard to get. I'll have to let him down gently after he's done all the donkeywork. I'll tell him I'd love him to do it, and know he'd do a distinguished job, but after that advance... They want my story in my words, not a biography. Sorry, old chap, but you're not even a well-known writer. No track record. They won't wear it, so I'll have to buckle down. Knew you'd understand. I'll promise him a generous acknowledgement. That'll satisfy him. Excellent.

Clive was innocently happy. Only now did he realise just how discontented he had been. His retirement had brought the bleakness of his life into full relief. He could now see what had been happening. He had locked himself up in the department, working longer hours there than he needed, in order to minimise his time at home with Celia. But the last few months had made him face the truth. They were not just strangers. They were avoiding each other. He did not hate her—although he worried that she despised him—but there was a cold gulf between them. What had he done wrong? She seemed resentful. He was clearly inadequate, but she would not, or could not, enlighten him. And was she inadequate? That was an odd, new thought. It had never occurred to him to think it. It was rather subversive. He had always been amazed that she had chosen him. To question it would be ridiculous. Well, he was questioning it now. It was icily polite between them. They did not row. They lived in the same house. They had been together for years, yet they avoided each other. He had felt, day by day, that life was seeping out of him, that he was being deflated in order to take up less room. He had been on the point of becoming existentially absent when he did actually leave. Roger's invitation had proved to be a line for him to grasp. He still did not understand his relationship with Celia, but now it did not seem to matter. He had interesting work, which sparked memories of his own youth. He was under the Provençal sun in a divine town. He could buy the local produce and cook the local recipes. He had Alain. He had a new friend. The thought of him made him smile. Being with him, pottering around the market, cooking, just hanging out, was heaven. They were like little boys together. Instantly he had become his best friend ever.

Alain had even found him a small flat. It involved walking up two flights of stairs, but that would be good exercise. It was in an old house in a terrace and had been modernised. It belonged to a German couple. Alain heard they wanted to let it from a friend of an acquaintance who worked in the building business. That was how anything happened in Hyères, so you needed to be plugged in, Clive was told. He was glad that Alain was plugged in. He seemed to know everybody and all the gossip. He was better informed than the Var Matin. The flat was furnished quite nicely and the kitchen was equipped. He moved in and promised to cook Alain dinner as soon as he was settled. He had not lived alone since before Celia. It was bliss. No mother, no Celia to tell him that what he was doing was wrong, or that he should be doing something he was not doing. Just silence.

***

Clive was not a Jesuitical disciple of Freud. As he often reminded his students, despite a scandalous theory and a controversial technique, Freud did not suddenly discover the importance of early experiences. Historians should always pay attention to the roots of behaviour. So he was professionally and personally interested in Roger's early life. Particularly so, because Roger himself seemed to dismiss its importance. As an historian, he must have known he was being disingenuous. Why? Clive decided it was his priority to open up the subject. In it might be the key to the biography, a way in to the contradictions of this man.

Roger could never resist a challenge, so Clive accused him of being inhibited. What was stopping him from being open about his early life? What unacknowledged secrets did it harbour?

The bugger's running in the wrong direction, as usual. I'm not inhibited. The truth is more pedestrian. I don't think my early life's particularly relevant. But he'll never rest until he's done his psychoanalytical digging, so I'd better indulge him.

It was not so easy. He could take his mind back to the late fifties, but it was just his memory and he knew how treacherous, how selective, and misleading that could be. He also felt detached. The boy he remembered was not him, nor was the boy's world his world. He could accept, intellectually, that the boy was being remembered, or re-created by him, and had no other existence. He knew that he used to be a version of that boy, but he did not know how close the memory was to the reality. In any case, reality is a slippery customer. It is always a perception. The experience of remembering was perhaps no more than an easily conjured up fiction. Had that boy actually existed in this way, or was he the invention of an old man—an invention that had been honed over decades? The historian considered this an important question. Roger actually did not give a fuck.

At Clive's suggestion, they took a stroll. Roger thought walking anywhere except to a necessary destination, like a restaurant, was excessive. But he complied, slowly, and began the speech he thought Clive would want to hear.

"On a hill at the edge of Rochdale is a terrace of council houses. It is called Spotland. It's by two cemeteries. One bunch of corpses in the ground, the other bunch of living dead next door, Rochdale Football Club. That's where hope used to go to die every other Saturday afternoon."

This was a well-worked riff, which used to get an appreciative smile from most audiences. It had been polished over the years. The truth was he had never been interested in football. He feigned an interest decades later as part of his working-class cred. Not Rochdale, though. That was for losers. Manchester United. He would talk affectionately late at night about the terrace at Old Trafford.

"No seats then. You'd be squeezed up, mill workers pissing in your pocket."

He had never actually been.

They made it up to the top of the hill, and Roger sat exhausted. If such an arduous adventure had been suggested before today, he would have looked at the precipitous incline and declared that mountaineering was not his hobby. But he had wanted to please Clive. He was surprised still to be alive. They sat in the garden of the Villa Noailles. The view over the town and the Med was indeed wonderful. After a few moments, Roger recovered his breath.

"Interesting, Clive, the higher you go, the more sky there seems to be."

Clive looked at him quietly. He had not come all this way to talk about scenery.

"We all invent ourselves as we go. What is the truth? I will try to tell you, stripped of subsequent layers of varnish. I was an only child. My mother adored me, even more than she adored my father. She obeyed him and indulged me. He was a cop. Yes, I know, get the prejudices out of your head. True, he was a big imposing man, physically, with a voice that stopped you in your tracks. But he was kind and reserved. He was strict. Dads were then, weren't they? I hated the bugger sometimes, but he was stricter with her. She took it. Even polished his boots. It was funny, he also worshipped her, and she was the boss, most of the time, except when he got mad and put his foot down. It seemed to work. But he was not a bully. I wasn't afraid of him. I think I intimidated him, actually, with my head into books, and the way I had with words. He was a sergeant in uniform. The most exciting thing he ever did was go on to the moors once a year to supervise the sheep dip. I don't think he ever arrested anybody.

"I took after him physically. I was a big, strong lad; I had never been bullied, nor ever needed to bully. I had natural authority, without being aware of it. It was just how I was, how the world worked. Good at sport, full of myself, but cack-handed with girls. You could say I was spoilt. My mom lived for me. I think I had supplanted my dad in her affections even before I was born. He didn't seem to resent this. He was proud of me. They would look at each other, amazed that they had produced this boy who the teachers said was clever enough to go to University.

"So I was a young god in suburban Rochdale, with the world my playground. Except that, like most teenage boys, I was obsessed with girls, with sex, and I wasn't getting any. Nor did I know how to. Nor would I have known what to do with it if it had been delivered registered post. The girls I saw were unavailable, forbidden, and indifferent to my desperate needs. This was a new experience for me—needing and having no way of satisfying that need. Constant, obsessive masturbation was no substitute for the real thing. I hated women—well, young, attractive women—for causing this suffering and wilfully refusing to cure me. All they had to do was recognise what I was going through and offer their bodies on demand. Not much to ask. But they chose to withhold, to ignore, and leave me to writhe in agony. My desire tipped into murderous fantasies of punishing them for their cruelty. Not so different from other lads, you may think. Not so different from you. Just an ordinary adolescent, no?"

Clive tipped his head in acknowledgement, but said nothing. He was horrified, not only at what Roger had said, but also at his assumption that it was so routine it hardly deserved comment. But he did not want this to become a conversation, let alone a dispute with moral overtones. He wanted it raw from the source. "When did you... lose your virginity? And in what circumstances?"

"I got lucky. It changed my life; I'll admit that. Mum was a hairdresser and did a few afternoons a week at Dorothy's Salon on the corner of the main road. Just helping out like; when it got busy over the weekend. Dorothy was a divorcee, a scandalous state in those days, with a reputation for being no better than she ought to be. She was subject to nods and winks, and meaningful looks behind her back. I thought she was old, but she was probably not even forty. She was well built, on the plump side, with dyed blond hair, piled up. She wore high heels, even though she was on her feet all day, and her nylons made a swishy noise as her thighs touched when she walked. She had lots of makeup. I thought she had intimidating glamour, the sort you only really see in magazines or on screen. She lived in another dimension. Not Rochdale. Another planet, probably. I was paralysed with shyness in her presence.

It was June and I had just finished my exams. Nothing was happening at school now. We were all demob happy. I was earning a few quid at Dorothy's sweeping up at the end of the day, generally tidying the place, making it neat for tomorrow. I was a bit embarrassed doing such a sissy job, but it was cash in the hand and mum was pleased. I was helping Dorothy out.

"Well, I'd just finished and was putting the cleaning things away. I sensed Dorothy had been watching me, standing with her arms folded, one hand taking her cigarette to her mouth as she looked me up and down."

"'You're a big lad for your age,' she said."

"I'm nearly sixteen."

"Are you now? Do you have a girlfriend?"

I mumbled "No," and looked down. I was not enjoying this. Was she teasing me?

"Why not? Don't you like girls?"

"I don't know any."

"You what? Look at me. You what?"

"I repeated that I didn't know any girls, not really."

"Is that right?"

Then, she took a last drag of the cigarette, damped it out in the sink, and dropped it in the bin. She looked at me again and said, 'Follow me. I've got something for you.'"

"She walked into the back of the shop and went up the stairs. I followed behind, watching her bottom swing as she went. She opened a door, which led into the living room of her flat.

"'Come in, Roger. I won't bite,' she said. She went over to her handbag, took out five pounds, and held it out. I walked over and took my wages. I thanked her and she said I was welcome. We were standing very close. I didn't move, could hardly breathe. Her perfume was paralysing. But more than that, she had somehow changed the atmosphere into something dangerous and exciting. I was out of my depth. She stepped even closer and traced her finger down the side of my face. This made me look up at her.

"You're a handsome lad, Roger. I've had my eye on you. You've been looking at me, too. I've noticed you."

"Have I, I said."

"Aye. You know you have. Do you think of me when you go home? When you're in bed at night, do you think of me then?"

I could only nod, and then she said, "Well, if you want to kiss me. Now's your chance. Kiss me."

"I moved the magical two inches forward and my mouth docked on hers. Her hand slipped to the back of my head and her other arm went round my waist. She drew us even closer. I stood like a statue, being kissed. I didn't dare move, didn't know what move I should make. She then relaxed and her face was just an inch from mine. I could feel her smoky breath.

"I'm going to have to teach you how to kiss, Roger. I'm going to have to teach you a lot of things, aren't I? Would you like that?"

41

I could barely speak."

Roger sat looking far out to sea, not even aware of it. His conscious self was the teenage boy, more than half a century ago. His focus returned to the present and he turned to Clive.

"And she did. Over that summer she taught me everything I would ever need to know about women, sexually at least. She supervised my research. Started with a relaxing vodka that burned my throat. Sent me home with a mint.

"She told me, 'Can't have your dad suspecting I'm leading you astray. Very suspicious, police are. Suspect you of doing summat even when you're doing nowt, so we may as well get up to summat.'"

"She had large breasts and a tight belt. That's all you need to know, really. My adolescent eyes were popping out. She was a fantasy, becoming real. When I look back, I admire her. She was loud, blowsy and fearless, took what she wanted. She was not dependent on a man. Had her own business on her own premises, housewives mainly from round Spotland coming in to be permed and glamourised for the weekend. She took no shit from anyone. And she was sexually liberated—in a Rochdale fifties way—where the respectable working class knew right from wrong and thought sex was dirty. Well, she had appetites and she went about satisfying them. She didn't just teach me the tricks of the trade. It was that women had an appetite for men. Men weren't the only ones who felt these dirty things. Anyway, sex was fun, and what was wrong with fun? I was hopeless, at first. I came before we'd even started."

Clive nodded sympathetically.

"She was patient and good humoured. It seemed to amuse her to train this gauche youth. She taught me what to do, and when. What to say, and how. She gave seduction its narrative, teaching me how to build to a climax and how to resolve it satisfyingly. For instance, she taught me that it's not just about making sure the woman has an orgasm. Coming is not the end. What you did afterwards, how you brought them down, and back to you was the test. Do that skilfully and tenderly and they won't just fancy you sexually, they'll fall in love with you.

"Evening after evening, that summer, she instructed me in the theory and the practice of sex. I was an assiduous pupil—you may imagine—quick on the uptake, and willing to practise. After a few months I was accomplished, but more important, I was confident. I knew I had an edge. Girls didn't intimidate me anymore. After all, I had a secret lover, an experienced older woman, and I was satisfying her. I felt like I knew more about what the girls needed than they themselves did, and I knew how to give it to them.

"I started to pick them up and seduce them, one after the other. Finding somewhere to have sex was more difficult than getting a willing girl. I still saw Dorothy. She was amused to know about my adventures, not a bit jealous. It was just a delicious game for her, and that's what it became for me."

Clive did not know whether to believe this tale or not. It certainly seemed too easy. He challenged him. "You were attending one of those boys' Grammar Schools, like I was. I remember what it was like. I never met any girls, not really. I saw them, at the bus stop, serving behind the counter at Boots, but I never spoke to any. Not that I would have known what to say. They all terrified me. They were mysterious creatures in their own world. They looked down on me, if they even noticed. It's one thing to be seduced by an older woman, Roger, who makes all the running. Another to get teenage girls to have sex with you. You didn't even have any sisters, whose friends would be available. How did you make the transition? You make it sound easy."

"Well, it was and it wasn't. This was the fifties, remember, and the sixties didn't really start 'til sixty three, at the earliest. Where, that was the problem. No cars, no privacy. The summer was easier, alfresco sex, but winter nights were frustrating, I remember. They weren't on the pill—terrified of pregnancy—and it took cheek to buy Durex, although it was easier when I got to know the barber. What I most vividly recall were the clothes you had to negotiate before you could say bingo. Girdles, slips, petticoats, garter belts, bras and nylons, panties. All erotic now, worn specially to excite you. Just impediments then. But Dorothy taught me to be patient, stealthy. Sometimes it took me weeks to get past the caution point, but then resistance collapsed suddenly, and you were in. A combination approach worked best."

"A combination approach? You've lost me. I never thought of this in a tactical way. Would you explain?"

"Certainly. This was war. It was all about how to make advances, take territory, and induce surrender. I used a combination of three approaches. Tell them you love them, and that they're the only one; gradually excite them physically, the wet test; and make them feel guilty if they refused; make them take pity on the suffering their refusal is causing you. Usually did the trick."

"You make it sound so cold, so clinical."

"Well, in a way, yes. It all had to be planned and worked at. But I enjoyed the chase, the winning. And I was obsessed with sex, always have been. Cunt has been the most important thing in my life. By far."

"Well, you've had plenty, by your account."

"Yes. And never enough. One is never satisfied. It just got easier, as I got older and the sixties loosened them all up. Being in the sixth form with no money, trying to work the Church Youth Club, with all those shy virgins, that was hard. But I had Dorothy, remember, to satisfy me and advise me. She would offer tactical advice, helping me to overcome any resistance from my current seduction target—what to say to them, whether I should back off for a while and give them time, or whether I should drive forward and insist on clinching the goodies. I learnt it was all psychology. The breakthrough came when it dawned that the key really was confidence. Most women want to feel they are in capable hands. Some even like arrogance and dominance. If you act as though you won't be refused, nine times out of ten you won't be, not eventually. They'll refuse at first for form's sake. They want to say yes, but don't want to seem easy. Most girls think it impolite to refuse, or don't want to hurt you, or are flattered, or don't want to lose you. Or they just give way in the end to insistence. The point to reach is *yes*. Tentative and overly polite men, who expect to get knocked back, usually are."

Clive said nothing. It was too close to his experience. He had been one of those men, too polite and expecting refusal. He had hardly dared to ask. "What happened when feminism began? That must have cramped your style."

"Feminism just affected their heads, not their feelings. When it came to actual sex, they always went for the confident bastard who would sweep them off their feet, who promised a good fucking from the first look. Eye contact was the key. It took some nerve, originally. But the girl who was not up for it, who hated you for your arrogance, who looked down at you like some aristo noticing a peasant, she would be the one to go for. She would come across, if you were confident enough. Nine times out of ten, you understand. Dorothy explained, you must play the averages, and not get too personally involved. If you ask for it, you might or might not get it. If you don't, you certainly won't."

Roger was on a roll now. He got up, and paced around, developing his thoughts, as though in a lecture theatre again. "You see, Clive, women are brought up to be sexually submissive. Not so much now, unfortunately, although it will take a long time for it to be squeezed out of the system. False consciousness, you've lectured around that idea. And attitudes are passed on early in life, aren't they? You Freudians know all about that. So when they got into feminism, it changed nothing, except their heads. They all still fell for a dominant, confident male, even if they hated him, and themselves, for needing him. Couldn't help it."

He's forgotten Celia. I bet she was on top when they had a fling. One of her disdainful looks could wilt your enthusiasm from fifty yards. He should have heard what she said about him later. I saw his chutzpah early on, but it probably didn't appeal to many women. Surely.

Clive said, "So by the time you started at Uni you were years ahead of anyone, further ahead than most of us would ever be."

"So it appeared. I was able to refine my technique, as I continued my researches, as it were. I realised that even the most respectable, refined, repressed girl, was a sexual opportunity. In fact, the tighter the lid, the hotter the furnace underneath. Prise open that lid, and stand well back—the heat will burn you. They still needed another reason, a cover story. So, of course, I talked to them of love. I behaved in ways that made them believe it was an

45

honour for them to give themselves to such a principled, brave man. I pretended indifference, or blew hot and cold, to make them doubt themselves. And I appealed to the nurse, the mother in them 'til they offered sex to heal my wounds. Always give them another narrative, Clive. Most of them would close up if you just demanded sex. Psychology, Clive, psychology. That's the key. They want cock, but for fuck's sake, don't offer it. That's the third act resolution, not the first act tease."

A revulsion rose in Clive as he listened to this advice. He knew he should continue coaxing him into more exposing reminiscence, but detached research lost out to moral distaste. The cold opportunism was what he found shocking. He had watched Roger, especially when they had been young and had marvelled at one lovely woman after another on his arm, but had not thought much about it. He had felt envy, certainly, and thought Roger full of himself, but nothing more. Looking at this old, broken man now—it occurred to him that most of this boasting was intended to boost Roger's own ego. The rest, to shock his old friend, whom he had always thought was staid and conventional.

He's teasing me. I think. I hope.

"Did you never wonder, have you never thought, of the emotional consequences, Roger? Some of these young women must have fallen in love with you, imagined that there was a promise implicit in the intimacy. You make it all sound like cold consumption. What about feelings? Did you never feel any responsibility? Did you never feel love or even tenderness for any of them?"

Roger raised his eyebrows and widened his eyes in a mocking stare.

"All's fair, Clive, you know the old saying. We are free. There are no little bastards running round without a father, as far as I know. I am not a rapist. I did not remove their knickers with alcohol. They were free, willing, and able and probably enjoyed the best sex of their lives, considering the boring men most of them subsequently married. Of course, there was hurt when these affairs ended. That's life. And regret. But spare me your hypocritical Victorian, faux protective sympathy for the fairer sex. Our society is so inhibited; it's a terrible waste. I'd like it to be sexual indulgence from early adolescence 'til senescence, a lifetime of glorious fucking. Is there a more enjoyable way to spend one's time? It's cheap, doesn't harm the planet, even disconnected from reproduction these days. An innocent, harmless hobby. What is there not to like?"

"I hardly think you would make many converts to this unrestricted hedonism in much of the world. It might appeal to the fantasies of schoolboys, but is not a serious idea." Clive knew he sounded prim, and that he was walking into Roger's trap. He should be humouring him and not rising to the bait.

"I'm not advocating compulsory sex for Muslim communities in Bradford, although we would have less terrorism if there was more fucking. Just freedom, that's all. Remove the constraints and let's all have some fun."

"I wasn't thinking of Bradford, Roger. More of Cheltenham or Tunbridge Wells. All societies temper licentiousness—you know that. As a matter of purely hypothetical interest, how would you go about instigating this paradise?"

"I would like it to be part of our cultural tradition, built into our sense of rights and obligations—an unquestioned given in society—that females from fifteen to twenty should offer sexual pleasure to men over fifty. Teenage boys should be discouraged from having sex with girls their own age—older women, yes, who could enjoy training them to be good lovers—but otherwise, their energies should be channelled elsewhere.

"Each generation of female teenagers would be off limits to all men under fifty. At twenty, they could choose who they like and marry if they wished. Clearly pregnancy would be discouraged before then, but if it happened and they insisted on keeping the baby, the older man would be expected to play his part. I'm not advocating anything irresponsible here.

"The whole point is that children are not brought up in an ideological vacuum. Religion and tradition and society's expectations actually shape what they think is right and proper, even what they feel they want. Most of them want approval, not to be cast out as sinful or weird. Even stroppy teenagers. People would conform. This expectation would become the new normal. And life would be more satisfying all around."

"Especially for the older men."

"Everyone."

"What about homosexuals?"

"What about them?"

"Where do they fit in?"

"Older men have always found boys. And vice versa. They would carry on as normal. Or abnormal."

"Wouldn't the fathers of these teenage virgins have something to say about the arrangement? Be a little possessive, not to say protective?"

"Not on the whole. They would be too busy swapping daughters with each other. And the mothers, who are so competitive with their daughters, would enjoy flaunting their cute teenage boy-friends. The world, I assure you, would be a happier place. When the young people were delivered to each other, as it were, in maturity, the girls would be skilled in the arts of pleasuring their partners, and the boys would be proper men, able to satisfy them, not callow boys unable to give them an orgasm. Why is it that one of the most important human activities, perhaps the most important, is left to chance—two completely bungling amateurs thrown together in the hope that they will work it out. Absolute nonsense."

This breathtaking proposal was even more shocking because it was presented neutrally, as though Roger was putting forward a policy document for discussion at a Labour Party branch meeting. Clive decided to assume that Roger was being his naughty self, trying to shock him into rising to the bait. He would not give Roger the satisfaction. He would pretend sophisticated amusement. What amazed him was how much effort he had put into imagining this paradise. He was now too old to enjoy such a world, should it ever come to pass, but he clearly thought the idea was attractive. Maybe it was connected to his age. Maybe Roger was finding the idea of senility—of waning attractiveness and sexual powers—so unwelcome, that he was prone to fantasies like this. In that case, he deserved sympathy. These ideas would not help the book. What Clive wanted was to move on to more details of Roger's actual private life and what connection he thought it had had to his feminist principles. In particular, he wanted the full dirt on the Anna saga. But that would have to wait for another occasion. "Well, that is an interesting idea. One out of my expertise, of course. It would certainly change our society drastically. I will have to think about it."

Encourage him to talk. Be a sympathetic ear and he will open up with the useful stuff. He always needed an audience.

Chapter 6

Roger had given little thought to his health. He had never been ill, not really ill. If health is the norm, decade after decade, what is there to think about? He also knew, of course, that he would die, one way or another, but that would be in some undetermined future. Meanwhile, others succumbed to terrible illnesses and gradually fell apart. He had been to enough funerals lately to make denial impossible. He vaguely knew a chap, a media leftie, who used to say that he enjoyed funerals. It was where he could catch up with old friends. Roger found them depressing.

These thoughts were spinning around one afternoon after his nap, when he was trying to have a pee. Lately, he had started sitting down for this, like a girl. It was a bit embarrassing, but no one could see him. The reason was twofold. One, his belly was so large that it constricted the view, making him shoot blindly. Two, it seemed to be just dribbling out lately, however much he was bursting to do it. Often, nothing would come and then it would suddenly go all over the floor.

Fuck, there's no flow at all. Wonder if anything is wrong.

He tried, and failed, to obliterate the thought. He would chat to Clive. He knew he was overweight, that he shouldn't smoke, that he drank too much, did not exercise, ate too much meat, and butter, and sweet stuff. So the experts said.

But it's like buses. If you don't want a nine, wait a bit and a thirty-one will come along. They'll change their minds. The most laughable sentence in the English language begins, "Scientists have proven that dot dot dot." Uncle Fred was ninety-six before he went, and he drank like a fish, smoked forty Players a day, and lived out of the frying pan.

With that definitive flourish, his internal debate concluded for the day. Pleasure, ten—Puritans, nil.

***

Clive wandered out of the documents room, seeking a glass of water, and faced a strange woman. She looked startled.

"Ah, Madame, pardon, je suis désolé… er." His French ebbed away.

Roger said, "Cut the cod French. Her English trumps your bloody efforts. This is Céline. Céline, my old friend Clive, who is helping me with my writing. He will be here a lot, so ignore him. Céline is my fiancée, the love of my life, the woman of my dreams, and she comes most days to rescue me from my own slutty untidiness. She is like my mother, but incomparably more beautiful."

Céline ignored his fanciful rhetoric. She put out her hand to Clive, who shook it warmly.

"I am happy to meet you, m'sieur. I help M'sieur Roger."

"Oh, hi, yes, good. And ignore everything he says, I hope."

"Oh, M'sieur Roger is… M'sieur Roger." She shrugged charmingly.

What a thoroughly nice woman, Clive thought, and said so to Roger after she had left. She'd had a no-nonsense decency about her, and good humour, which drew Clive to her. In her fifties, he guessed, sturdily built, with a quite delicate face for someone so plump, as though the face and the body did not go together, quite.

"Best thing to happen to me for years, Clive. Keeps this place neat and tidy; as honest as the day is long; a fine woman. Often tempted to give her one, but I shouldn't. Small town. I'd be wading into complications. Don't sleep with the help. Always good advice. But she'd be a goer, I reckon. Must be gagging for it. Husband died, quite suddenly, I believe. Must have been a shock. Son in New York, I think. Lonely. Would welcome a bit of excitement. Fancy a tickle yourself? No? Oh well. So how's it going at the pit face?"

"It's all starting to behave, Roger. You know how material cowers under my cruel whip."

"Excellent. By the way, how's your waterworks?"

"My what?"

"Your peeing. I've been meaning to compare notes. How often do you pee? Any problems?"

"You sound like a keen GP, Roger."

"Well, I used to pee like a horse. Lately, I wait and nothing happens. Then an apologetic dribble. I think it's all over, put it away, and more dribbles out. I'm up four or five times in the night. Is this normal? Is it what we have to look forward to?"

The conversation flummoxed Clive. He was not a doctor.

"Mine's okay. Not as copious a stream as in my youth, but no problem. Have you seen a doctor?"

"No. I wouldn't trust a French medic."

"Why ever not?"

"Clive, French wine, yes, French food, by all means. They have a natural gift. But I don't trust any foreigners with my health. The language barrier could lead to fatal misunderstandings."

"Well, if I were you, I'd check it out. Probably nothing serious, but still… for peace of mind."

Roger was persuaded against his better judgement to visit a doctor in Hyères, whom he was assured spoke excellent English. Dr. Dupont was smooth, charming, and thorough. He spoke English laboriously and with a heavy accent, but in impeccably grammatical sentences. He listened to Roger, sent him off for a blood test, and told him not to worry. When Roger returned he was told that with his PSA—whatever that was—at seventeen, he should have a biopsy. "As a precaution," the doctor said.

When the procedure was described, Roger blanched, said thanks, he would think it over and rapidly left.

If anybody is going to stick anything up my arse, it will be an English doctor in London. I'll think about it.

***

Clive had never met Anna Chisholm, so could not say that he knew her. But he certainly knew of her. She was famous beyond academia and feminism. Through her journalism and public speaking, but particularly her regular appearances on television, she was a celebrity. There was therefore, an aura about her, created by the gulf between thinking you knew her intimately and realising you did not know her at all. She was unavailable and unknowable, living a glamour-plated life with other celebrities, on a planet you were not allowed to visit. Yet she was so often chatting easily and naturally in your sitting room, sharing her thoughts, smiling coquettishly, reprimanding authoritatively, that she was almost a close friend. In reality, she might always be protected behind security in the roped-off area of the club, but you referred to her by her first name, and people knew whom you meant.

She intrigued, dazzled, and frightened Clive, so much that he was glad she had never been within striking distance of him. She had made mincemeat of tougher men than he was, Gunga Din. But he was also drawn to her. The combination of her physical beauty, fierce intelligence, and fearlessness was very interesting. There was also an unspoken class element. She had a sense of entitlement, a sure-footedness in a world she had inherited, which was effortless. In fact, she was so sexy, Clive thought, one would not survive; like that insect, which died after intercourse. Roger clearly had not been intimidated. He had won her heart and seduced her. They had lived together and been a famous couple for some years. Then it had gone spectacularly and publically wrong. Clive looked forward to hearing the match analysed, ball by ball, by the man himself.

First, Clive set down what he knew of Anna. She had been in

her mid-forties when she and Roger had linked up together. He had been early sixties. Had she been affected by him earlier? Had their paths crossed? When she had gone up to Cambridge, he would have been nearly forty, famous, handsome, magnetic, and adored by impressionable young intellectual women. He had a pop star following in the Universities. His passionate feminism, his oratory, and his looks were a heady combination. She could not have been immune. If they had met, he would have been drawn to her. Did they have an earlier affair?

Before she took up with Roger she had been alone. Her son was doing post-graduate work at Cornell. An early relationship had dissolved without fuss. When still in her twenties, she had made her name with a precocious book that placed the sixties and seventies wave of feminism in an historical context. It was learned and clearly written. What took it into the bestseller list was its furious tone and wounding wit. It became an inspiration and a manifesto. It saw the progress of women as a series of historical surges, meeting deadly opposition, and it called for a ruthless fight against the male oppressor. But it was not separatist thinking. She did not side with the dungarees, much to their bitter disappointment. Anna therefore found herself attacked by the supercilious male establishment on her right and a powerful branch of the women's movement on her left, in a time when the tide had gone out on the entire question. It no longer resonated. It was yesterday's obsession. None of this crushed her. Her qualities thrust her into the public gaze. The media fed off her gratefully. She was young, photogenic, assured, quick-witted, and brave. Her enemies were easily caricatured. She never looked back. Although keeping an academic career as a base, her real work was the cultivation of her own celebrity.

Clive had seen her on television recently. He had remembered that up close, at a pre-conference drink soirée, she had looked slimmer. He remembered reading somewhere that the screen puffed people up a little. But either way, your eyes were drawn to her. Even the camera seemed to be trying to start an affair. She had a ripe figure, but was tall and could carry it off. Her hair was long and abundant. Her face was handsome rather than pretty. She seemed to look down on the world with a hauteur that made you cross enough to want to slap her. Then she would dip her head and smile like a shy adolescent, acknowledging her opponent's point, disarmingly. She would look serious, thinking it through for a moment. Just as one warmed to this divine child-woman, she would zap him with a reply, usually in the form of an un-answerable question, leaving him in intellectual tatters. Not a woman to mess with, Clive was sure.

But Roger had felt differently. Maybe it was the challenge. How had it come about and what was the real story behind the implosion?

***

Roger knew that he would have to spill the beans about his relationship with Anna, or at least enough of them to feed Clive's prurient curiosity. He thought his best tactic would be to underline the romantic element and admit the infidelity. It had ruptured their relationship, and gone on public record. It could not be denied. The main object was to convince Clive that apart from this silly, suicidal slip, they had been deeply in love and happy.

What Roger admitted to himself was that when he and Anna had appeared at the Camden Conference, the idea had popped into his head that he could use her as a ride back to the centre of things. By then, over sixty and staring at a looming academic retirement, he had become yesterday's man. It had happened gradually. No committee had summoned him and stripped him of his celebrity, telling him to return to the forgotten past and await death. It had crept up on him in stealth, until one day it suddenly dawned—he was not hot anymore. She was. Hitched to her, he would have access to parties and those casual dinners, full of media types from the Guardian, the New Statesman, and BBC4, who might realise he was available and interesting. He could then become a living legend, back from the dead, available to entertain and inspire a new generation. He did not aspire to be a national treasure. That was too cosy and unsexy. But he wanted to be a star again. Enough of her dazzle would rub off on him. He needed her imprimatur.

You weren't optimistic were you? She'd already knocked you back, about twenty-five years before. Nobody knows that, but I knew she'd remember. It was before THE LONG WAR came out and made a star of her. Written on the back of my stuff, though nobody acknowledged that, least of all her. She was just another student groupie, or so I thought. Very tasty. I walked straight into a brick wall. Definitive. No second try. Do not pass go. Do not pick up the cunt. It's not on offer.

"No, I will not come to your room. And take that hand from my bottom. I am not interested. One, because I am involved with a man already, and he is quite sufficient. I do not cheat. Two, because I think you just want a fuck, one of hundreds no doubt, and I am not anyone's fuck. Three, you are an arrogant, self-regarding cocksmith, a type I never fancy."

She just stood there, I remember, gazing at me as though dismissing a servant from the room. I couldn't believe this kid had just cut my legs off. Afterwards, I wanted to slap her. I managed to raise an eyebrow in an attempt at insouciance and walked away to the bar. I'd been well told.

So my chances of pulling her now looked bleak. A mature middle-aged woman, who was an international celebrity. My stock was in decline. She probably ate men for breakfast by now. But I was up for a try, got to give myself credit there. She was a challenge I could not resist, I suppose. This was my chance.

***

They were sitting outside the Excelsior. It was a calm, sunny day. Clive resisted the impulse to make notes. He hoped to encourage indiscretions. Roger was in an expansive mood, talking about his specialist subject, himself.

"The invitation was a surprise. Somebody obviously had the bright idea to disinter me. It was a panel. It was me and Anna, with two uninteresting kids; one fat and oozing with self-righteousness, the other one a dyke, rather sensible actually, but with her own agenda. It was called, *The New Feminism*. Things seemed to be stirring again, after years of lipstick careerism. Another false dawn, but there you go. Anna was the big established name, the star attraction. I was, I don't know… continuity, a relic of the sixties, the token male, fuck knows. But I knew what I had to do. The trick was not to be too obvious. So I maintained a posture of difference, whilst making sure I agreed substantially with Anna, praising her work. Gruffly, not smarmily. Everyone loves praise. I could see her melting. I ended with saying the next generation should find its own way forward, but hoped it would embrace feminism as a global problem. I knew that was one of her main riffs.

"Afterwards, they lay on drinks, but the student wine was piss, so I suggested to Anna that we could skip away and find a real drink. She agreed and I began to think I was in. We settled in a quiet bar and I was encouraged to see her accept a large whisky. Promising. We looked at each other. For once, I didn't know how to play it, but thought I had to stamp out our last encounter, even though it was ancient history.

"I'm surprised you are having a drink with me. I remember my gross behaviour the last time we met. I want to apologise. I am embarrassed."

"It was a very long time ago, Roger."

"Yes, but it burns in my memory. I have improved."

"By all accounts there was much room for improvement. Your reputation was incendiary, among the women I knew."

"Oh dear. I pick out the word *was* as a lifeline."

"She smiled warmly. Encouraging. "Actually, you were an important source for me when I wrote, *The Long War*. And an inspiration. You were an inspiration to many of us then. I thought of getting in touch with you, to offer my gratitude, but held back, after our little frisson. I thought I might be misunderstood."

"Even more encouraging. The evening progressed smoothly through dinner and a walk. I behaved modestly, listened respectfully, and asked questions as though I wanted to hear her thoughts. I looked into her eyes and refused to allow mine to wonder south, where they wanted to go. I did not touch her, even fleetingly. I said it had been one of the most interesting evenings of my life, what good company she was and I asked would she consider seeing me again. I was quite the gentleman suitor. She gave me her mobile number and hailed a cab. Bingo. I knew it would only be a matter of time. I was playing to my strengths now. I texted her within minutes; she must have still been in the cab. Hoping she slept well, doubting if I would, and thanking her for an entrancing evening. Then I didn't call for three days.

"We did the usual things, meals out, movies, walks in the park. After three weeks, she invited me home, and cooked some pasta. I did not even try to kiss her, but was warm, attentive, and entertaining. She became more girly, not exactly flirtatious, she was too austere for that, but available, less locked up. She had already begun to wear prettier clothes. She clearly was wondering why this horny stud had not made a lunge at her. Was he losing his mojo? Or was she past it?

"So then I found a moment and talked very earnestly to her, about how my feelings had been growing, how I thought I was falling in love with her, and please if it was hopeless, to tell me, it was just too painful, etc. I laid it on, going for broke.

She flung her arms round me, telling me she felt the same, that she had found her soul mate, had always admired me, and now she knew she loved me, too. I took her to bed to clinch the goodies and we were a couple. Mission accomplished. I moved in. It took six weeks. Pretty fast going, I think you'll admit.

"I did actually fancy I was wildly in love with her—it was what I always felt in the first hot flush of romance. Men call sexual desire love, if it's hot enough. But this time it was something else, too. I was in love with her world; her contacts and her reputation. Life seemed perfect. The little house in Kentish Town was cute. Nicely modernised. Close to the tube. She had bought it with an inheritance from her parents. Suited me nicely to be in comfortable digs. To have this star as my lover, re-authenticating me, pulling me back into the limelight, was a career saver. As I'd predicted, with her help, I was soon back on board. I enjoyed the cruise. I enjoyed her. She seemed potty about me. She had spent too many dry years on her own. Keeping her satisfied played to my strengths and although she was already middle-aged, it was not a chore. She was generous, even grateful, and encouraged me to work on a new book. A book which would point the way for a new generation, a new generation I had no connection with."

He knew that he could not deny to Clive that he had fucked it all up. What he needed to do was convince Clive that his feelings for Anna had nevertheless been genuine. He needed to make Clive sympathetic to his weakness.

"Now I'm telling you all this in my usual style, Clive, you would miss it if I changed, but it's partly so I can detach myself from the later hurt. The fact was I loved her and desired her and it was not a calculation. I thought she was the one I could spend my life with, what was left of it. About time you might say. It was very good between us."

"Until...."

"You know the rest, Clive."

"I need to hear it from you."

"Another time. Possibly."

Roger gave Clive a steely look. Clive decided to retreat. He left Roger with his coffee and regrets. He had shopping to do. Alain was coming round for dinner. He was nervous and excited.

***

Roger ordered another coffee and a large cognac. He was lost in the past and in danger of becoming maudlin.

Why did you fuck it up? You stupid cunt. Dick led and accident-prone. Mad. You had it made. What a result. She was potty about you. When she gave it up it was for real, hundred per cent. The sex was amazing, surprisingly. I never thought an overweight middle-aged woman could turn me on like that. But she was ripe and fleshy and gave herself in such a trusting way. In bed, she was not the ball-breaking Commissar. She would cling to me after she'd come and tell me how much she loved me. I think she'd been lonely, actually, before I came along. And horny. I think men were scared of her. Hadn't had one dare come near her for years. So you had a nice home, a luscious woman who took you every-where, just as you'd planned, introducing you, and authenticating you; so proud to be on your arm. Your rehabilitation was going so well, you had a new book coming out, and what did you do? You fucked it up. You couldn't resist an opportunity to get it up.

59

Why did you think you could get away with it? You knew the bitches would stick together. You knew you couldn't humiliate a woman like that and survive. You stupid, stupid cunt.

Each time he went over the events, he beat himself up like this, and achieved nothing. He knew he was self-destructive—the evidence was burned into him—but he did not know why. All he knew was that he had become yesterday's man, again. She had rescued him and given him a better life than any sixty-year-old could hope for, and he had pissed on it. But even now, he could not fully acknowledge his own guilt. His predicament was all the fault of a contingent of women, who had overreacted and conspired to destroy him. It had been excessive and unjust. It was absolutely necessary to convince Clive of this. The effectiveness of the biography depended upon it.

Chapter 7

The next day, Clive woke early, pursued by a puzzling mix of feelings. The walk down the narrow streets, the early sunshine, and the clean smell of the town gave no pleasure. He bought his breakfast from the pâtisserie and sat on his usual bench. It was a tart filled with a cream custard, on top of which was a selection of fresh fruits, raspberries, blueberries, wild strawberries, all lined in careful circles and standing proudly, shoulder to shoulder, waiting to be admired and eaten, daring him to be indulgent. Each morning, the first heavenly bite made him shudder with sensual pleasure. He had been brought up in a restrained, parsimonious family, which had an instrumental no-nonsense approach to life, believing in the virtue of hard work. They distrusted decoration. Unnecessary pleasure was unnecessary — at that moment, sitting in the sunshine, feeding his face in Provence, he was not sure what they would have regarded as a necessary pleasure, but this would not have been one of them. Putting the paper bag in a bin, he strolled to the Excelsior, ordered a coffee, and sat outside. The puzzling thoughts crowded in, followed by feelings he could not quite grasp or identify, as though they were just out of focus. They were disturbing. He had no idea just why he should feel so disturbed.

Alain was the subject. Last night Clive, almost paralysed with nerves, wanted to cook a successful dinner for his friend. But awareness of the quality of Alain's cooking had threatened to strip him of what little skill he possessed. He so longed for the evening to be perfect that he nearly worried himself out of enjoying it at all. But within five minutes Alain had waved away the anxiety. He was warm and relaxed, complimenting the smells from the stove, sliding himself into helping without intruding, making the evening a joint adventure. He gossiped about the town's latest scandal. He admired the cut of Clive's shirt, saying he liked London tailoring. Clive was not used to anyone complimenting his appearance, but was thrilled. He refrained from saying the shirt was actually from Marks and Spencer.

The meal was a success. Not perfect, but good enough to escape humiliation. He had put what he thought was a lot of garlic in the Puy lentil soup, but this was what Alain said made it work. He had then simply grilled some flattened quail, having made a sauce of anchovies, black olives, and olive oil. He served them with a baguette and a salad. The actual grilling, which he had to do at the last minute in front of Alain, unnerved Clive, but Alain cheerfully kept an eye on them as they chatted, and turned them over at the correct moment. Clive had bought a fresh fruit tart from the pâtisserie, partly because it was customary, but mainly because he felt he could not manage to cook a dessert as well. Alain was complimentary and said how well chosen the meal was. Clive suspected he was being nice and assumed it was an expression of his kind personality, but he felt grateful. He certainly seemed uncompetitive, rejoicing in the food and the conviviality. He had a way of simply celebrating life, which Clive envied.

Around eleven, after two coffees, Alain rose and thanked Clive. At the door he hugged him, touched his cheek and left. Clive, who had refrained from coffee on the grounds that it would keep him awake, could not sleep. He was disturbed. Stirred up. Almost uncomfortable. He could not find the exact word. In the end, he decided that he was having difficulty in adjusting to French ways. This was his first close friendship with a French person—the physical intimacy and the emotional openness took some getting used to, if you were an inhibited Englishman, and Clive admitted he was in that category. The French were less restrained than the English were; especially, it seemed, down here in the South. That must be it. He would adjust. This conclusion was only partly satisfying. The French he had come across before, mainly at academic conferences, had struck him as being the opposite; intellectually superior and personally distant. Very confusing.

Whatever the truth of the matter, here he was the next day, the mix of feelings still swirling and refusing to settle.

Never mind, duty calls. This morning I will go over what I can find about Anna, and then confront Roger again.

***

He found some copies of the Guardian neatly folded in a box, indicating that Roger had originally intended to fire back at Anna and those he called *the dungarees*. Clive steadily read through it all again, making notes.

The ostensible subject of Anna's review was Roger's new book, which Clive noted was not actually new. It was largely a collection of speeches and articles, going back to the sixties, interspersed with new material, explaining, excusing, and putting his ideas into a modern context. Clive was very impressed by its cumulative power, even though he had been contemporaneously aware of each piece at its inception. Collectively, it amounted to an eloquent and rallying defence of the rights of women, learnedly planted in the historical record; and a fierce denunciation of the feet dragging, intellectually dishonest and sexist conservatives, on Right and Left, who just wanted to retain their privileges.

Anna's dismissive and contemptuous review was distasteful to Clive, who thought it intemperate and embarrassingly ad hominem, but he had to admit it was witty and wounding, even entertaining in a scandalous way, to everyone but its target.

She had three lines of attack. The first had some grip, in Clive's view, and he wanted to hear Roger defend himself. She was scathing in noting that Roger, during forty years of writing about women, had scarcely mentioned children. He had merely commented in passing that, of course, both parents should be equally responsible for their nurture, as though it were not just a given, but almost a detail. He had been careful in his own life to avoid allowing the sex to lead anywhere. His Utopian project was a world without children. The messy, dependant things had to be nurtured, taking one away from the really interesting stuff, like your own ego. What a bore. So his own world of equality was really a world of male adolescent fantasy—of boys having fun—except that half of the boys happened to be girls. No doubt very generous of him to award these girls equal status but completely irrelevant to most women. His forty years of mouthing off was like the Pope talking about sex. He just did not get it.

Clive was unsure about her second point. Roger certainly had confined his work to the place of women in developed Northern Hemisphere countries, Europe and North America. Anna claimed that this was parochial. He had ignored the global question, which was not just a weak omission, but almost criminal in the light of what we are witnessing on a daily basis. It was inadmissible to know and then to turn away. A few socialist slogans, warmed over from the Nineteenth Century, were not enough clothing to cover a moral nudity. He was a beached colonialist, indifferent and anachronistic. He prided himself on his grasp of history but he had a limited knowledge of it. He had nothing to contribute to the urgent, current debate.

But her review really steamed with venom when she took up the relationship between private behaviour and public beliefs. She began by asking whether we have a duty to connect them, or whether how we behave is irrelevant. Can you be, say, a mass murderer, and yet be taken seriously as a moralist? She invited him to justify forty years of public, lucrative, feminist argument, taking into account his treatment of individual women. Did his cold seductions, his sudden rejections, his rutting, his betrayals, his using women as instruments of pleasure, and his commodification of them, incessantly over forty years, fit well with either his feminism or his socialism?

She concluded that he was outdated, reactionary, dishonest, and irrelevant. He was in the dustbin of history, a mere footnote, and the women's movement had spit him out. His ambition had been for the book to erect him as a role model. Instead, it had exposed him, and it would lead to his detumescence. It was not a celebration of what had been accomplished. It was a warning of the fight ahead. Beware the enemy who says he loves you: he entices you close, in order to stab you.

The effect on Clive had not diminished on this second reading. What word could pin it down? Annihilation, perhaps? Manslaughter? Clive had lived all his life among the feline back-biting of academia, the spitefulness and character assassinations that were routine between colleagues. All that meanness flowed like a polluted underground stream beneath the oily courtesy and conventional politeness of the Common Room. But this tirade, openly in a national newspaper, made no attempt to sugar the bitter pill. Its gossip quotient was increased by the back-story, which elevated it above mere academic or political disagreement. Everyone knew, or was soon informed, that Anna and Roger had been lovers until very recently, although only a few knew the details of their parting. The story was so dramatic, it spilled out from the Saturday Guardian, to news pages and gossip columns.

It got worse. The following Saturday, half a dozen letters were published from women in support of Anna. Each claimed to have had a sexual affair with Roger, to have been betrayed by him and testified to the accuracy of Anna's indictment. One discarded lover wrote calmly, in regret and apology, maintaining that she would never have considered him, but he had assured her that his affair with Anna was over—had burned out and they were now just friends—so he was free to start an affair with her. If she had known, she would never have betrayed Anna, and wanted to say sorry. This letter seemed to skewer Roger even more clinically than the bitter ones. How could this rat hold himself up as a fighter for women? He was a fraud, and at last he had been exposed.

Clive underlined a few of the choice phrases.

"For him women are not humans, they are receptacles."

"He has narrowed his own humanity down to his lust. The triumphant role of women, in his Utopia, is to open their legs, and receive his benediction. Then shut up and disappear."

"Like a heroin addict who will lie, cheat, and steal to get a fix, he will say anything, betray anyone, and destroy all human trust, in order to satisfy the insatiable—his lust."

"We should be careful. Just as all men are not rapists, not all men are like Roger Burton, either. He is the enemy in our midst, but that is not an argument for separation."

So it went on. Clive thought some of them were undergraduate and intemperate, but cumulatively they were devastating. After two or three weeks, it was forgotten. The letters and the editorial comments dried up. At no point was there a public word from Roger. He did not defend himself. He disappeared. This puzzled Clive. His old friend was a combative personality, who was always spoiling for a dust up. Why the silence? That would be one of his questions.

***

Clive knew it would be painful for Roger, so he arranged the conversation with some thought. He chose mid-morning at the Excelsior. Roger, fortified by a coffee and a cognac, was alert and still sober. He looked relaxed enough. Wary, but not hostile.

Clive decided to ease in gently.

"I've read the Anna stuff in the Guardian again, and I think she comes out of it very badly. I imagine you could answer anything substantive in her review, if you can call it a review, and the rest is so ad hominem, methinks she protests too much. It might have been good knockabout stuff for some of her sillier sisters, but anyone with a serious academic, or political, interest would find its excesses distasteful."

Roger's wariness faded. Instead he adopted his brave put-upon face, waiting for Clive to massage him further.

"My first question is, why the silence? No one has heard a peep out of you throughout. That is not the Roger I know."

"What would have been the point? It was obviously a put up job. She was close to the Guardian apparatchiks. They had conspired together, just as she had with those other women all lined up as reinforcements."

"All of whom you had known, intimately."

"Well, there was one who puzzled me. I wouldn't have fucked her with yours. I always thought she was a dyke."

Clive let this go.

"This passivity is still puzzling."

"The Guardian did ask me. Posing as offering a right to reply. Very liberal of them. But really wanting to extend the fun. I decided a dignified silence was appropriate. I would reply in my own time, and in my own way. A dish best served cold; or whatever the saying is. Which is where you come in."

"In that case, some questions. What about the global dimension. She says you are parochial."

"You don't need me to help you deal with that. Yes, I have studied the UK, and the US, in more depth than, say, India, or Saudi Arabia. So what. My socialism has always been international in outlook. And we should be wary of this conscience-redeeming liberal interventionism. To you and me, clitoridectomy is barbaric and cruel. What does she expect as a response? Find a girl so abused and send a gunboat? Who does she think she is, Palmerston? How to intervene is a subtle question. So is whether we should. Are we confident that our ways are always superior? Is overwhelming force the answer? Who is being colonial here? You can make mincemeat of this rubbish before breakfast."

"I'm bucked by your faith in me. The next point is more delicate and personal. You never married and you are not a parent. Celia and I know from personal experience just how central this question is; just how deeply it goes in the renegotiation between individual men and women, and what a challenge it presents to our society's economic and institutional arrangements. The next generation seems to be making a better-tempered fist of it, but the forces of reaction in society are still resistant and make it difficult. What is your response? Do you understand or are you just a male, giving the problem lip service?"

"Twofold. My socialist analysis warned way back that under capitalism, women of all classes would be drawn into the workforce with the result that they would have the doubtful privilege of two full-time jobs, one in the public workplace as wage slaves, the other in the private workplace as domestic slaves. Although seemingly liberating them from the domestic prison, it would prove a poisoned chalice. I argued that the primary task was not to get women into equality at work, which the pushy middle-class careerists wanted, but to get men into the home. The last thing we wanted was to masculinise women. What we needed was to feminise men. Men who want children must stay at home to look after them. I didn't invent the messy trap women now find themselves in. I warned against it. The fact that I am not a parent is irrelevant. She can't win the ball, so she kicks the man. Need I go on?"

"You would be on stronger ground if you had lived you convictions a little more, dirtied your hands in real life, as it were. You have never changed a nappy."

"No. Nor cleaned a toilet. Or used an iron. Or done any cooking, more than make a bacon sandwich. I pay others to do that sort of stuff. All jobs can be dignified and worthwhile. I use my mind and my pen. I teach and speak ideas. The problem is pay. It's a class question. How many times do I need to say that?"

Roger was shouting now. He waved his arm imperiously and ordered two more coffees and another cognac. Clive thought it prudent to close the conversation for today. Anna had got behind his armour and really hurt him. But there was something quietly persistent in Clive. He had Roger in the raw and took advantage.

"So, to get back to your relationship with Anna. You were living together, as partners. For how long? Three years or so? And contented? Yes. So what precipitated all this?"

Instead of exploding, Roger gave a long sigh, sipped the cognac, and looked vacantly over the square. His voice was low. "I fucked it up. Literally. I got the itch. I resisted for ages, but there was this Ph.D. student. She was based at Royal Holloway, so seemed safe enough, no connection with Anna's crowd as far as I knew. Sought me out, flattered me, and asked for help. We met. One thing led to another. I know, Clive, don't say it. I should have known she was trouble. I shouldn't have been playing away, certainly not with her. Highly emotional, neurotic, a bit unpredictable. But tasty as hell, especially after I'd had a few drinks, you know what booze can do for a woman's looks. So I went for her. It led to an affair. Went well for a while. Thought I could get away with it. Then, stupidly, I sacked her. Getting on my nerves, too clingy, and I didn't manage it well. I look back and kick myself. She went hysterical. That made me shut her out completely. I was actually breathing a sigh of relief, thinking it was behind me, a close shave, you know, when it happened. She must have got in touch with Anna and spilled the beans. I came home one evening to find my stuff packed on the front step and a new lock on the door. What a fucking cliché. Two suitcases. No lights on. I banged. No reply. Called her mobile. Message service. Then I saw an envelope. Oh, shit, do you really want me to continue this drab tale? You've got the picture."

"Yes."

"I called a cab and repaired to the Savile. The note said, far as I remember, 'You are fired. Your remaining stuff will be sent on. Do not communicate ever.' Anyway, my other bits and pieces, personal stuff, were delivered to the Savile. I tried all ways to speak to her—if I could get to her; I thought I could talk her round—but I only got through once, using another guy's phone. She rang off as soon as she heard my voice. Absolute silence until the Guardian blitz. Should have been suspicious. Like those war movie sketches. You know the ones. 'It's quiet out there, Sir.' 'Yes. Too quiet.' I should have known she was planning something. Should have known she would punish me. No right of appeal, guilty as charged, get out. My whole world went south from that moment, climaxing, if that is the right word, in the Guardian debacle."

He looked beyond self-pity. Resigned was the word that popped into Clive's head. Resigned and drained. A sad, but not surprising denouement, Clive thought, knowing Roger as he did.

"I think I have all I need. Thanks, you've been a great help. I now have some context for that review, if we can call it a review. I will think it through."

He left Roger, knowing that a quick exit would save him from a long and maudlin lunch. He went back to his apartment, where he planned to make himself a salad. A glass of red with his lunch lifted his spirits and he sat quietly making notes on the morning's conversation. At the end of the afternoon, he decided that Roger's—and Anna's, for that matter—private life was no one's concern but theirs. He would judge her review merely as an appraisal of his book, which it purported to be. Others may judge him as a person, friendly or hostile, but Clive was writing about Roger's life of ideas, about his life as a public intellectual. It was the quality of this, and its place in history, which should mark the boundary. Otherwise, the biography would descend into gossip. History was full of examples of people whose lives may not have been exemplary, but who were interesting for their intellectual and political contribution. He was an historian, not a moral arbiter.

Do I care that Lloyd George was a goat? What possible relevance could that have to an assessment of his contribution to social welfare or the Great War? Dr. Martin Luther King was not a dutiful and faithful husband, by all accounts. Did his cavorting with sundry women have any relevance or legitimate interest to anyone other than his wife? Did it affect his fight for freedom, for the human rights of black people? And even John Lennon. He said women were the niggers of the world, remember—slaves of the slaves. Very good feminist stuff, even though it may have been Yoko talking. But was he a nice chap? Did he treat women well? Does it matter? What relevance does it have to the stature of his work?

Clive pulled himself up short. This internal rhetoric was not like him. He realised he was jumping too far ahead with his fantasies. This was Clive rehearsing the defence of his book on Newsnight. He told himself, in some embarrassment, that preparing for a bout with Jeremy Paxman was rather premature. Nonetheless, as he remarked to Alain, this stance would be a neat way out. He recognised it was more complicated than that. For those who thought that the personal was political, Roger's work could never be understood in isolation from his private life. At the very least, the question of its importance, even its relevance, had to be put. If he avoided that, he would be accused of sanitising him, even of an academic failure of nerve, certainly of protecting an old friend. He would be endangering his own reputation by protecting Roger's. He would have to think this through carefully. Alain had looked puzzled and not a little amused.

"You Anglo-Saxons. You and the Americans. For us, it is just normal. A private life is just that. Why do you become so agitated? It is just sex. People have sex, all kinds of sex, even people in public life."

He shrugged, in what Clive thought was a self-consciously Gallic way, and smiled. He looked superior. Clive decided not to continue this conversation with Alain. He regretted bringing it up. Alain did not take it seriously.

In any case, his private life and feelings were proving quite enough to cope with on their own. He felt alive now. It was exciting and uncomfortable. Was it being away from Celia? That was an uncharitable thought, but possible. Was it the magic of Hyères? Was it to do with Alain? He certainly felt younger than he had ever felt, even when he actually *was* young.

***

Roger was sure he had navigated the Anna problem skilfully. Clive would be on his side now and relieved to be there. So why, he wondered, did he not feel better? He had rarely felt lower. Going over the Anna story so forensically with his old friend had opened the wound. It was the first time he had talked about it with anyone. He ordered another cognac, knowing that the alcohol was an anaesthetic, not a cure. At twelve-thirty he walked up the hill. Marius was closed. He sat at his usual table and a waiter appeared. He ordered a bouillabaisse, partly in the hope that the food would be a balm, and partly to accompany a bottle of the local rosé. When it was finished, he felt no better. He walked unsteadily up the hill, finally wrestled the key into the lock, and sank into his armchair, filling a tumbler with cognac. He drank steadily and professionally, without pleasure. He felt lower than ever. He refilled the tumbler and staggered upstairs, took off his shoes and trousers, an achievement that took all his concentration, and collapsed into bed. At least, he thought, if I can't stand up, I'm in the right place. He was half-sitting and half-lying, his back supported by two big pillows. His head felt like lead, too heavy for him to support. His eyes closed, giving up the struggle, and his head capitulated next, dropping forward, his neck unable to bear the weight. This jolted him awake. He extinguished his cigarette. He had finally reached his nicotine limit. He knew that smoking in bed was unwise and smoking in bed when drunk was possibly suicidal, but he had been doing it since his student days. A cigarette after sex was as necessary as one after dinner. It rounded off the experience.

What experience? Chance would be a fine thing. Anyway, need a splint to keep it upright. Do you live to fuck, Roger? Think you do. I can see the wanker who said that now. What was his name? Wanker. No, I fuck to live. He didn't get it. Oh fuck, need to pee.

He levered himself off the bed and staggered towards the bathroom, holding on to furniture, steadying himself, carefully measuring up the distance before the next lurch. It had become an obstacle course. He passed the wall mirror and confronted his image. It petrified him. He stood motionless and studied this half-naked creature. He wanted to deny all responsibility. This was a drunken fantasy. But he well knew that he did not suffer from the DTs. Not yet. This is what he had become. He was an old, bald, drunk with a grotesque belly, large breasts and a double chin. His face was bloated, his eyes dull, and his hands were shaking. His back ached. So did his left knee. He did not just feel like shit. He looked like shit. This is what he had become. Even he, a practised master of silver-tongued deception, could deny it no longer. The evidence, my Lord, is before you.

He shuffled away in self-disgust and sat gratefully on the loo

Peeing like a girl. Or not peeing like a girl. They go tinkle-tinkle. I used to love watching them having a pee, knickers round their knees, looking cute, waving me away. I sit here and nothing comes for ages, then a few begrudging drops. I'm bursting. Fuck it. I can't go on like this. I'll go to London, few days at the Savile, see the doc, and get it fixed. Have to. Nothing for it. Definitely.

The decision was made. He felt better. Though the thought about what they might do to him made him cringe.

Chapter 8

Roger walked up Brook Street in Mayfair, past Claridge's, and entered the Savile. It occupied two early Georgian houses and was both warm and elegant, a combination managed by few buildings, and even fewer people. He felt a discreet welcome, which comforted him. It was more a nod of acknowledgement than a warm hug, but it confirmed that he belonged and was valued in this exclusive world. He looked about him at the other members. He rarely dined there, but he recognised the same old faces. The long, communal table seemed convivial enough. The food had improved, he was told, and was now rather dashing. The stodgy institutional days had been abandoned. He wondered if they had also bothered to improve the conversation.

Is this where old men come to die? Maybe the younger ones are at home with their wives, enjoying domesticity. The men here will be escaping their wives, having had their fill of domesticity. Get 'em on their special subject and they'll bore the arse off you, but at least you'll learn stuff. Off their special subject, they'll bore the arse off you with prejudice and ignorance. They're all pub bores with money. This may be members only, but it's just a Mayfair saloon bar. Wonder how many here have prostate trouble. Probably most of them. So, correction, this is a place where old men fail to pee.

His ambivalence towards the Savile still prodded him. In his youth, gentlemen's clubs were an easy target. They failed the socialist and the feminist test. He had remembered saying in a speech once that the only way he would ever pass through the front door of one would be with a machine gun. The gag did so well he made it part of his stump speech. There was a gasp, followed by a laugh and then a round of applause. But when old Jeremy, a philosophy don he had palled up with, took him to the Savile for lunch, and suggested he put him up for membership, Roger had been pathetically pleased and flattered. By then, it was the nineties and the symbolism had lost its radical energy. Roger saw a beautiful Mayfair building. What it meant was inclusion, acceptance, and recognition. Membership was a balm to his sensitive ego.

What he now told himself was that, living abroad, it was a sensible place to stay and to meet people in Central London. It was merely a practical matter. The world had ceased to be exercised either way. He looked around expectantly, but his entrance had not caused a ripple. The days when he could expect to be the centre of admiring attention were over. To be the object of polite attention was not enough. The membership had changed. Now it was full of businessmen, hustling deals with their laptops. The artists and writers seemed outnumbered. He took a cognac up to his room.

His first call after arriving in London had been frustrating. His intention had been to let Dr. Grant's surgery know that he would pop round the next morning. But no, it seemed that he was not allowed to make an appointment. These days they granted one, and only after a humiliating interrogation.

Last time I wanted to see him, I just popped along. Now, you bloody well have to beg. How urgent is it? Very fucking urgent. Cheeky sods. What's happened to the National Health? Or am I getting grand? It'll give me time to see Celia. Been ages. I'll give her a call. That's if I'm forgiven.

The call began disconcertingly. Having said it was Roger and asked after her—rather warmly, he thought—there was a long silence. He guessed they had been cut off and blamed his mobile, but after a few seconds she said, "Roger," rather flatly, and left him floundering. He started to speak, pouring on the charm. Her refusal to bat the ball back, to have a conversation, made him feel he was grovelling. In the end she decided that a point had been made, and invited him round, out of curiosity more than a desire to see him.

***

"Marvellous to see you again, Celia. My, you look amazing, ravishing. How long is it? How could we have let the time go like this?"

"Well, that's rich, considering it was you who dumped me. So cut the crap. In fact, you didn't actually dump me. There would have been some dignity in that. A closure, at least, an acknowledgement that something had actually passed between us. What you did was disappear, without a word of anger or regret, no end of chapter, no that was then this is now, turn the page. Did it really mean nothing, Roger? Were you leaving nothing behind? No memories? Do you spend your life walking away from what you've done, from who you are? Or was it just me?"

She was tart, too disengaged now for bitterness. That was all spent, or so she thought. But being alone with him again, or at least a man who movingly reminded her of Roger, was disconcerting. Her exterior was a cool front. Her balance was precarious.

It was not Roger himself. She had always known he was a shit. The truth was it had never been just sex; a pastime she tried to convince herself was over rated. There had been something about this greedy little boy, his selfish neediness, combined with his testosterone-driven masculine aggression, which had forced her to surrender her being, to give herself up. It was beyond rationality. It was demeaning. It was against her principles. It was animal and impossible to fight.

A look across a room, a brief phone summons, even a terse note in her pigeonhole had been enough for her to drop everything and run to him. She hated him for having this power and she despised herself for submitting to it. Yet the arrogant assumption of his right to use her for his pleasure was the very quality that subjugated her. No other man would have dared to speak to her like this, or even imagine treating her the way he treated her. Well, maybe imagine. That was safe. She had never understood what need in her was being satisfied. She could not admit its existence; such was the dissonance between its expression and the beliefs upon which she based her life. Even her most intimate friends would have been shocked, or so she thought. Her reputation with them was important to her.

She looked at him now. Old, paunchy, balding. He had not worn well. His manner was the same. The voice that used to throb through her. The arrogant, charming grin when he wanted something; and the sadistic, cruel face when he was getting it, no doubt. Well, she doubted he was getting any now. But you never know.

"I'm so sorry you feel like that, Celia. I apologise if I hurt you. I don't remember it like that. I remember being consumed by guilt. Wanting you desperately, but too guilty to continue. God, you were beautiful. Are. But you were a family. A lovely daughter. How is she? And Clive, devoted Clive, my best friend, I couldn't bear the thought of it coming out and breaking you all up. It would have been too painful. My conscience couldn't have born it. So I faded out. Cowardly, I know, just to disappear, as you put it, but I didn't know what else to do. I'm sorry, Celia. Can you forgive me? It was a long time ago."

She looked at him like a critic assessing a performance.

Not bad. At least he tried, even though he didn't mean a word of it. Clive, indeed. He didn't give a shit about Clive. Always walked all over him. Oh well, this is the best I will get.

"I'll think about it and let you know. Maybe. Emma is fine, thanks, as far as I know. Living in Canterbury. She comes up with her two little ones, who are enchanting, if you are interested, which you are not. But you know children. They grow up and leave. She was very fond of you. Couldn't get enough of her uncle Roger."

It warmed up after this jousting start. The drink eased matters. She put out some supper and they chatted about the past and moaned about the present; the political work of their youth and the disappointments in the modern world, which had not turned out the way that their youthful idealism had promised. They meandered down memory lane, Celia bringing him up to date with who was dead and who was divorced, who had come out and who was still in the closet. Sharing gossip and scandal drew them together again, despite her wariness.

The wine was going down nicely. He was feeling mellow but had to have a cigarette. He asked meekly if she would excuse him, knowing in advance that it would be prohibited in the house. He stood in the dark garden with an ashtray in his palm. It was spitting with rain. Thinking through the evening so far, he knew it had been a good move to look Celia up again. She would come round, he could tell. Lonely, clearly fed up with Clive—well, he was an old woman—and probably horny.

Hasn't had any for years, probably. Nothing wrong with her that a good fucking would put right. But, God, no thanks, there comes a point when you have to draw a line, not even pissed and in the dark. Not even a Braille fuck. Couldn't get it up, afraid. She was such a great fuck once. Gorgeous. And gagging for it. Women are either moaners or screamers and she was one hell of a screamer. Out of control. Very gratifying. A man likes his work to be appreciated, but embarrassing. Dangerous, considering it was supposed to be secret. But what a turn on. Not now, clearly. Her face all puffy, tits facing south, arse like a carthorse—how did that happen? Why do they let themselves go like that?

He looked back at the house and thought it was a nice little place, convenient for town. He no longer had anywhere in London apart from the Savile. Could be a useful pied-à-terre. Clive and Celia back in his life would be just the ticket.

He lingered past midnight, finishing the bottle of red he had brought. Both of them had demolished hers. He was more than hinting that he wanted to stay, assuming that he could. She was not going to give in like that. The prospect of his drunken weight on top of her, trying to repeat their sexual past, did not appeal. She briskly called a cab. When it arrived, he put his arm round her in a maudlin show of affection, murmuring how wonderful it was to renew their friendship, and how they must get together again very soon. She remained rigidly cordial, her body showing no give. She wanted to get him out, not to encourage him. She knew him of old. He was the type to read encouragement into the smallest gesture.

She left the clearing up, which was unusual. The truth was she missed Clive, who was meticulous. He would never go to bed unless the kitchen was pristine. He cleared up as though he was erasing all signs of a crime and expected a forensic team any moment. Cosy in her bed, her mind was full of the young Roger. He had been a big part of her life, but she remembered her attachment to him as if it was madness or an illness, like the flu. Or an addiction. Yes, that had been more like it, she thought. He had been a need. But she knew what he was like, so why had she allowed it? He had a reputation of being dangerous. She saw through his ideological earnestness and into his vanity. She knew that he was what her mother would have called a rotter. But she had still succumbed. Thinking back on it now, she could not understand. It was embarrassing. Even more embarrassing was how long it had lasted. Was it because all the other women were competing for his favours? Was it female competitiveness? Was it his attentiveness, making her feel special, the centre of the universe? Was it that he seemed to take her seriously, was ready to argue with her, as an equal? That had flattered and disarmed her. The first fateful evening she had torn into him fiercely.

"How dare you pretend to be an expert on women and what they want? Typical man, taking charge. Well, back off, we'll do it for ourselves."

It escalated. For hours. It got brutal. Then he told her he could not live without her, took her to bed, and gave her the most thorough sexual mauling she had ever imagined. More than she had ever imagined, actually. It was the intensity, the urgency. Nothing polite or considerate. No asking permission. She had become used to them minding their manners, showing their tender, respectful sides, being almost apologetic and anxious to please. He took her breath away, leaving her weak and roughed up. It was not rape. She had fought at first, but she had not wanted it to stop and when it did she wanted it all again. She had been making herself come since she was fourteen. One or two men had helped her over the brink. Too many times, they had brought her there and then given up, not having the staying power or the oomph to push her over. There was nothing quite so frustrating. But with him, it was a firestorm. Roger would drag her over and keep going. Afterwards, she would feel calm and more than satisfied. She felt self-satisfied. Cats and cream came to mind. She spent a lot of time smiling, as though in possession of a great secret.

She never understood how giving herself so completely... no, more correctly, allowing him to take her like he was on some raiding party... how that could have been so fulfilling. It went against everything she believed in about herself and about what was proper in the world. She had suspected, without getting too psychoanalytical about it—Freud himself being suspect where women were concerned—that there had been some abuse in the past, probably in her early childhood, which she had repressed and eroticised. So this behaviour was a repetition, a compulsion she had to indulge, and he was another abuser. She had been helpless in the face of it, unable to refuse. She now thought, all these years later, that she had just been horny, and marrying a complete wimp had not helped. She needed a good fuck, which was why she even had him back. Not an explanation she would prefer to put to her sisters.

On that basis, young men like Roger should be chained up like studs, fed red meat, sent to the gym, and brought out when needed to serve their mistresses. You would not have to listen to their whining or flatter their sensitive egos. They would exist to do what they did best.

She smiled happily at this, turned over and went to sleep.

Chapter 9

"**O**h, just a design fault, Roger, I'm afraid." Dr. Grant drew a diagram. "This fellow here, the prostate, not much bloody use at the best of times, expands as you get older—we don't know why—and squeezes into the bladder and on to the urethra. Makes peeing, shall we say, less efficient because of the constriction. No problem. There's a simple procedure. We get at it by pushing a device down your penis and core out a larger exit route for your urine and in a few days you'll be peeing satisfactorily."

Roger looked at him as though he was a mad sadist.

"A rotor rooter... device... stuck all the way down the middle of my penis, reaming through the route the urine takes coming out. Are you fucking serious?"

"Roger, you'll be under an anaesthetic. After you come round you will need a catheter for a day or so. Then, right as rain. We do thousands of them."

This sounds like a medieval torture technique. He's so matter of fact. I've never understood medics. But what else am I to do? I can't go on like I am.

"What happens next?"

"I'll fix you up with the consultant. He will take it from here."

***

Mr. Galloway was in his late fifties, which was reassuring to Roger. He did not want a lad just out of med school practicing on his penis.

I know they have to be trained, but not on me, thank you very much. This chap looks quietly competent and his hands are not shaking. That's good. The medics I remember at Uni were all piss artists.

Roger listened as he purred reassurance. He did so many of these procedures, it was routine. Nothing to worry about. "But before we sort you out, your PSA being... what is it? Yes, seventeen... we'll do a biopsy, just to eliminate anything more serious. Merely precautionary. Nothing to worry about."

Shit, why did I think I could get out of one of those?

***

He was taken into a basement and told to undress. He put on one of those gowns that tied at the back and was told to lie on his side on a medical bed with his legs tucked up and his arse facing two matter-of-fact white coats, one male, and the other female. As he obeyed, he saw a frightening piece of gear attached to what looked like a TV screen. They then started to fiddle with his anus, poking at it in a disconcertingly familiar way.

Are they lubing me up? I never could see the thrill. Looks like I'm about to find out. And all on the National Health.

He felt a probe go right up inside him, suddenly. It was very cold. He gave a sharp intake of breath. There were then six or eight, he lost count, crunching clicks, which did not exactly hurt in a screaming way, but were very uncomfortable. The probe was taken out, his arse wiped and he was told it was over.

"Thank you, Mr Burton. All over. We'll be sending the result to your consultant."

"Could you see anything? Everything where it should be, is it?"

"Well, we have to go through the results, Mr Burton. As I

said, we will be getting them to your consultant, hopefully by the end of the day. He will explain them to you."

***

Roger turned up again to see Mr. Galloway, obediently accepting his secretary's suggestion of a time, with the thought that they can keep you waiting but you are expected to adapt to their diaries.

I wonder if we put up with it because they could legally kill you on a whim and get away with it. Far wiser not to piss them off, just to be on the safe side.

He kept this hypothesis to himself. He had decided to submit to the rotor rooter, horrible as it sounded, get his peeing back to normal and go on with his life. It was all bloody irritating, and frankly scary, but he could not go on like this. He would bite the bullet. Not literally, thank God, not these days, but figuratively. He felt better for having made the decision.

As he sat down, Mr. Galloway looked up from his desk. "The biopsy report is back. Always a wise thing to have one done. We did find something, I'm afraid."

"What do you mean? Find what?"

"I'm afraid there is some cancer."

"Shit, I've got cancer. God. You're telling me I've got cancer?" Roger felt sick and panicky. His heart raced. This could not be true.

"Well, yes, there is some. But you're lucky. We've got it early. All confined to the prostate, we're pretty sure. So, easily dealt with. My advice is that you come in as soon as I can arrange it and have the prostate gland whipped out. Better out than in. If it spreads, you're in real difficulties."

Roger had recovered his composure, putting on an empty face, giving no clue to the turmoil and panic inside. Afterwards, he could not remember much, just the cruel fact, the recommendation, and the consultant's calm reassurances.

Well, it wasn't his fucking prostate, was it? Just his bread and butter.

Mr. Galloway had said something about the risks of

82

incontinence and impotence. A grisly warning about how horrible a death awaited him if the cancer escaped outside the prostate. The fact that some men decide against intervention. "Watchful waiting," it was called. That did not sound very dynamic and decisive. Then he got confused about the options: open surgery, laparoscopy, or something called brachytherapy, which entailed radioactive pellets. Roger did not fancy being bombarded with radioactive pellets. He finally said, "If you were me, what would you do?"

"Well, Mr. Burton, I know a lot of men die of other causes and have cancer in their prostates doing them no harm. But I would hope to go on a long time. I wouldn't take a risk. I'd get open surgery, because we've had the most practice at it. I'd take my chances with the after affects. There are some cases of impotence, less of incontinence, but even those men are alive and well. And I am very careful. I know how important these matters are to one's wellbeing. That's what I'd do. But you may want to think about it. I do open surgery, so you may want to consult elsewhere and talk to your GP."

"Fix it up. Thanks. Soon as you can. Let's get the bloody thing over with."

He went out into the street. It had felt good, that decisive moment, as though he had taken back the initiative. He knew that if he returned to the Savile he might have to be congenial, so he found a bar and started to drink. Some hours, five large scotches, and two sausages later, he felt mellow. Then he did go back to the Savile. In his room, he put *prostate cancer* into Google on his laptop and spent an hour getting more confused and depressed, trying to make sense of the amazing amount of opinion, and fact pretending it was above opinion. The stuff about impotence rocked him back. It was not a small risk. How could he live with a limp dick? The only sex he'd been getting for a while was from internet porn, but a hard on was part of his life.

Be honest, getting one has been harder and harder, hasn't it? As it were. But not to get even a soft hard, to be limp and useless, that would be... Oh fuck, what a prospect. That would be just... Senility.

But the stuff about the cancer running wild was so scary; he knew he had made the right decision. Go with the medics.

Let's hope that bugger has a good eye and a respect for another's manhood.

Things moved surprisingly quickly. He was glad to be caught up in the process. It gave him no time to dwell on it and change his mind. He was told to be at some hospital he had never heard of, in South London—somewhere near Tooting —the following Tuesday, and be prepared to stay a few days. He did not know if this was a stroke of luck caused by a cancellation or if the consultant was a surgeon short of clients. He imagined him standing around, scalpel in hand, urging GPs to find him some victims. Anyway, the train had left the station and he was on it. He had been sent to this man by the GP, who presumably knew his track record, unless he was on a backhander, which could not be ruled out. The man was mature. Lots of experience but still young enough to have a steady hand.

A surgeon with Parkinson's would not fill one with confidence. Do women surgeons do this op? Not on me, that's for sure. Imagine being knocked unconscious and having a ball-breaking career woman with a scalpel getting stuck into your privates. Not a week at Butlins, as my dad used to say about anything even mildly unpleasant.

He decided to call Celia. He knew lots of people in London, but faced with a serious illness he could not think of anyone he wanted to call, or could not be sure of anyone who would welcome the call. He had no friends. This had never occurred to him before. Celia, despite her sharp tongue, was still fond of him, he hoped. They shared a long, secret past. Confessing vulnerability, especially attached to the taboo word, cancer, was a risk, but this was not something he could easily deny. The decider was the thought that he might be dead in a few days.

Instead of Celia, he got her brisk, say-what-you-have-to-say-and-don't-waste-my-time instruction. "Celia Hopkins is unavailable. Please leave your name, number and the time."

"Oh, hi, Celia, Roger here." He would leave his message, giving her enough of the facts, avoiding self-pity, and she would respond or not. He knew her well enough to know that she would despise self-pity and be attracted to courage in the face of danger. That was the tone he aimed to achieve. "Sorry not to have called. I so want to see you again. It was great the other evening; you looking so wonderful. But there's a little problem I have to deal with. A date with a surgeon. Just a little local difficulty, as MacMillan used to say. Hope to be up and about very soon, take you out to dinner. Hugs and kisses." He then added the details of the hospital, as though an afterthought.

That might be enough to get her to visit. Didn't sound too needy. She'll come out of curiosity, if nothing else. Be nice to have someone I can rely on in there.

He packed his case, called a cab, and set off to meet his destiny in an operating theatre somewhere in south London. He could not remember the last time he had ventured south of the river. He had never been inside a hospital, except occasionally with a box of chocolates as a visitor.

***

Celia had spent the day at the British Library, irritated at the overcrowding and the noisy behaviour of the undergraduates.

They shouldn't be allowed in. It is a place for serious research, not the bloody Students' Union. Or, maybe I'm getting old. More likely.

She put down her rucksack, poured a gin and tonic, which she had been looking forward to all afternoon, and flicked on the phone. Roger's message surprised her. His rich baritone, arrogant and presumptuous, tugged her, being attractive and irritating, irritating for being so attractive. The content, as usual with him, provoked questions and was thin with answers.

An operation? He gave no hint of being unwell. He's over-weight, disgustingly so; is it his heart? Knowing him, it's probably an ingrown toenail. It's other people's hearts that get damaged. Surprised if he had one. Ignore the bastard. He ignored you enough. He expects you to go running to him, bringing gifts and sympathy, like some little wifey. Well, fuck him. I've no obligation to Roger.

The gin and tonic did its good work, and she mellowed, mixing a salad and grilling a fillet of lemon sole. She ate, with a glass of Marlborough sauvignon blanc and Jon Snow for company. Even he was starting to look old. It seemed to be happening to every familiar face.

We'll all quietly disappear soon. No one will miss us. The young ones will be too busy, just like we were. The young never take it seriously. It's never going to happen to them.

Later, she lay in bed, unable to sleep. He had rarely been in bed with her when she needed him. Now that she wanted to get rid of him so she could sleep, the bugger was stuck in her mind. Finally she gave up. She knew she would have to go to him. He might be seriously ill. She hated him and loved him.

Love him? Love is not a useful word. It tries to cover so much of the map of human feeling that it's lost its traction. But he's an old man now. He's not the Roger who made me ache with desire. We're all old and we'll be dead soon. I bet that swagger is just an act. He's terrified of incapacity, of his body and mind disintegrating, of death and nothingness. Or is that me, really, projecting?

She did feel lonely and increasingly redundant. Her retirement had made it worse. The world was leaving her by the roadside.

I will visit the bastard. I bet he has nobody else. Discover what's being cut out. Hope it's his dick. The WMD so many women ached for. Get it neutralised, I say.

She smiled, pleased with herself, and went to sleep.

***

"Why go, if it's so irritating?"

Celia had no answer. Maggs always went simply to the point. "Well, I'm under no illusions. My research won't light up the Orange list, won't even find a publisher. Not fashionable, and I'm not young enough or photogenic enough."

"Youth and beauty sells, darling."

"I don't know where else to go. I've been going there so long, well before the new building, which I rather like. It punctuates my day, takes me out of the flat, gives me the illusion I'm doing something productive. What do you expect me to do, walk aimlessly around Tesco in a tracksuit and trainers? I'll do that when I'm finally doolally. I go to the gym, which is more than you do, you lazy cow, but it's so boring. I need to work out the mind, what's left of it."

They were sitting in the shade outside Maggs' French windows, looking on to her long garden. It was late afternoon. The white wine spritzers were refreshing in the heat. Their affectionate bickering had been honed over decades. They had seen each other through crises and managed to be generous with each other's triumphs. It was a friendship that allowed unguarded intimacy.

"What do you think is wrong with him? An operation could mean anything."

"Well, I'll find out. That's why I'm going to visit. I'm curious."

"Are you still crazy about him? Truth now."

"Absolutely not. You haven't seen him. I hadn't seen him, not for years. I hardly recognised him. He is disgusting. An old man, Maggs. Shocking, the change in him."

"Mmm. I think you want to find him vulnerable and dependent. You want to take him home and look after him. You want a tame Roger, at last, that you can have all to yourself. Old or not. And just be careful what you say, I'm old. So are you."

"Maggs, first, we are not old. We are mature and well preserved. Two, I am over him, and if I weren't, one look at him now, and I would be, I assure you. I just think he probably has no one and I can't refuse go to visit."

"Very noble, Celia, and totally unconvincing."

Celia looked at the garden. It was lovely. She did not want a row. "Do you do all this? It must be a lot of work."

"I do the interesting, gardening stuff, and Mark does all the heavy digging and mowing and clearing up stuff. It's called the division of labour."

"You've got him well-trained."

"The key is to pick one who's trainable. Mark came to me like a lost child. I knew he would shape up. The Rogers of this world only take. They are roaming Cossacks. To be avoided."

Maggs had form, Celia knew, and talked from experience. Mark was a sweet bear of a man, ten years younger than Maggs. Potty about her like an obedient Labrador, and just as boring, in Celia's view. He was the third man to get the job. Maggs had divorced number one, the father of her two boys. The second had died of cancer. That had been a bad time. Then she found Mark at a conference in Geneva. He did not stand a chance once she had decided he would do. She reeled him in and they both seemed very happy.

"You don't understand. You were always immune to Roger. Or maybe he didn't try with you. Not really. Is that it?"

"Oh, he tried, as you well know. He kept trying. Even when he was shagging you and disappearing, and coming back and driving you into despair, he was trying me. Couldn't understand why I said no. I clearly like sex, but not with him, somehow. He didn't want me, especially, probably, just didn't like being turned down."

"Well, he wasn't your type, Maggs. We can't help who attracts us."

"Oh, I could see his attraction. I didn't want to be used. I want affection. If they worship me too, for the pleasure I give them, I'll take that. I offer mystery. Men are simple, Celia, they just must never be given the upper hand. It's about power, psychological power. If we have it, we have civilisation. The men are happier, the children cared for, and the world is liveable in. If they have the upper hand, no one is happy. Not even the men. We have to protect them from themselves. Roger was beyond rehabilitation. But you wouldn't listen. You won't listen now."

"Oh, that's the new twenty-first century feminism, is it?" Celia sat taller and her tone was tart. "Train the wild animal or he'll bite? Not exactly the searing class analysis of power relations I've been used to, I must say. And Roger, for all his selfish faults, was very good and brave when we were young. He inspired us."

"He did. True. I admired his brain. But his cock had another agenda. I wasn't going to be on it. Not even as Any Other Business."

They grinned. That was enough of Roger for one afternoon.

"So what's Clive up to, exactly? Is he coming back?"

"I don't know. On balance, I hope not. It's lonely without him, but when he's there he drives me mad. Now he's retired, he just gets under my feet. I used to laugh at that phrase when I was a girl. My Aunties used it. It's the wanting to please with Clive which I find wearing. His dependency. He's down in Provence helping Roger sort out his files, God knows why. Maybe we can expect the Authorised Version. *Horny Feminist; the True Story.* Who knows? Who cares?"

"Poor Clive. I always thought you gave him such a hard time because he wasn't Roger. He couldn't win. The more he tried to ingratiate, the more you beat him up."

"I never beat him up. What a thing to say."

"No, not literally. Though he might have liked it. There's something funny about Clive. I could never put my finger on it. He's not happy. Let him go. He was never for you."

"A lonely old age. Is that what we have to look forward to?"

"No, we have each other. The men will die off anyway, before us. We have each other." She raised her glass.

Celia laughed and raised hers.

Chapter 10

Roger had hoped the hospital would be one of the new PFI extravaganzas, a cross between a glass and steel head office and a Holiday Inn, all white and futuristic. What he saw was worthy Victoriana, a relic designed to intimidate and confine, but which had passed its prime. It was doing its best to keep up and entreating him to make allowances. As he negotiated the signs, filled out forms, and walked corridors to find his ward, he felt like the new boy at school. He decided that rebellion would be punished, so he would hand himself over to authority quietly, his body at least. He would hide his soul and smile.

His ward had eight beds, and six were occupied. He changed into one of those gowns designed for embarrassment and got into bed. He had never even considered private health insurance. A man with his politics—living off those politics, his cynical opponents would say—would be fatally exposed if caught in a private room at the Wellington in St John's Wood. The Daily Mail would have put him through the mincer. But he looked round with disdain at this green ward, smelling of stale stew, and longed for private luxury. He was not rejoicing in the camaraderie of the NHS. Instead, he fondly remembered visiting an old girlfriend at the Wellington.

*Breast cancer, poor kid, dead now. The place was like the
Dorchester, but with doctors. Lovely private rooms and little
balconies, attentive and polite staff. The menu alone was worth
the subscription. They even had a wine list with some decent
choices of claret. I could have just moved in and stayed, knowing
that if any health problems occurred, experts were to hand. Could
be the medical staff were no different from the NHS. The
atmosphere certainly was. Oh, the price of left-wing principles.
Discomfort and poor service.*

"Hello, cocker, I'm Jim. Just come in? Op in the morning?"

A little old man with energy pouring out of him was holding
out his hand. Roger took it in his. It was shaken vigorously. His
manner irritated Roger, who wanted to be left alone, not join some
Senior Citizens' club, but he thought he should humour him.

"Oh, hi. Roger. Yes, I think so. Don't know when, in fact. They
never tell you, do they?"

"Don't worry about it. They know what they're doing in here,
no worries. They're doing me tomorrow. What's yours?"

"Er. Prostate."

"Cancer?" He said the word with a grim relish.

"Yes."

"Same here. Bowel. He's going to cut it out and join me up
again. Explained everything. You're just like me, I told him. How
come, he said? Just a bloody plumber, really. But I don't have to
give the pipes anaesthetic before 'and. I just have a go at 'em. He
laughed. Marvellous what they can do now. Marvellous. Just a
job of work to him. He said I should be out and about in no time.
Good luck, Roger. You'll be all right. They're good as gold in
here."

Having delivered this morale-boosting homily, Jim went across
to the bed opposite and began a cheery conversation with a man
who was dozing off.

***

Roger lay tucked up efficiently in the hospital bed, longing for
a drink. Whisky, cognac, even wine. The evening meal, served
around his usual teatime, had been disgusting, but he now wished

that at least he had eaten the potato. It was early evening. His pubic and stomach hair had been shaved in a detached matter of fact manner by a middle-aged woman who thankfully was not seeking empty conversation. He was now Nil by Mouth, and the chart informed everyone of the fact. He was first on the list for theatre in the morning.

How can they concentrate that early? I hope the bugger doing me is in bed too, and not out on the piss.

The ward was full of sorry old men, some already survivors of the knife.

Well, they wouldn't be here if they weren't, would they? They'd be in the morgue. Can't believe they've put me with all these decrepit sods. It'll be hacking coughs all night. Two doing a snoring duet already. Fuck.

He wanted to go straight back home. He had never felt so low.

I could be dead in a few hours. It happens. Slip of the knife and an artery goes. Heart maybe won't survive the anaesthetic and the trauma of it all. One of those deadly hospital bugs. Read about it all the time. They reckon on killing a percentage. Shit.

He stared around him at the drab, institutional ward. A nurse was checking from bed to bed—a woman commandant with no sex appeal. Actually, it wasn't sex appeal he needed. His dick had shrivelled up, knowing what was planned. It was trying to hide. He craved affection and reassurance. He wanted his mother. But he could not conjure up the young mother he had known as a boy. He kept seeing the old lady in the nursing home, after her stroke, rattling on like a lunatic, her eyes looking but not recognising, her humanity confiscated by Alzheimer's.

That had been a bad way to go. Then he thought of his grandma. He remembered coming home from school to an empty house. The woman next door popped round.

"Where's my mum?"

"You're to go to Oldham, to your Grandma's. Your mum said to go over there."

When he got there, five of his cousins and two of his uncles were sitting in the kitchen.

"What's up here?"

"They're all with her. All the sisters."

His grandma had done the washing, tidied up, and said to her youngest daughter, who lived two doors down, "I'm going to bed now. Fetch your sisters."

She bloody well knew she was going to die. How do you know something like that? They sat round her bed all day and us kids were allowed in for ten minutes to say goodbye. Say goodbye. I didn't know what to bloody say. "Have a good trip, grandma. Hope the weather's nice?" "See you later?" But she didn't look worried. I'd have been panicking, like I am now. Mind you, she believed in heaven. "There's no washing up in heaven," she used to say. But I don't believe that claptrap, and even if I did, I'd still sooner stay here, thank you very much, God, if it's all the same to you.

He badly wanted a strong drink and a ciggy now. He realised that he had never thought about his own death. He was seventy, so he had clearly been in denial.

But what would be the point? It's inescapable. You don't even know the when or the how. What would thinking about it achieve? Get me into a state of mind to welcome it? Well, I don't fucking welcome it. I want to go on enjoying life. I have appetites. I want to eat and drink and smoke. I want to fuck; chance would be a fine thing. Oh shit, what if I wake up after and can never fuck again? Limp dick forever. And have to do everything in a nappy and knickers or whatever they give you. Would I want to live then?

The stark truth hit him. Yes, he would. Even though he would hate life like that, infantilised and pathetic, he would still cling on to it.

He started to weep. It surprised him, the tears just welling up. He gave way to it, quietly. It was even comforting. What was going on? Was he just sorry for himself? Lonely? Was it deeper? Was he in mourning? He realised there were many ways of dying, before the definitive final one.

He drifted off into an uneasy sleep as the tears subsided.

***

Early next morning, he was woken into brisk action. He felt terrible, and to his knowledge had never been awake at this hour in his life. Certainly not since adolescence. It was a shock to his system. He had always been a night person, and would have voted for the abolition of mornings altogether. But the staff had a routine and a schedule. He had to play his part. He knew it was pointless to ask for a drink of water, let alone a crisp bacon sandwich, so he meekly obeyed when a nurse gave him an enema.

They then came and laid him down on a wheeled contraption. He knew that this was the last chance to run. He had no courage, he realised. He was passive and scared and feeling very sorry for himself. A tough, cheery young man towered over him. He looked as though he could hold his own in a pub brawl. He was saying something about an injection. Roger felt a jab. Not too painful, he thought. Then he started to disappear. Oblivion beckoned.

Is this what death feels like? Is this death actually happening now? How are we to bloody well know?

***

He woke suddenly, immediately after losing consciousness. For him, the time in between had not happened. It might have been a century. It might have been an instant. He opened his eyes, wriggled his fingers and toes, and felt surprisingly well. A nurse towered over him, fiddling with things, as they do.

"Hello, sir, how are we feeling?"

Patronising cow. We, indeed. Who does she think she is, the fucking queen?

He gave her a faint smile. She did not wait for an answer.

"All over now. Went very well. No problems. Just lie there for a while and we'll have you up to the ward. Well done."

What did she think I did? I just provided the body. Maybe my exceptional prostate provided the inspiration. I'm alive. You're alive. It's over. Thank God. You're through and out the other side, and the other side feels great.

The euphoria lasted. The relief made him lightheaded. He felt as though he had survived D-Day. He also felt surprisingly well, under the circumstances. No energy, but bright in himself.

Is it relief, or am I on something? If I am, I want the name.
Maybe I could get some on the internet from one of those dodgy
sites in Canada.

The mood ebbed away. He had a drain and a catheter in his
penis. He was exhausted. He was also starving, he realised, but
the lunch smelled disgusting. Far from wanting to eat, he wanted
to wretch. By mid-afternoon he regretted his abstinence and by
the evening he was cursing himself for not bringing in a supply of
chocolate at least. He felt depressed. Or was it melancholy? He
had never been quite sure of the difference, or which applied to
him when in this mood. Anyway, it felt terminal. He knew that a
stiff drink would take the edge off it. But there was not a stiff
drink within reach. Plus, he knew he must face the whole question
of stiff drinks. He had made a bargain with himself, or with the
God he did not believe in, before the operation. Now he had to
keep it.

***

Celia paused as she entered the ward, looking round to make
sure she was in the correct place. Sitting up in a corner bed was an
old man who caught her eye. It was clearly Roger, yet she could
not believe it was him. He looked shrunken and grey, diminished
in a way that marked the invisible transition between a mature and
an old man. He was not the Roger who had been her lover for so
many years; not even the bloated caricature who had recently spent
the evening with her. He was a man she did not recognise, a man
who reminded her of Roger. What moved her was his look of
defeat, the absence of arrogant swagger that used to so anger and
excite her. He just looked forlorn. Was this place the anteroom of
death?

She was upon him before he noticed her. He looked up and
his face broke into a grateful smile, which gratified her. She sat
sideways on the bed and took his hands in hers.

"So, you survived whatever it was. You probably refused
anaesthetic so you could coach the surgeon through the moves. Or
did you dispense with all that and do it yourself?"

He said nothing. His smile was teary. He looked at her fondly and enjoyed the way she squeezed his hands. No woman had ever made him happier than Celia at that moment, just touching him and smiling kindly. Her rough tongue was like a balm.

"Now tell me everything. You were tantalisingly mysterious."

He thought he had nothing to lose now. She listened in growing horror. This was no ingrown toenail. It was cancer, and a serious operation. As he rounded off the story, his style growing in cocky understatement, she realised that another step towards death had been taken. Life was not continuous. It was a series of qualitative moves, each marking a stage. This event was symbolic and literal, not only for him, but for her, too. Seeing him so ill made her full of kindness, a feeling she had never felt for him. She had felt fury, yes. Overwhelming sexual desire, well, that was an understatement, however unbelievable it seemed looking at him now. But not kindness. She realised that he was like a sick little boy who needed mothering. Men are always hopeless when there's anything wrong with them, and he was an archetypical male.

She could see how tired he was. They sat for a while saying little. She asked him if he needed anything, and he said he was starving. She told him that satisfying a gourmet snob was not the NHS's priority, and to eat the breakfast and stop moaning. She would call Clive and let him know. Her manner was brisk and unsympathetic, as usual, but Roger knew her well enough to be warmed by her rough concern. He was not so low now, but felt sleepy.

I'm so tired, couldn't knock the skin off a rice pudding. Hmm. Another thing my dad used to say. Why am I thinking about him? Oh, I'm aching with tiredness. Don't know why, I've done nothing all day.

"I'll pop in tomorrow, and if you're a good boy, I'll bring a treat. Now go to sleep. You look terrible." She smiled, patted his hand and left.

He did as he was told and went to sleep.

***

The moment Celia got home she put the kettle on, sat down, and wept. Both the tea and the tears after a while made her feel better.

Poor man. He does look terrible. Ghostly grey and diminished, somehow smaller. He's old now. No life in him, not like the old Roger. Just deflated. As though life has been drained out of him. Might be the after-effects, he's just had a big op. Maybe he'll bounce back.

Was the ghost in that hospital the same man as the beautiful young God she had loved? Even the air in there had been full of age and decay. You could smell the imminence of death. She would go on losing people, one by one, and then lose her own faculties. In the end, she would disappear like the rest of them. Her grandchildren burst into her head. Their energy and life force so abundant it could be spent with reckless abandon. She thought of Emma as a baby, so miraculous, despite the horrendous forty-eight hour labour. How stubbornly ideological she had been about natural childbirth, refusing even an epidural, just sweating it out in agony and exhaustion. That had put her off having another one. But watching Emma grow was wonderful. Now she was watching others die.

She thought of Roger again and laughed at herself, remembering how much she had hated him at first. But then he had left her and she really did hate him. He had disappeared without trace. Off to New York and no call, no letter, no acknowledgement of who they were for each other. She missed him terribly, but it was the cold rejection that hurt her pride.

I wanted to kill him. Slowly. I had always been angry, but I'd never felt hate. Like that. It was terrifying. He was wise to stay three thousand miles away. Was that why I took up with Clive? The number of times I've asked myself that one. I still don't know. Did I do it to piss Roger off? I hope not. Clive deserves more than that. He was very sweet and adored me. Just worshipped me. I liked that. He couldn't believe it when I pulled him. I'd have waited forever if I'd waited for him to make a move. Came to me like an obedient child. I liked the power. He would do anything to please me. Still would. Irritates me now. But it was balm to my wounds then. I had Emma. Suddenly, a traditional family unit: I remember realising that. A surprise. Clive actually wanted to marry me, begged me, but I thought he just wanted to please his parents.

97

They were prissily hostile to us living together, I remember. I wouldn't take it seriously, which hurt him, but did he really think I would consent to be called Mrs. Kettle? Mrs. Kettle? Good God. But it was a nice time. I did feel fulfilled for a while, I remember. Then Roger came back. Just swanned into town. "Hi." Just like that.

I wanted nothing to do with him. "Fuck him," I said to Clive, "I'm happy, we're happy. Who needs that shit?"

It was Clive who patiently brokered it. Poor sap, he didn't know what he was inviting. "He's an old friend."

I held out for three months, was it four? I enjoyed that, frustrating the bastard, he could never bear not getting what he wanted. Then I gave in. Clive was sitting Emma. I was supposed to be in the library. I was with Roger. It was like the very first time, but wilder. I hit him, hard and often. I fought him, except he wouldn't fight. I drew blood with that ornament, and then he begged to be forgiven, said what remorse he felt, yes, he was a terrible shit of a man, but he couldn't live without me. He made tender love to me. Incredible. Affectionate and delicate, murmuring apologies like a mantra. I melted. He made me come. Only Roger ever made me come like that. With Clive I've never been close, face it. Just a spectator, really, waiting for him to finish. It never took him long, poor pet. He was a trier. I'll give him that. But I was glad when the sex just faded out. So was he, probably. We never talked about it.

She took the tea things into the kitchen and washed them up, putting them on the drainer, not noticing what she was doing. She was on autopilot. Her mind was on Roger.

Looking back now, Roger used me for comfort and sex. When he was lonely or at a loose end. Mainly for sex. I could never say no. Without the excitement of that affair, without him, I would have gone mad, locked up in all that boring domesticity. Funny, he drove me crazy and kept me sane. I didn't want to hurt Clive, or disturb the status quo. We managed it, year after year. Amazing, come to think of it. There was me, the principled feminist, being something on the side. My friends would have been scandalised. They would even now, but no one will ever know. Maggs is loyal, she knows but it will stay with her. It's in the past. It would hurt Clive, and Emma. No need for that. Sometimes, the past should just be in the past. Huh. Fancy me, a historian, thinking that. I'll be up in front of the Central Committee.

***

"Emma sends her love."

"What?"

Even after all the years, he was suddenly alert and on guard. Celia, who had been true to her word, was again sitting on the bed. She grinned. He put on his neutral face.

"She was always in love with you, even as a little toddler. I used to say to Clive, another female falls for his charms; and he would say, a little young, three, don't you think? Then we would laugh at her flirting with you, shamelessly. And you, I might add, flirting with her. But you had to be liked; to capture and charm. You were like that with students, children, dogs, anything with a pulse."

She was still grinning indulgently. Roger relaxed. He smiled, acknowledging the ribbing. "How is she?"

"In unaccountable good form. She actually seems happy, in a boring uncomplicated way I never managed. The marriage seems sound, you can never know, of course, what's going on, can you? But from the outside it's harmonious. He's a good, steady chap. What we used to imagine a new man would be like. Truly. Don't smirk. You could never understand. She's still working. They've found a way to share it all. And the children are divine. I don't deserve it, I know. Probably Clive, all down to Clive. She's terrific. We clash, of course, mothers and daughters. She keeps me at a remove."

There was regret in her face. Roger decided to lift her. "You should take credit with Clive, love. Give yourself a break. You were always a good mother. She was a lovely child."

"Well, she got my looks and Clive's temperament."

"Tough on her if it had been the other way round."

"You are in a vulnerable position, lying there, Roger, and I

99

could give you a smack you would remember."

They were comfortably silent for a moment, looking fondly at each other.

It's true; Emma's body was so like Celia. The long thin legs; in fact her whole torso. Thin arms. The divine bottom sticking out. Celia's face, no, she reminded me more of Clive in the face. And his personality. Easygoing. But Celia's mettle, no doubt about that, you knew about it if you crossed her.

"I'm glad the kid turned out well, Celia. Always thought she would."

"She wanted to come to visit."

"She did?"

"Yes, she's so fond of you still. Uncle Roger. She was upset. But I told her to wait and come to see you in a little while, when you're a bit better."

"I may be in France."

"You're in no condition to go anywhere. You're coming home with me when they kick you out of here, which—with the way you probably behave—will be very soon. I'll look after you for a while."

"Celia, I can't ask you to… You've been a good friend already. I really couldn't…"

"Be quiet. It's not a matter for discussion. You'll do as you're told for once in your life."

She relaxed her stern face, looked at him warmly, and took his hand. He returned her squeeze, moved and worried it would show in a tear. He looked away, down the ward. He so wanted to get out of there.

***

"Is that all she said?"

Alain and Clive were making their lunch in Alain's kitchen. He was almost cutting through half an avocado in thin slices, then fanning it out on the plate most elegantly. Clive did not know which to admire more, Alain's skill or the perfect ripeness of the avocado. In London, their ripeness was sneakily elusive, one moment like bullets, the next black and unappetisingly over ripe. Life was just easier down here.

"More or less. Celia is not one to gossip and speculate. It was not so much a conversation. More a briefing."

"Well, it is serious surgery, Clive. Let us hope the after-effects are not bad for him. He may be... how do you say, not the master of his urine?"

"You mean, incontinent?"

"I think, yes. But also, maybe it is the end of sex for Roger."

"Good God. I'd heard of this, of course, I had colleagues who... but no one went into too much detail."

"He may be lucky."

"Well, I hope so, Alain. An impotent Roger would be a walking corpse"

Alain looked puzzled.

"Never mind. Let us hope the old rogue makes a full recovery. But if he has to give up sex, or at least its possibility, well..."

They both smiled. Clive did feel sorry for Roger and hoped it would go well for him. But he still smiled.

They prepared their lunch. Or Alain did, with Clive the eager apprentice.

Chapter 11

An SS guard, masquerading as a nurse, told him to go for a walk round. He sulkily started a listless shuffle down the corridor, not entranced by the scenery. At the side of the lift shaft, by an open window, he saw a cabal of men, looking round in a furtive way. It was not a place to plan a robbery or even a revolutionary insurrection. His curiosity was sparked. As he drew near, they seemed to relax, and began chatting again. They clearly thought he was no danger to their enterprise, whatever it was. His nose was the lead detective in solving the mystery. Cigarette smoke wafted his way; not all of it had been swept out of the window. Beautiful, sensual, sublime cigarette smoke, blue and cool and sexy, wafting into his soul and sparking the desire he knew he must refuse to satisfy. That was the moment he realised how difficult it was going to be, holding on to the letter of his resolution. Each day from now on, he would be faced with cigarettes, giving their nectar to others, tantalisingly. No whisky at six or cognac after dinner. No extra helpings, all that excess butter, and sugar, and potatoes, and pasta, and... God, was appetite to be denied this man of appetites? Would it be worth extending a life like this, if the very means required to extend it were what made it tasteless? Sex was the appetite he most valued, the primus inter pares, and it was not fattening or dangerous to health. But what if sexual competence had been removed surgically, with his permission? That would be a cruel hit. No wonder he chose not to believe in a God who would do that to a man. He turned round before the furtive slaves to addiction could invite him to join them. He wanted to be given a cigarette, have it lit by a fellow addict, and then breathe the heavenly smoke deep into his lungs. It would not have been as good as the smoke with an espresso, or anywhere approaching the satisfaction of the one after sex, but it would have been undisputedly the highlight of his stay there—a post op smoke, as opposed to a postprandial or post-orgasm smoke. He returned and sat on a chair while she plumped up his bed. A pretty fat thing, officious in a detached way. As sexy as a Union branch meeting. An entirely hypothetical matter anyway, the way he was feeling.

He climbed back into bed and quietly dipped into the bag of goodies Celia had brought. He was starving, despite having picked at the hospital offerings during the day. There was a rare roast beef sandwich with horseradish. Poilane bread. Some green seedless grapes. He would reveal those to the NHS diet police. A piece of fruitcake. Above all, some quite decent claret, sneakily decanted into a Ribena bottle. Bliss. He had not forgotten the resolution about reforming his life. He really would stop smoking, lose weight, and give up alcohol. But that meant spirits. To give up wine, on top of everything else, would have been impossible, and he was not going to attempt the impossible, even for God. An old girlfriend came to mind. She had been lusciously pretty, but an unusual physical type for him, rather plump. Although constantly fighting and losing a battle with her weight, her powers of rationalisation never left her. His favourite was her grave, and incontrovertible, assertion that chocolate was a vegetable.

Well, wine was a food of ancient pedigree. It was health giving. He drank and savoured. Amazing, the effect of a good claret, he thought. Within minutes he was mellow. He settled down in the pillows, shutting out the surroundings. He knew he would sleep soon. Maybe his health would gradually improve. Maybe life was not over. Not yet.

He thought of Emma. All through her childhood she had been a delight. He had enjoyed her flirting outrageously with him. He had enjoyed being the favourite uncle, part of her family, bringing her presents slightly too old and daring for her, to her great delight; and the disapproval of her parents, to her further delight. Celia and he had kept their affair for other times in other places. It was only in adolescence that Emma had become a torment. From about fifteen or so, he could not stop fantasising about her, even when fucking Celia, who by then was in early middle age, the freshness having left her. He knew Emma was out of bounds. Incest almost. She was truly forbidden fruit. This beautiful virgin, innocent, untouched by human hand, nubile… he would just have to bear the longing, leaving her for another man's pleasure. It was like God's justice. He had never longed like this, and he knew it was not possible.

He had watched her become more desirable each month, her clothes more adult and provocative. She was innocent and knowing, a paradox that killed him. An hour in her company, especially alone, was coveted and excruciating, like an existential death.

Pull yourself together. She's eighteen, just going up to Uni, and you're nearly fifty. You're a dirty old man. Anyway, she would never be interested in you sexually, thank God. You're a wrinkly Uncle Roger. So leave it at that.

But it was not easy. She kept seeking him out. Rows with her parents drove her to him. Well, not with Clive, he was too conciliatory. But Celia *did not understand*. That old chestnut. But Uncle Roger would. She also came to his public lectures, even though she was at Queen Mary's and he was at the LSE. He spent hours with her, taking her through the history of the Labour Party and its relationship with the Trades Unions. She hung on his every word, thanking him profusely for his time. He was still quite famous, which helped, he supposed. He had a groupie but he was not allowed to clinch the goodies. God, he concluded, had a mean sense of humour.

Then it happened. He did not seduce her, did not lay a finger on her, nor even chat her up. She came on to him so strong it should have been embarrassing. First, she contrived to insist they meet at his flat. Then she would arrive in clothes that might have led to her arrest. She would sit very close to him and stare into his eyes. It was so obvious and crude, so lacking in guile, so much an adolescent's idea of how you do it, he knew he should just laugh it off. Certainly ignore it. Or, of course, give in to it. Roger, being Roger, gave in.

As with every other time when he was hungry for something he knew he should not have, he pretended he would not, whilst edging towards it, and then reached a point of no return, when nothing could stop him. It was practiced bad faith turned into an art form.

"You're looking attractive today."

This very light and avuncular.

"New boyfriend?"

"No."

She looked into his eyes, one hand under her chin, like an invigilator. She was so close he could feel her breath.

"Do you have anyone, Roger? You never talk about her if you do. Celia says you don't—that you're on your own. Is that true?"

Christ, I'd like to have watched Celia's face in that conversation.

"True."

There was a silence. She continued to look straight at him. It was unnerving, but he could not edge away. This was what they meant when they said pain was exquisite, he thought.

Whatever happened to the male gaze, when I need it? She's killing me here.

"Do you really think I'm attractive?"

"Sure. I always have. The most attractive in the whole world. My favourite. You know that."

Keep it light and affectionate. Uncle with little niece. That might steer us through, give us a bit of distance.

"Then why haven't you done anything about it?"

Roger pretended to look puzzled, managing to shift in his seat and move a little away.

"Clive says you are a ladies' man and smiles knowingly."

"He does, does he?"

"Yes, he does. A quaint expression, but…"

I'd better put a stop to this.

"It's just not possible, Em, you know that. Stop teasing."

"Why not? It wouldn't be incest. You're only a pretend uncle."

"Yes, but I'm old enough to be your father. You should be with a boy your own age."

"Don't tell me what I should and shouldn't do. You are not my father. Are you? Unless…"

Her smile betrayed her mock serious voice, which aimed at mere curiosity.

"Oh, don't tell me… Fuck, Roger, maybe you are my father. Are you? Does Clive know? Have you and Mom been doing the naughties and slipped up? Was I the result? Well, I'm glad you told me, at last."

"Don't be ridiculous."

"Well, if you just don't fancy me, say so. See if I care." She pouted. She was looking upset now, which made her even more desirable.

He made one last pathetic effort, knowing it was a token gesture, but he hoped it would be taken into account, m'lud. "What would your parents say?"

"Fuck my parents. My life is none of their business. They don't have to know, if that's worrying you."

"Oh, Emma, oh my God, Emma."

He was out of ammunition. They had been blanks, anyway, from the start. Token gestures. His heart was revving up on the grid. His hard on was agony against his pants.

This is the most delicious transgression and it's begging me.

He started to stroke her hair delicately. His other hand lifted her chin. She closed her eyes, waiting for the kiss that would irrevocably change their relationship. He kissed her, tenderly, and kept kissing her. She made little, animal whining sounds.

Jesus fucking Christ.

His body was in a hospital bed, and the bed was in a NHS ward, but he was reliving the first time with Emma

That has to be the best fuck of all time. It was the youth; that had to be it, above anything else. We are drawn to youth. The skin, the firm flesh, oh God. The forbidden...

His mind went away from Emma's body. He was in the pantry and his hand was in the biscuit tin. He had to have a chocolate thin. He knew he would be spanked if caught, but the fear and the desire and the high from being so naughty were intoxicating. Almost as intense as the pleasure of the chocolate thin in his mouth.

Emma amazed him. She was not a virgin. She seemed to have no hang-ups about sex, none that he could tell. Although cautious—being, in Roger's view panicky about STDs—she thought sex was recreational. She discussed it in a matter of fact way, keen to learn all she could. This threw Roger off his confident game. It was refreshing, in its way, but it upset his dominance. He had been used to women who, however assertive in their daily lives, carried residual negative and guilty feelings about sex. It was mysterious and forbidden for nice girls. In furious rejection of this conditioning, some decided to take control, but their denials did not convince. They insisted too much. Emma was very natural. She did not claim knowledge of techniques she did not know about, but was ready to try anything. She just really seemed to like sex. It was a marvellous invention and she was glad she was old enough to enjoy it.

"You're a very good lover, Roger. I knew you would be. Practice, I suppose. Or is it just natural genius?"

She looked down on him, smiling, looking relaxed and happy.

It had all been so ridiculously easy. He had feared complications, impediments, risks. The result was simplicity. They were lovers now. It would be their secret. They would do ordinary things together in public as devoted uncle and niece. They would do other things together in his flat.

"Where, Roger, you will pleasure me and educate me in the

fine erotic arts. Well, you're a teacher, aren't you? You have a duty to pass on your knowledge to the next generation."

I was besotted with her. I wonder now if that was my first hint of mortality, that life is a cycle and I was starting the downhill ride to oblivion? I was nearly fifty, an age I dreaded reaching, for some reason. She was a child. Well, a fresh adult. It was as though I was drinking her. There's a phrase, fountain of youth. Yes, as if I could have her, and her youth would reinforce my life, renew it. Mad. Me being with her mother, going from one to the other; that pointed it up. There was enough similarity in their bodies to remind me of the inevitability of aging. You don't want to notice it in yourself.

How on earth did I keep juggling them? Months. And not get caught? I feel good about that, but it was Emma's doing. She did not want her mother's tut-tutting to spoil her fun, and she liked the conspiracy side to it. Lucky me. At least I did not have it on my conscience. God knows what it would have done to Celia. Clive would have just hurt inside, forcing himself to admit that Emma was now an adult. Wimp. Celia would have gone barmy. Maybe dangerously so, knowing her. And I wonder what Emma would have had to say if she had discovered that I was fucking her mother at the same time. Just different days of the week. Take a shrink to work that out. It was close, too. Like a bloody French farce. In one door, out the other, changing bedclothes. It's their perfumes; they're the dead give-aways. Bits of jewellery, especially Celia, fucking earrings lost in the bed. God, I had to wipe the place clean, everything but fingerprints.

And Celia talking to me about Emma, mother confiding in Uncle Roger.

"Do you think she has a boyfriend?"

"I've no idea."

"She talks to you; thought you might know. Never talks to me, says it's none of my business."

"Well, it isn't."

"Suppose not."

"Did you want to tell your mother anything?"

"No, you're right."

But what a time. Alternating those two. Either of them a result, face it, but mother and daughter, that was the turn on. The only thing I never did was have the two at the same time, in bed together. It's happened; some lucky sods have done it. Not a proposition I was tempted to put to these two.

The ward was dark now and deathly quiet, except for the familiar duet of snorers.

They can't even snore in time.

An old man at the other end was whimpering like a lost child.

Poor chap. Hope he's asleep. It feels like a morgue in here, no, the waiting room.

He shut his eyes and Emma came back, wearing a T-shirt. He watched her pull it off over her head, exposing her naked breasts. Her hair was askew and she grinned, asking him to help pull off her tight jeans. That went on for months. Two terms and a vac.

Then she chucked me. No warning. None that I had noticed, anyway. This didn't happen to me. I was the one who got bored and moved on. Served me bloody right, I suppose, but it didn't feel like that at the time. I was furious. My pride, really. I was still mad about her. She was kind, and nice, and warm, and thanked me, it had been brilliant, but she didn't want to do it anymore. We can still be friends, can't we, Roger? I'll always be fond of you. I remember trying to swallow it, pretend insouciance, retain a bit of self-respect, and keep my sangfroid. Fucking hell, I could have killed the bitch. No, we can't still be bloody friends. It was never quite the same after that. She moved out of my orbit. I'd lost her. I took it out on Celia, I know. I was cruel to her. Slapped her, abused her, and fucked her in a rage, as though the fact that her daughter wouldn't fuck me anymore was her fault. Not proud of that now. Celia's a good bird. I think she really loves me. Got a sharp edge to her, but I think she really loves me.

He drifted off into temporary oblivion.

***

He was relieved when they told him he could go home. It was disconcerting to realise that he was not being given permission. It was an order. He was sacked.

I've got stitches, well, more like the work of an office stapler, a bag hanging down and a bloody great pipe sticking out of my cock and you tell me to fuck off out of here, we need the bed. I only had a serious operation a few days ago, in case you have forgotten, and now I'm supposed to cope on my own. Come back next week to outpatients. In the meantime, fuck off out of here. Thank you very much.

The only bit of this he said out loud was, "Thank you very much."

No point in pissing them off. They've got the whip hand. I'll call Celia and see how much of a Florence Nightingale she turns out to be.

Chapter 12

Celia played the role with aplomb. She put him in a mini cab and took him home, giving him the bedroom next to the loo. He felt humiliated, being so helpless, and embarrassed by the medical apparatus, the catheter, and the bag. He was physically weak and depressed. She was brisk and cheerful, having adopted her new role as though her secret ambition had always been geriatric nursing. She enjoyed his dependence. She undressed him and tenderly washed his fat naked body with a sponge. His little cock drooped into the catheter. It, like him, had relinquished its imperious independence. He wept, quietly, looking at the floor. She kissed his forehead and gently helped him to dress. Then she fed and watered him. Every day, she made him take exercise round the small garden and was strict in the enforcement of the rules. No smoking and no spirits, just a little wine.

I didn't need God. She's in charge.

But she was kind. He thrived on the routine and the abstinence. Within days, his skin had colour and some of his old bounce came back. He even started to cheek her, but he knew she was the boss. She savoured this. They would chat in the evenings. They talked about the last fifty years; about socialism, feminism, and their place in it all.

She had fought the good fight as a feminist in the Trade Union movement. She had watched helplessly as the Labour Party had been hijacked and handed over to the enemy.

"There is no movement, Roger, just individual women fighting the glass ceiling. They don't notice the sinking floor. We went from short skirts to manly power suits. Then gay male fashion designers made us look like anorexic boys. Now it's porn-star glamour models and fucking pole-dancing—liberating, apparently. Socialism and feminism? You used to say you couldn't have one without the other. Well, we have neither. Anyway, you were hardly an example. Your brain told us one thing, your cock wanted another."

He felt the sap rise in him again. She was still the same good comrade. He looked at her with affection, certainly gratitude, even though she had not lost her asperity.

"My heart, Celia."

"You never had one, far as I could detect, or it was facing in, not out."

"That's harsh."

"Face it, Roger, have you ever thought of anyone but yourself? Except tactically, to get what you want? Why do you think you have no children—well, none that you know about? Anna left you. How many friends, mm? Real friends? You've loved humanity. Bloody useless with people. A socialist in theory and a fucking exploiter in practice. Your books and speeches will live on after you, and people already talk about and mythologise your teaching. But I have friends, Roger, real friends, and a daughter, and two grandchildren."

"Who you said were a pain in the arse?"

"And so they are. Emma's welcome to them. But they're magic, too. Magic out of me. I look at them in their innocent perfection, so vital, and I want to cry. They would not be in the world if it wasn't for me."

Roger looked at the ceiling. There was a pause. "Men make.

Women create. Men envy the women, cannot forgive them for having this gift, the gift that they have with God, so subjugate them. Then, believing that what women create, they have *really* created, they feel better in their dominion. But it is lying self-deception, and they know it—beneath the posturing, they know it. Oh, I could go on, but shut me up. I'm not in a lecture theatre. I'm just wittering."

"Did you just make that up?" she asked.

"Yes. But I've probably dredged it from stuff other people have thought."

"Well, tidy it up. It's rubbish, of course. But when did that stop you? You could use it."

"What's the point? I've done that all my life, it's what you were just castigating me for."

"I know. But you were good at it. You slick conman. And it was all just to get knickers off wasn't it? You horny sod." She was grinning indulgently at him. Their eyes met.

"Not any more, alas."

She was glad to see his old fire return. It reminded her of how much he had inspired her decades ago. They chatted companionably, sharing the disappointment and puzzlement about the retreats of the last thirty years. He was trenchant about the failures of the left. They argued to and fro on the question of women and how much progress had been made. He said only by the middle class.

"I predicted this and the dungarees and the careerist posh shouted me down. The working class woman has two jobs now. One in the factory gutting chickens, and the other back home cleaning the house and wiping kids' arses. A lot of bloody freedom that's been, where one wage isn't enough, and the women are bigger slaves than before. Late capitalism has just absorbed the women's movement and said thanks very much; we'll have some of that."

"You're like a one club golfer, Roger. You've been pushing that argument since I've known you. It's more nuanced than that. Capitalism won. Socialist ideas disappeared. Young women made what gains they could in the world that appeared. We shouldn't be too hard on them, even though, shit, I want to be. What else were they to do?"

She was glad to see him engaged, even if he seemed to be a throwback to an earlier time. He was alive and looking more like the old Roger.

***

Celia did a last check in the bedroom mirror. She was wearing a tight skirt to the knee.

Am I too old for it? I know what my mother would have said. Even now, I always know what my mother would have said. About everything. Ridiculous. I'm nearly seventy and she's been dead for years. Mutton dressed as lamb, she would have said. Is Emma burdened by me in the same way? She doesn't seem to be but you never know. I hope not. Well, Mum, I'm still slim enough, my legs are my best feature, and I'm going to wear it. So there.

She was aware that she had taken extra care preparing for tonight, trying on different clothes, and spending ages on her hair. For what? She told herself it was normal, that she enjoyed dressing up before a night out, and that one is never too old to be smart and attractive. She was doing it for herself, for her own pleasure, and it had nothing to do with the man downstairs.

He's not even coming with me.

She had prepared a light supper on a tray and she took it in to Roger, who was sitting gloomily in the armchair, in front of the TV. The ads were on and he had dimmed the sound with the remote. He looked her up and down.

"Girls night out, Celia?" The days when he could provoke with the word *girl* were in the past, but he still tried. "You do scrub up well, I'll give you that. Very tasty. Off on the pull? You girls always hunt in packs. Who's going?"

"Just three old friends. You know one of them. Maggs Caldwell."

"Oh, my God. The men'll be running to the hills."

"The evening has nothing to do with men, Roger, difficult as that might seem. South Bank, maybe catch a film. A civilised evening with no male distraction. Enjoy yourself. Be a good boy."

She kissed the top of his bald head and left him. He sat morosely, longing for a whisky and a cigarette. Celia did not stock the former and had strictly forbidden the latter. Maybe it was her willpower rather than his that was keeping him to his resolution. He looked at the Guardian's TV page.

Fuck all on, as usual. What's happened to it? More channels and all crap. Is it me? Or has it been taken over by morons?

Even reading a book seemed too much effort. He thought about Celia and how she looked tonight.

Old woman now. Her bottom's expanded, as they always do, don't know why. I used to love her little bottom. Loved slapping it. Not too hard. Just a bit kinky. Begging to be buggered. Not sure she liked that much, but the submission of a stroppy woman, God, used to turn me on. Never had much in the tit department, but I was never a tit man. My first had huge tits, though, big woman all round. Didn't know what I liked then, really, just amazed it was on offer. Celia's little bottom and long thin legs always got me going. Oh, well, all in the past. She's a good woman. My only long-term relationship, when you think about it. Just known to us. Funny that. She's a trooper to look after me here. I couldn't fancy her now. Do they do it, old women? Doubt it. Into grandchildren.

He thought of the first time he had seen her and remembered the effect this tall slim girl with the beautiful long legs had made. The skirt was short enough to be superfluous, as the fashion demanded. They were in separate groups in the bar. It was agony but he could not take his eyes away.

"Fucking hell, Clive, look at that one in the blue thingy. It shouldn't be allowed. There ought to be a law against it." He poured the rest of his pint down his throat and burped. "There probably is a law against it. God, what wouldn't I give for that? Who is she? Looks posh. Do you know her?"

"No. Never seen her. She's certainly very beguiling. A mischievous smile. Looks arrogant, though. Don't you think?"

"See what she looks like after I've licked her little clit, Clive. I'd fuck her into the next county."

Roger saw her next at his Women's History lecture. She sat near the front, legs demurely crossed, and looked earnest. It almost threw him, but then it inspired him. The lecture took on more fire and passion. It earned a round of applause at the end, which he modestly acknowledged.

They then found themselves opposite each other in a very crowded room, debating tactics for a demo. He had forgotten now what it was about. They disagreed, the disagreement turned into a row and she kept coming back at him, rather tartly. He was used to carrying all before him.

"You could out argue the Brain's Trust, you could, lad," his dad would say. "I say, he ought to be a lawyer, Ada, the way he's going." His mother would smile proudly.

He almost lost his temper with this angry girl, but instead asked her out for a drink afterwards. He had said, "We need to sort this out."

The drink turned into a curry and they went back to his place, still arguing. She maintained that being a man disqualified him from understanding. He could not know what it felt like to be discriminated against. He tried to educate her in class politics. It got very heated, fuelled by the booze.

He could still remember, all these years later, how it had turned him on. He could not stand it. He grabbed her and started to kiss her, trying to get her to open her mouth in his usual way. They struggled for a few moments and then she gave her mouth to him and returned his passion. Clothes were discarded and he was on top of her. Afterwards, they lay in a daze, amazed at the turn of events, although they should not have been, he now thought. That was what their whole fight had been about. She whimpered a little. He cuddled her. She went to sleep. After a while, he was horny again, but decided not to push his luck by waking her. He went to sleep, too.

He woke early the next morning to see her at the end of the bed, dressing. They stared at each other. She looked very grave. She came over to him, looked down, kneeled, and kissed him gently on the mouth.

"That wasn't fair," she had said.

She then left. He lay there, thinking about her. He knew he had to have her again.

And I did. I'd never experienced such passion. It didn't seem English, somehow, yet she was home-bloody-counties English. When we weren't rowing and screaming abuse at each other, horrible abuse, we were fucking like wild animals. It would turn on a sixpence, instantly. I couldn't get enough of her. I think she resented me, hated the effect I had on her, as though it was my fault she needed me. I think now, looking back, that her body and mind were at war over me. It was like that for years. She tried to give me up, flush me out of her, but she couldn't. I used her, I suppose, her attachment to me. But what was I to do?

Why was it so easy in those days? Was it because I was young and good-looking? Probably. But lots of girls like older men, so it can't only be that. I think times have changed. Girls have become savvier now. Can't call them girls anymore, either. When I first got started, it was a golden age for sex, they were all so naïve. Now they know the moves.

His mind wandered with nostalgia to those early days, a whole campus at his mercy. He left behind his present humiliating situation and relived that time. He rehearsed a favourite line, one he had used often. It had never let him down.

"You never had a childhood. You had a girlhood. Think about who your mother wanted you to be. She was training you, in her image. Your father wanted you to be as submissive as she was. Oh, she ruled her kitchen, but who brought the money in? Girls still get married and their fathers give them away. They walk them down the aisle, in front of everybody, and give them away to a younger bloke, called the groom. Very fucking generous. Think. About. Yourself. I want to be your friend. I might want to be your lover. I don't want a girlfriend. I want a woman. A full, equal person. Step out of the girl's clothes and be a woman with me and I'll be a man with you. And I don't want to marry you, and I won't have you even if your bloody father wants to give you to me, because you're not his property, and I don't want you to be my property."

I'd give them this sort of talk in the pub, or over a pizza, or walking in the park. I wouldn't make a pass. I'd listen very seriously and ask for their opinions. Then I'd see them home, telling them they were interesting, and maybe we could meet up again, soon. Then I wouldn't call. Maybe meet them casually around the college, say Hi, and move on, pursuing my busy life. Leave it a week or so, and then suggest a meet. A few of those and she would be softened up, really puzzled about my interest in her. Was I interested sexually? New for her, other men would have made an early lunge. I'd wait until I was sure she was asking the right questions. Aren't I attractive? Is he involved with another woman? And then come to the right conclusion. I want him. I have to have him. Then I'd step forward and claim the prize. Sure thing. Just needed a bit of patience.

He recalled all the demos he went on. The Vietnam ones were the best. Lots of police action, in front of the American Embassy. Expecting to be rewarded with a fuck and some comfort for bravery in front of the pigs. The warrior seduction. That was a good one.

What with the pill, the breaking down of the fifties conventions and Women's Lib, he could not believe his luck. There was sex everywhere and plenty to go round. Thinking about it now, he guessed that it was best from the middle sixties to sometime in the seventies. Then the separatists and the lesbians—the dungarees—had taken over. Men were looked on with caution. Women had got savvier, somehow.

The more he thought back from this distance, the more he realised that the trip to New York was crucial. When he returned, the opportunity seemed obvious. Be a D. H. Laurence for the militant feminists. First be on their side and get access, then be earthy, masculine.

I saw too many blokes get all wet and feminine, thinking that was correct and would ingratiate. Great mistake. Women didn't want men to be like them. What they needed was a right seeing to. A comrade on the demo and a cocksmith in the bedroom. That was the winning combination.

Well, yes, it was, for a while. Look at me now. Why did I think this would never happen to me? I would see old farts around.

Why should I be an exception? Now I couldn't pull and couldn't fuck, even if I could. The thing is, you don't know it's happening. It creeps up and then ambushes you.

***

Celia, Maggs, Audrey, and Sally were on the South Bank, enjoying a drink in the NFT bar, and trying to agree on a vacation out of all the offers in that week's Observer.

"I am not going walking in Crete. Plus, you do not go to Greece for the cuisine. I want to relax and eat well." Sally was firm.

"Well, that's Greece out. And the Baltic tour. That's cured fish and vodka, probably." This was Audrey's negativity.

"This one's favourite, though I can't even pronounce it. Aeolian Islands. Too many vowels, somehow. Anyway, off Sicily, Stromboli spouting off, warm weather, Italian food and wine, dangerous Italian men to look at. What's not to like?"

Everyone agreed with Maggs. Celia would book it and the others would settle up with her. Audrey was a widow, but Maggs and Sally were happy to leave their men behind. They went back a long way together, and valued their friendship, which was surer than any they had experienced with a man. You can lose a man at any time, they used to say; either from illness—so vulnerable—or to another woman. You can fall out with your children, especially daughters. But friends like these were steadfast. Celia and Maggs had met at the Camden Women's Group in the seventies. Audrey and Sally had met even earlier, at the Ruskin Conference. They had drifted apart as their lives got complicated, but now were close again. Maggs had said that their friendship was like fine claret. It changed over the years, but lasted, and in the end improved so much it was unrecognisable compared with its youth. There was a mellow satisfaction to its maturity. They had all liked that.

Audrey was fascinated by Roger and impressed that Celia was looking after him. She only knew of his reputation, which was high but scandalous. She did not know now whether to admire him or despise him. As a young woman, she had admired him from afar, but the recent revelations disgusted and fascinated her.

"What's he really like?"

"He's a total shit and a pompous bore," Maggs said.

The others ignored Maggs and looked expectantly at Celia. They had no inkling of her long affair with him.

"He's an old man. This operation has knocked the stuffing out of him. He's pathetic now, really. He has no family. Clive and I are old friends. We go way back with him—student days—so I'm looking after him. He's not an easy patient."

"None of them are," said Sally. "Do you think all that stuff in the Guardian was true?"

"You bet," said Maggs. "With knobs on. Good for Anna. They don't like it up 'em. He had it coming."

Sally was clearly entranced by the scandal and glamour of Roger's life and felt short changed by Celia's reluctance to indulge in gossip. If only she knew the half of it, thought Celia. She concluded that Audrey was just one of many who had a crush, not on him, but on their fantasy of him. Audrey should see him now.

Chapter 13

By the following week, Roger was much improved. Because of this period of abstinence, he looked and felt better without his prostate than he had felt with it. He still tired easily, but the graph was trending upwards and he marvelled at his powers of recovery. Even at his age, it augured well and he felt optimistic. In a few days, he was due to get rid of the catheter and bag.

Celia looked appraisingly at him over the breakfast things. She was proud that he was progressing so well under her tutelage. Celia had been brought up with the precept that if a job was worth doing, it was worth doing well.

She said, "I have a surprise. Emma's coming up to see you."

"Emma?"

"Yes. That was her, calling to say she was just leaving. Jon will be there for the children. She's been awfully worried about you. She'll stay for lunch. I had discouraged her before. You looked like you were on your way to a funeral. Yours. It would have upset her. But you look almost human now."

"Thanks, Celia. From you, that is a vote of confidence."

He spent most of the morning in his room. He shaved carefully. There was not much he could do about his hair because there was very little to play with. He was liberal with sprays of deodorant and toilet water. He put on a fresh shirt, pale blue, which had just come back from the laundry, and the pants from his suit. They were a little baggy now, but he did not mind. He wanted to disguise the humiliating apparatus attached to his cock. The fact that this elaborate preparation was that of an adolescent boy preparing nervously for his first date entirely escaped him. He told himself it was a sign of his accelerating recovery.

Emma arrived, in a whirlwind of, "Hi mum," and, "They are fine, wanted to know why they couldn't come, think it's not fair, send their love," all in the hall. Roger waited, practicing his nonchalance in the armchair with the Guardian, as though Polly Toynbee's views fascinated him.

"Roger. Mum says you had a fight with a surgeon. No doubt over a woman."

She was in the room with a large grin, her hands on her hips, looking him up and down. She was older, clearly a confident woman now, but still slim, in tight blue jeans and a sweet little blouse, her small breasts breaking the long thin line of her body. She was so beautiful that Roger was thrown. He managed a little smile.

"Hi Emma. Good to see you."

Celia fussed in with some coffee and said she would leave them to talk. She was popping out to the shop, having forgotten the salads to go with lunch. It was a clumsy wheeze to leave them alone to catch up and it amused them.

After the easy stuff, about how he felt now and how awful it must have been; after the ritual of coffee, pouring, and sipping, and biscuiting; after, "Yes, I knew you were married with two children, I talked to Clive, so glad, you look well and happy," there was an awkward silence. They were like two actors who had dried up, the script beyond recall. They were panicking, as they sat paralysed, waiting for the prompt.

Roger realised he was in a state of controlled fury. It hit him from deep inside and came at him in a leap. It was fury he had bottled up years ago. He decided to release it. "Emma, now you're here, maybe you'll tell me why you broke it off. I thought at the time I deserved an explanation, a proper explanation. I didn't get one, nice as you tried to be. Superficially nice. You just chucked me, charmingly. But it was out of nowhere. It was cruel."

What he really meant was that he was not a man to be chucked, especially by an eighteen-year-old girl. She looked at him as though she was trying to decide how to handle one of her children.

"Roger, it was a long time ago."

The implication was, *get over it*. Roger clearly had not, and did not want to. He spoke to her precisely and loudly, as though he was correcting a student in a tutorial. "Emma, there is at least a protocol in these matters. The one who is chucked deserves a credible reason, some sympathy—a sign that the relationship was not worthless. What I got from you was, I won't be seeing you again, and then silence. Are you proud of that? Did I mean so little to you?"

It was only when driving home, esprit d'escalier, did she think that he was a fine one to be giving this homily, considering the way he had callously chucked women, by all accounts. She looked at him and decided to tell him the truth.

"I had missed a period and went for a test. I was pregnant. It was the wrong time and place, and you were the wrong man. I had an abortion. I knew it was time to move on."

This shook Roger. He could hardly believe it. He had never trusted women to take responsibility, despite the pill. He wanted the control. They were treacherous little bitches, often unconsciously, and a pregnant girlfriend was one with cards to play. He used condoms. Without fail. Drunk or sober. But it was possible.

"Was it mine?"

"Of course it was yours, you idiot. What do you think? I was giving it out all over the Students' Union?"

"Then don't you think I should have been told? Don't you think I had a moral right to be part of the discussion?"

"No, I don't. Gosh, this is a surprise. Roger the proud father?

Sticking by his girlfriend and bringing up baby? I never saw you as father material, Roger, and I still don't. You would have thrown some money at me and run."

He knew she was probably right. Her poise and directness was straight from her mother.

"So what did you do? You must have felt very lonely?"

"Lonely doesn't come into it. You're a man. You wouldn't understand. You're disqualified."

"Patronising bitch. Try me."

"No point. I told my mother and she organised it and went with me and looked after me. She was brilliant."

"You told Celia?"

"Not about you, silly. She wasn't curious about the father, just assumed it was a drunken fling with another student."

"I see. So. Neatly done. No consequences. That's something."

"There were consequences, Roger. The sense of loss, the hurt retreated only after I had my babies with Jon. I still sometimes think about it. But you wouldn't understand. As I said, you're disqualified."

She looked gravely at his hurt face. Thinking what a self-pitying baby he was. But she did not blame him for what had happened. She had never blamed him.

"Are you sulking?"

He looked at her with dignity and raised his eyebrows.

"I'm sorry I hurt you. I was in a bit of a panic. I do love you, Roger. And I was potty about you for a while. Don't be cross with me. Let's be friends. It's all years ago. Our lives are different." She looked pleadingly at him.

Yes, you patronising little cow, they are different. Yours is full of everything you want and mine is nearly over.

"Okay. You're a heartless little bitch. But okay."

She laughed in relief. This was the old Roger. Uncle Roger. That's who she wanted.

***

Lunch was convivial. Celia was told about the children. She demanded details and was clearly fascinated by the minutiae. Emma mentioned her own work, in passing. Roger did not understand what it was exactly, except that it was to do with websites and she could do most of it from home. Jon was going to stay in charity work, even though his IT skills were in demand elsewhere. He was comfortable doing it. In fact, things were going well for him, except his football team was facing relegation, which filled him with gloom. Emma had no interest in this but knew she must dance around it sympathetically. Celia and she smiled in that girly way, which infuriated Roger. They agreed she had three, not two, children to look after, the patronising cliché of which infuriated him even further.

What she should really be asking is why she's with a grown man who likes football at all. He has to be a twenty-one carat pain in the arse. Fucking hell, this is bizarre. A stranger coming in here would think we were one happy nuclear family. A few years ago, these two would have been in my bed. I'd have the mother in the afternoon, the daughter in the evening. Now I'm having a cosy lunch with them. Good thing neither of them will ever know. I wouldn't want to be around when that shit hit the fan.

"To your full recovery, Roger. It's lovely to see you." Emma raised her glass of white wine spritzer.

"It's marvellous to see you again, Emma. You're almost as beautiful as your mother, who I have to thank. She missed her vocation." They enjoyed his gallantry. He thought it was the least he could do to round it all off.

After Emma left, Celia wanted to talk about her. "They seem to be more grown-up than we were. More together. We were a bit of a mess, emotionally. Confused. They're more assured. They manage relationships better. Infuriating."

"Why should that be infuriating? It should be a matter for celebration. And self-congratulation. Who brought them up? Don't you think their parents should take a bow if they've turned out well? I suspect you're envious. We're getting old. It's their world now. If they're making a go of it, good luck to them."

None of this gloss even hinted at the twisted views he had of the younger generation, and particularly of this little bitch who had discarded him years ago, but he wanted to make Celia feel better. That was the goal of this conversation. She deserved that.

"Mmm. She's got no politics."

"You did that for her. She's enjoying the world you changed."

"We did so little. It's still a shitty place for women."

"Yes. But not as shitty. Not for women like her."

***

Later that night, he lay in bed thinking of Emma. She was even more aloof and confident, which made it so satisfying when you did nail them. He remembered her at eighteen, watching the passion scarring her face and listening to her sounds; her, "Oh Roger, oh, god Roger, oh."

She loved it then. Couldn't get enough of it. Bet the sex is milquetoast now, by the sound of him. Maybe she's found a version of Clive. Could be. They say they often marry their fathers. Well, if she has, there'll be no fireworks. Just please and thank you. Bet he's polite. What a fucking waste. Will I be up for it again? Ever? Not the way I'm feeling now. Not even a stir.

It was a while before sleep overcame him.

***

He always felt younger again after each return to the hospital. The improvement had been like weights lifted from him. No stockings for clots. No staple. The relief he felt after they removed his catheter made him want to cry. No bag hanging down, nothing sticking up his dick and the biggest relief of all, he could pee on his own, just as he used to. Better, actually. There was no prostate in the way. He could hold it in and let it out. Hallelujah. At the back of his mind had been the fear of having to wear a nappy for the remainder of his life. The ultimate infantilism. Bucked by this, he allowed himself optimism about sex. They gave him some pills and an appointment a few weeks hence.

"Don't worry, sir, see how you do with these. If they don't do the trick we can talk about other ways to help, when you come in to see us again."

Roger had no idea what these ways might be, but he would Google around and see what was what. He was bucked by the air of confidence and would start on the pills and try to have sex. The problem was that he had no one to try it on. A few practice runs on his own would be a good idea.

He called Clive, who said he was making progress with the material, but would not give a timetable.

"There's a lot of it, and it is in a shameful mess. I am trying to turn junk into an historical source, Roger. That takes time. Anyway, how are you? Celia says you are much better. It must have been awful. Poor chap."

"I'm fine and raring to go. See you soon."

Over dinner Roger and Celia had a last intimate chat. She had mixed feelings about him leaving. She had liked his company but wanted to be on her own again. She had concluded late in life that she preferred loneliness, which she occasionally felt when alone, to the daily irritation of having someone else under her feet, having to adjust to them and make the effort to talk to them. But this experience with Roger had been good. She had been crazy about him years ago and now realised she actually loved the old rogue, for all his faults. Or, considering how suspicious she was of the idea of love, she certainly cared. She was proud to have been there for him and to have nursed him through. That was what friends were for. That is what he is now, she thought, and none of us has many friends. But he was only bearable in small doses.

He got sentimental as the evening wore on, which embarrassed her. His gratitude seemed real, though. She looked at him, so different from the young man she had first met, and wondered if age, if not bringing wisdom, at least made us all more appreciative of others, less self-obsessed. Maybe it was dependency. Was that what made little children and very old people more sympathetic than all the rest of us?

"I must get back to my book. See what Clive has made of the material while I've been gone. I think I have one last big piece of work in me. I am so grateful to you, Celia, you are the best. I never deserved you then, and I don't now. But thanks. I promise to keep to the diet and everything. No more excess. That way, I'll live to be a hundred. What do you think, eh? A life of abstinence, but a long one. A hundred?"

"You? A hundred? Does the world deserve to be punished for quite that long, Roger? Keep up the good work if you can. You won't have me to nag you."

Chapter 14

Roger presided like a mafia don at his usual table outside the Excelsior. There was a coffee, but no accompanying cognac, before him. He waved graciously at those who came to welcome him back and enquire about his health. He was touched by this, but hoped no one knew the details of his operation, which lacked glamour and smacked of senility. His new slimmer version was noticed and favourably commented upon, which gave him encouragement. He questioned Clive, rather too imperiously, about his progress on the book.

"The basic organisation of the material is nearly done. A few boxes to go. Some of that looks miscellaneous. I glanced at it. Doesn't seem important, mostly odd notes in your execrable writing. I'll get to it, but there's nothing substantial there. I can see a book, in fact more than one. The question is what book do you want? How far should a subject's life be part of, and inform the account of the work? Childhood creating the man, and so on."

Roger had the expressionless expression of a man in a poker game. He was not sure where Clive was going, so decided to let him get there and reveal himself.

"We don't need to rehearse the arguments. As historians, we

demand everything. We are as curious as any door-stepping, phone-tapping tabloid hack. We want the ideas, yes, and we also want the dirt. But when you are the subject, rather than the object, what do you say? I'll tell you what the book is, after you answer that question."

"What question, precisely?"

"Well, you have had sex, but no relationships. Interesting. Never married. No children. Why? Considering your special subject, as it were, all that is relevant. And your childhood. Even I—I've known you for most of our adult life, and I think we've been close, as close as anyone—what do I know of your background? Only child, Rochdale, working class, council house. Introduced to sex by an older woman. Not much else. Is it relevant? Roger, I'm not suggesting you get on the couch, but as a fellow historian, you know that a book about your life that excludes everything but the library and the activism will be deficient. It will ask more questions than it answers."

"Nice try, Clive. Don't you think Anna and her dungaree friends have said enough? First, I won't stir those dying ashes into flame again and second, I may have been a shit, certainly in their warped vision, but I am discreet. Who I shared a bed with, and what happened there—that's between me and them. End of discussion. My personal history is irrelevant and of no interest."

"You may not be the best judge of that."

"No, but I will be the only judge. Because either I write it myself or whoever does, writes it to my spec."

"Which is?"

"A book of ideas, a history of one man's struggle with those ideas and his wish to propagate, to disseminate, to persuade. A man in the middle of the great political fights of his age. An academic historian who popularised. A polemicist who took the fight to the streets. A history of that struggle for ideas told through the endeavours of that man. A book to inspire the young today. To show how far we have come, and how far we have to go. Part history, Clive, part manifesto."

Roger had assumed his public persona, the baritone voice

rising and his gesture rather too grand for a quiet café conversation. People at neighbouring tables had looked up, noticed that the source of all the noise was the eccentric Englishman, and returned to their coffees.

"So, a book about you, but without you. Just an account of your journey through ideas. An academic book, then, not a popular book. Not one that sells much beyond fellow historians and a few activists. I see."

"Yes, Clive, your sour disappointment perfectly expressed the views of my publisher. What they want is an orgy of sex and scandal, of naming and shaming, of gossip and tittle-tattle, wrapped up in mock innocence as a serious contribution to knowledge. The equivalent of reading a book of porn with a cover and title of modest rectitude. A book that you can buy without embarrassment, read on the tube openly, but that you can actually get off on. That, they think, will sell. They don't put it so crudely, of course; they still pretend to be gentlefolk. They don't say they expect it to fly off the shelves at Tesco. But that is what they think they paid the advance for."

"Which you have already spent."

"Which I have already spent."

There was a long ruminative silence. Roger ordered more coffee. Clive looked out over the square. It was another lovely day. He was having lunch with Alain, who said he knew a restaurant Clive would love. It allowed one to sit outside among some trees, on top of a cliff, and look out to the sea. Clive was happy just thinking about it. It was good to be here at all, but to be shown these little secrets hidden to casual visitors was a privilege. To be shown them by Alain was heaven. He kept pushing away the thought that he had never been happy before, because it was too painful. He did not want to face the implications of the irretrievable loss that an acceptance of that thought would impose. How much life was left, and how much had been wasted?

Roger looked carefully at Clive over his coffee.

Let him stew. Plenty to weigh up. He's a careful, slow thinker. The problem is what do I want? Now? You decided to write it, and then thought it would go down better if you didn't, but James was no help, was he? Said they would jib at a book by Clive, never heard of him, especially a book with no dirt, and as he said, that was not the book he had sold them. Fuck it, what do agents know? Maybe I could promise two books. If my publisher thought they were getting a book of bedroom confessions, the bad boy stuff, which would sell, maybe serialise, then they would hear the ching of the cash register and be content to go on waiting. Another publisher could then do the serious none-seller by Clive in a limited run. A University Press. Clive could get on with that, which is the one I want out there, and I would go on promising I was doing the other. Fuck 'em, I could promise for ever. They can live in hope. I'll have the book that I want out on the shelves carrying the imprint of my reputation. What could they do? Sue me? Wouldn't be worth it. That's the plan. That's the way through it.

"Leave the publisher to me, Clive. If you agree to write the serious, academic book, I can think of no one with more status or qualification. The publisher problem is mine to solve. You won't get an advance, I'm afraid, they won't come up with another one, not in this economic climate, but the definitive book is there to be written. There is the material, open only to you. You've lived through those events with me. I know you said weeks ago that you wanted to think about it. I respect that. But how about it, Clive? One last big book from you. Crown your career. What do you say?"

"Well, our previous conversation had left it open on both sides, as I recall. But now you are formally inviting me to write a professional biography, with full access to all those papers and to you?"

"I am."

"And you will speak frankly to me, without dissembling? I still want warts and all, Roger."

He's like a prick-teasing girl. Little sod. He knows he'll say yes. I know I've got him. But he loves the tease. Turns him on. Oh well. Just like fishing. Give 'em plenty of line, and then haul 'em in. The landing net is waiting, Clive, and you know it.

"Of course, Clive. You already have access to all my papers, the contents of which, I remind you, are unknown to me. I haven't looked at the damned things. God knows what they will reveal about me. I will speak to you in the same unguarded spirit. I trust your academic nose, Clive."

Clive looked at him; trying and failing to preserve a poker face. All this was too much temptation. A reason to stay in Hyéres and a last chance to write something important. What a way to go out. What a way to spend his retirement. He smiled broadly. "Then, Roger, I accept and will start work immediately."

He put out his hand and Roger shook it.

"Good. We should celebrate. Any plans for today?"

"I'm having lunch with Alain. He's taking me somewhere."

"Taking you somewhere. Mm."

"What does that mean? That tone of voice? If you're interested, he knows a lovely restaurant. You sit among trees on a cliff, overlooking the sea. He says it's magical. He is kind enough to want to show it to me."

"I've told you before, Clive, watch that merchant. He's a poof. He'll have his hand in your flies, I'm telling you. Don't encourage him."

"Roger, you could find sex lurking anywhere. He is a friend. We have similar interests and I like him. Really, Roger."

Roger waved his hand. "Okay. I'll say no more. I'll say no more."

***

The restaurant was indeed magical. They had the local fish with some tapenade and a white wine from Bandol. The trees filtered the sun, offering shade and a dappled light. The sea glittered. Clive did not want the afternoon to end. Alain broke the spell abruptly, saying as he rose, "Come Clive, I have something to show you." They went back to the Old Town and walked up the hill. Clive thought they were going back to Alain's place, but after the church, they turned left along Rue Sainte Claire. Ahead was a dead end. They approached a wooden door. Alain confidently opened it and they walked into what looked like a private estate. Ahead was an old house. It overlooked the town.

"Edith Wharton lived here."

They started to climb the hill behind the house, sets of steps offering choices; some to the side and some steeply upwards. All round them was the garden, and its varied magnificence entranced Clive. He had never been a gardener and barely knew the names of anything there, but the clusters of flowers between the different trees and exotic leaves, in a casual excess spreading all over the hill, combined to calm him into a reverence. They sat on a bench and said nothing. Clive listened to the call of the birds, subduing the distant rumble of the town beneath. The clay roofs looked like rustic corrugated iron. There was an enormous sky, clear blue, and cloudless.

Alain took his hand in his and squeezed it gently. He did not return the squeeze, but neither did he withdraw his hand. Was this a French custom? He had watched rough middle-aged workmen greet each other heartily in the street, exchanging kisses on each cheek, so he thought it might be. It felt right, which surprised him, and Alain's warmth, in this setting, made conversation redundant.

***

The next day, Clive got to work with Roger. He had not decided what personal freight the book should carry. He would squeeze as much as he could from Roger and then see. They talked on the way up the hill, avoiding admitting the need to pause for breath by turning to look at the tiled roofs of Hyères and the calm Mediterranean. They made it to the top, sweating, and smiling, like proud athletes breaching the tape, and sat in the garden of the Villa Noailles. Clive looked at Roger.

"You okay?"

"Hundred per cent. Matterhorn next."

"You certainly look so much better already."

"I'm going to keep up this regime, Clive. You've seen nothing yet. This is the start of the new me. I needed that cancer to shake me up. I was getting older, going downhill. Well, now I'm going to get younger."

"I wanted to ask you about regrets, looking back. We have talked about sexual pleasure. You've had more than you deserve of that. But what about the heart, feelings, other people's feelings. Have you ever given thought to those?"

"That's the one thing that worries me about you. Your prissy conventional morality. Distorting your judgement. I've spent my life fighting for women's emancipation. You know that. Equal pay, opportunities, freedom from oppression, childcare, you name it. But the necessary link between sex and pregnancy has been broken, in case you hadn't noticed. So why not fuck? It's the best thing in life. Fun, free and slimming. Why the fuss?"

"Because for some people, not only women, sex is bound up with love, and the idea of fidelity, even babies. A life together. Sex is not separate, a lust which is over in minutes."

"Minutes? Speak for yourself, Clive."

Roger was enjoying this, and to Clive's irritation, he could not make him engage. "The personal is the political. Surely you remember that? Don't you even believe in love?"

"You mean feelings which last longer than an erection?"

"What about Anna, and some of the others, the one with the daughter you mentioned, for instance, you said you were crazy about them. Wasn't that love?"

"No, Clive, it was sexual obsession. That longing is not love. Do you think I'd feel anything if I didn't want to fuck them? I had to go on fucking them, they became an obsession. And you know what they say about a standing dick. Lust is about appetite and satisfying it. I'm starving, I need that lamb chop, I'm going to fucking eat it. You could say I love that lamb chop, if you like. Okay. I've loved women, then. But that's not what women call love. And they're right. It is lust, power, sex—whatever—but it's not love. I don't do love. Doubt if many other men do, either. They pretend to, it makes them more acceptable, more domesticated. But they don't know, really, what it is they're pretending to feel."

"What about family, friends even? It's not all about sex. If I said I loved you—or Celia said she loved you—what would be the difference? It wouldn't make me gay, or her want to have sex with you."

Roger thought he would let this run its course. He did not know where he was going.

Clive asked, "You had no siblings. But did you not love your cousins?"

"I liked one or two."

"Well, your mother? Before adolescence, before sex—or I should more precisely say, as a boy unconscious of sex—did you not love her?"

This was leading Roger into difficult terrain. He had been close to his mother. Rather, she had devoted her life to him, and he had drawn from that well of love since before he could speak. It was a natural given. He remembered how he had felt nothing at her death, acting his part at the funeral, pitch perfect at the wake, being grave and brave and solicitous of others. Then, a week later, he became depressed. It happened one night in the pub. One moment, a convivial evening with admirers; the next, deep despair. It had been like falling over a cliff, into a dark, hopeless place he knew he would never escape. It lasted for eight months. Immobilised. Staring at a wall. Physically heavy. Emotionally black. Then it started to lift bit by bit, two steps forward, and one step back. By the next year, he seemed back to his old self, but that was superficial. He felt older. Alone. He was not the old Roger. He was acting. It was not life being lived. He went on every day, automatically, and knew how to play the role, but it was different. The difference between being and doing. He was brilliant at playing Roger. Convincing. But something had died inside him.

"Yes, of course I loved my mother, Clive, when she gave me what I wanted, and hated her when she didn't. Then I became independent and sentimentality crept in. I did not need her. It's about needs, and sexual need is the cruellest. I suppose it has to be that intense to ensure we propagate, but it subordinates your whole existence. People like us are never dying of thirst, or starving, so we don't know. But I've been so desperate for a fuck that I've thought the lack of one would kill me, or I would sooner die just to escape the suffering. Haven't you felt like that?"

"No, I've felt acutely lonely and longed for love, well,

warmth and affection. But I haven't needed sex, not like that. It's always rather intimidated me, you know? A skill I didn't possess. Like flying an aeroplane, fearing I would crash."

Clive looked pathetic, though he smiled, trying to turn his confession into worldly self-deprecation. "I guess we are talking about the capacity for empathy. You have too little."

"And you have too much."

***

Clive spent the evening alone, letting his thoughts roam. Lately, away from Celia and his London routines, he had felt freer to think about himself. It was no longer indulgent or embarrassing. He sat ruminatively with a glass of wine and some olives, admitting that he had never come to terms with sex. He had grown up in a contradictory age—first, at home where sex was a dark and evil temptation, but never mentioned. Then, in late adolescence with a group of people who openly discussed sex, as though it were just another appetite or interest, like dinner or films—something to be enjoyed, either discerningly or indiscriminately. That's what everyone seemed to be telling him. But he could not. He had sexual feelings, though not as strong as Roger's seemed to be. They were confused and confusing, he now thought, because he had never been honest with himself about them. He secretly wished they would go away and stop complicating his life. Or better, that he had been born in a more discreet, well, yes, repressed age. Victorian, say. Then, sex was unmentionable in polite society, safely repressed. He would have just lived his life.

As luck would have it, he had been young in the sixties, after the pill, in the middle of terrifying feminism. Sex was obligatory. His life had not been made free by all this openness. It had been made false. He had buried his true self from the world, even from himself, and he had gamely tried to play the game. He had done so until very recently—uncomfortably and unconvincingly. As he now sloughed off the studied bad faith of a lifetime, here in the sunny anonymity of Hyéres, he felt lighter, freer, and more optimistic. He still did not know who he was—that old self-indulgent, existential question—but he felt good, as though the sun was relaxing his inner self. He walked differently. He indulged himself with delicious pastries and wine, even at lunch. There had never been a friend like Alain. He had not felt like this about anyone in his life, male or female, even though he could not put his finger on just how he did feel, and did not particularly want to analyse it further. It was wonderful, and he did not want it to end.

Chapter 15

Roger had dined alone at Marius. Clive was at Alain's house. He and the poofter were playing gourmet chefs, no doubt mincing around a bunch of chives. He had enjoyed the daube a la Provençale, and then a Livarot, strong and piquant. A single half bottle of wine had vanished, and left him feeling teetotal. As he walked back up the hill, his need for a cigarette and a large cognac tormented him almost into capitulation. He had never been trained in self-denial. Giving in to temptation had been his life's sensual commitment. He now felt as if he knew what it would be like to go cold turkey off heroin. But something was steeling him. The stay in hospital, facing that surgery, had forced him to look at the physical wreck he had made of himself and he was determined to stay on the narrow path of virtue. He certainly looked and felt fitter. The weight was dropping off, he walked up the hill without stopping to catch his breath, and he was sleeping better. He felt younger and sharper. Just a cigarette and a cognac would make life bearable. The house lacked either, now. He was afraid that late at night, especially, temptation plus opportunity would be his undoing.

It had been raining hard, in that dramatic Provençal way, and the rivulets of water were streaming off the hills and down the streets, but it was fine. The moon was up and the rain had released divine smells, woody and sweet.

A cat shot across the street and dived between his feet, pursuing a rodent. Roger had never liked cats, not even the one at home when he was a child. They reminded him of the most frustrating women, sleek and elegant, self-admiring, seducing with their noses in the air, rationing out affection parsimoniously in exchange for material benefit. Completely independent. Unlike a dog, which always knew its master, you could not own a cat. Instead, they used you. He could never see the point of having anything to do with them. They were for old maids and poofters.

The cat was in the streetlight for a second and then disappeared, but it was enough to throw Roger. In trying to avoid it, he lost his balance and fell. Attempting to break his fall, his upturned arm slammed against a door, his feet slipped on the wet stones and he crashed heavily and awkwardly onto the street. He howled in pain and irritation as he went down, and then lay still, unconscious. The owner opened his door in response to the unexpected knock and discovered the body lying awkwardly on his doorstep. He looked down sourly at the pathetic drunk, deciding whether to leave him where he lay or call the police. His wife eased past him and bent down to inspect the body. He looked like a corpse. She instantly recognised *le professeur*, told her husband to call an ambulance, and ran to Clive's house in the next street, assuming that the other Englishman would stand in for next of kin.

Both Alain and Céline were with Clive, so all three came running. By this time, other neighbours were in the street, tutting over the body. It was turning into a theatrical event, but of little use to Roger, who was now regaining consciousness. Céline took charge. Her Monsieur Roger, the man she looked after every day, was hurt. She made everyone retreat, and called for a pillow and a blanket. She refused to allow any of them to move him. She wiped the blood from the cut above his eye, and talked to him tenderly.

By the time the ambulance men arrived, she was able to tell them that he had been unconscious, that his shoulder hurt, and that his breathing was also painful. Otherwise, he felt bruised and shaken, and feared he might faint. They strapped him up and slotted him into the ambulance. Céline absolutely insisted on accompanying him. Clive and Alain were told to go home and she would call them. They obeyed.

Roger was given an injection that made him feel great, and the pain receded in defeat. He was patched up and stitched. His shoulder was put back and his arm placed in a sling. He was x-rayed. He would be given a brain scan later. Within an hour, he was tucked up in bed, pain-free and comfortable. His suspicion of Frog medicine was giving way to grudging respect, on this evidence.

Not Frog cats and treacherous streets, but what else do you expect.

Céline was by his bed, looking solicitously at him.

"Where did you come from?" he asked.

She talked him through the damage, as far as they had established it. She told him that he might be feeling a lot better now that he was comfortable in bed, because he had been given drugs to ensure this. They would wear off. He would most likely take a little time to recover.

"You are in shock, Monsieur Roger, in addition to the physical injuries. You must take life very quietly for a while, give yourself time."

He smiled. "I'll be fine, Céline. Don't you worry about me. And I wasn't even drunk. That's the pisser."

They kept him in for a couple of days and did a few more tests. He could go home, but only if there was someone to care for him.

Céline said there was. She was as good as her word.

***

Clive arrived and offered yesterday's Guardian. Roger looked at him with a pained expression.

"How are you feeling?"

"Like shit. How do you think I'm fucking feeling? My head hurts, my shoulder's on fire, I'm bruised and grazed all over, and worst of all, two ribs are cracked, the x-ray revealed, thanks very much. But don't worry. It only really hurts when I laugh, so as you're no fun, I'm not in any danger. I could murder a large Scotch. Think that's allowed, under *prescription medicine*?"

Clive smiled happily. This robust complaining and abuse must mean he was in rude health, even though a little dented.

"That would come under self-prescription, Roger, and is therefore up to you."

"You prissy bitch. Does that mean you will bring me a bottle, instead of these editions of Pravda?"

"No, it does not."

Roger stared glumly at him.

***

After about a week, he did start to feel better. He had to be careful with his strapped up ribs and the shoulder sling was a nuisance, but the superficial injuries were clearing up, even the cut above his eye.

His mood was lightening. This was a result of Céline's ministrations. She washed him with a cloth dipped in warm, soapy water, very tenderly, as though he were a big new baby. He watched her serious face as she concentrated on her task. His embarrassment receded and he gratefully gave himself up to her care. She even helped him to the loo. He struggled, leaning his weight on her arm, but insisted on going in alone. He needed to manage that operation solo, however tricky. He had to draw the line somewhere.

She was warmer than Celia, more attentive and a much better cook. She made him tea, strictly according to instructions, although the French milk always messed it up. She made the most delicious dinners. Michelin baby food, he called it, and he spent the afternoons pleasantly anticipating the evening treat. She would bring in a deep dish and place it on a tray before him. As she lifted the lid, the smell would cause saliva to pour into his mouth. He would almost faint with desire. How she did it was above his pay grade, he decided. In Rochdale, it would be just called stew, and he remembered them with affection, but these dinners were more subtle, tantalising, and satisfying in elusive ways. She would sit on the bed, close to him, and feed him, spoonful by careful spoonful. This physical proximity and dependence infantilised him. They talked quietly and intimately. His manner softened as he regressed.

Sometimes you need a fuck, you get a fuck, and you don't need a fuck anymore. Very nice, thank you, ma'am. But sometimes, it's a work of art. It demeans the experience even to call it a fuck. Sometimes what a woman promises, and then withholds, and then offers up with such artistry—it's so deeply satisfying you want to cry, to worship, and long for the need again, so that you can gorge again. Céline's cooking is like that. What's puzzling is it seems so simple. Not many ingredients that I can detect. Pretty ordinary ones. It's not caviar, not even prime rib. Maybe she's a witch, goes out up the hills, and picks wild herbs not known to any cookery book. God, she's good. This is what I've always wanted. Or missed. She's the kindest person I've ever known. To be cared for like this… never wanted a woman fussing over me before, got irritated, too bloody domestic, and suffocating. But this is bliss.

There was a rabbit casserole, carefully deboned, full of creamy, mustardy sauce; a coq au vin, but with the chicken in bite-size pieces, tasting of thyme and mysterious, half-remembered ingredients he might have just been imagining. There was an unctuous potato puree, what he still called mash, which he would have gladly traded a heart attack for.

She doesn't come from Lyon for nothing. That's her secret. She combines that richness with Provence simplicity. Oh shut up, you poncy cunt, you'll end up in Pseud's Corner. Just eat the stuff and be glad.

He lay in bed and remembered his mom deciding to keep him from school, overruling his dad, who would have sent him on the cross-country run with pneumonia. Feeling sorry for himself, but tucked up in his warm bed with his comics, he enjoyed her physical intimacy. She would bring him toast and jam and pieces of homemade fruitcake. Even when he started to feel better, she still sat on the bed, close to him, chatting quietly and seriously, as she watched him eat. It was transgressive in a way he could not articulate, but the fact that its meaning was beyond his

143

understanding made it even more treasured.

He felt this way with Céline. He did not know why this kind, simple woman, virtually a stranger, an employee, was devoting herself so attentively to his recovery. He was brimming with gratitude. He extracted the word hospital from hospitality and especially in the early hours, feeling alone in the world, he quietly cried.

The prostate surgery, which had seemed to ambush him out of a clear horizon, had been a shock. But to be further struck down so soon after, just as he thought he was starting to reap the benefits from changing his life, had shaken him to his core. It was not the superficial damage. That was painful enough, and irritatingly inconvenient. It was his inner self that had been shaken. He knew he could no longer deny the years or their implications. He was now in the last stage of his life. He was winding down. This was depressing. It was the impotence, the inevitability, which made him angry. He was lonely. He had hardly any friends, real friends. No wife, no children, or grandchildren, no family he was in touch with.

Oh well. You reap what you sow, as they say. Stop feeling sorry for yourself.

But here was Céline. He could not imagine her motive, what she might be getting out of it, devoting her life to his well-being.

***

Time, aided by Céline's ministrations, allowed the life force to grow again, despite his distemper. His mood was nakedly exposed by the absence of his usual supports. No more whisky. No more cognac. No cigarettes. Nothing to punctuate the day and fill it out in a haze of cushioned half-life. These indulgences had anaesthetised him and given him the illusion of contentment. When his spirits flagged, he would revive them with another shot. The mornings had been rough, but for the rest of the day, he had floated. Now the pit props had been removed, he feared the roof would cave in.

He was physically recovered. The superficial wounds had healed, his shoulder was right, even the ribs were nearly mended.

Just a twinge when he coughed. No brain damage. In fact, it had been years since he felt so well.

But Céline had returned to her previous regime, and he only saw her three times a week when she came in to clean and do his laundry. The relationship had lost its unspoken intimacy. It was now employer and employee, friendly enough, but it did not assuage his loneliness. Clive would come to the house, busily and promptly, retreating to what was now called the Documents Room and only spending time with Roger to interrogate him about some past event, like a courtroom lawyer trying to discredit him as a witness. Socially, he seemed to spend all his time with the poofter, as Roger, delighting in his incorrigible incorrectness, insisted on referring to Alain.

He feared the future, now there seemed to be a chance of one. A future of lonely old age, forgotten, waiting for debilitating and painful afflictions to overtake him. None of that was going to be tea at the Ritz, he thought. Depression hovered.

***

Céline and Alain were gossiping intimately over coffee, huddled over Alain's kitchen table. They had quickly become intimates, these lonely immigrants, and trusted each other's discretion.

She was not boasting about her nursing of Roger, but she was openly proud. "He is so handsome now, a new man, slimmer; no cigarettes, the filthy things. So charming, And very clever, no? The professor? "

"I think you are falling in love with him, Céline."

She smiled at Alain's teasing. "I only said he was a very charming man."

"Take care, Céline, he should have a warning sign on him. Women beware. Danger. He will break your heart."

"Oh, Alain, we are too mature for this nonsense. Break my heart! I am not a teenager. I do not think a man like you can understand what he does to a woman. You know what he is? He is a real man. But lonely and sad. He needs to be cared for. Men like him cannot look after themselves. He needs to be loved. He has no one."

Alain was too wise to continue his warnings. He knew little of Roger. He should not judge second hand. Clive had problems with him. That was obvious, if not to him. She would follow her heart. What else should humans do?

Chapter 16

Now that Clive was on top of the material, working through it was not drudgery. He was fascinated. The journey brought back his own youth, even though he was a spectator and not a player. He and Celia had been Roger's close friends, Celia first, having had an affair with him. What woman then had not been involved with him? Clive had marvelled at the compulsive energy needed to keep at it like that, but Roger always had been a man of appetite. He was still the same. Even before ordering in a restaurant, he was wolfing down a roll and pining for a drink. No doubt he had broken hearts along the way. He was a selfish boor, certainly. It was unimportant historically. Mere tittle-tattle. The fact was that Roger had been right about important matters, and had been courageously eloquent in arguing the case. Despite everything Clive learned now, he did not expect to change that view.

In fact, the more he dug into the articles and speeches and interviews, with the advantage of a fifty-year perspective, the more impressive Roger seemed. Above all, he had been right to link women's rights to the fight for socialism. He saw it as a class issue, one about property rights. Roger knew that technology, like the pill, had driven things forward. But he continued to hammer home the central connection. "If that is lost, then socialism loses, and feminism loses," Roger used to say. He was scorned and abused by large sections of organised labour. The male Trades Union mind set had been very backward. And since the late seventies, whole sections of middle-class women also refused the political connection, and they had turned on him for being a man—that was a disqualification.

The women that Roger, somewhat incorrectly and provocatively, called the dykes, had kicked him out. Clive made a note—that would be a turning point in the biography. He was looking at reports of a conference in 1975 where Roger had clearly spoken in a way designed to attract hostility. Diplomacy had never found even a niche in his arrogant personality. He had ended by calling them separatists, determined to create an ineffective cult, which historical forces would smash. He had called them political illiterates, and bourgeois reformists who would end up with glittering careers. They would exploit other women—women from the working class—to clean their loos and change their babies' nappies. Having hired other women to be their servants, they would join the men. He had told the dungaree dykes to go fuck each other, if they could, but not to fuck the movement. After he told them that all men were not rapists, but the capitalist system was one big rape, and they were colluding in it, they threw him out.

Looking back on it now, it seemed to Clive that Roger had enjoyed seven or eight spectacular years, not just of fame, but of being in the eye of the storm. He had delighted in this, and used it as a currency to buy the use of women, to flatter his ego, to polish his self-image. Although he continued in academia, eventually being awarded a chair, his life had exploded and faded after the mid-seventies. The spotlight had moved elsewhere, the media constantly needing new sensations. Even through the nineties, he would still be wheeled out occasionally as a rent-a-quote, but he was yesterday's man.

In his compassionate way, Clive thought this slow decline was quite moving, particularly considering the broken old man before him now. The arc of the book was naturally revealing itself as he worked through the material chronologically. That was pleasing and unsurprising. Clive knew that the secret was in ordering material. Then patterns revealed themselves. Hard, systematic work yielded results. There was no magic. But as a man, rather than an historian of ideas, he was curious to hear more about Roger and women. He did not know if it was envy, disgust, or disbelief, but he decided to press him further.

"Women were your downfall. Do you agree?"

"Well, one, yes, Anna. Bitch."

They were walking sedately behind the main square, idly watching a group of solemn French men play pétanque.

"There were innumerable others, Roger."

"But I adored them. I adored Anna once, God help me. The need was terrible all my life. That was the problem. The need for sex. It was like a physical pain. Anything could trigger it. There was no pattern, no physical type. A smile, big eyes, thin legs. Sometimes that long torso you get on slim girls. Then a plump one. A voice… whatever. I was hooked; I had to have her, like it was life or death. All my thoughts would go into seducing her. Some used to fall like ripe fruit, some were agonisingly elusive. I needed to fuck them, Clive, I just had to. I sometimes look back and think that has been my life's work."

"It must be easier now. One of the compensations of growing old."

"What are you talking about? It's worse. I can't pull like I used to. I haven't had a fuck for ages. There's cunt all around. It gets younger. Look at it here, walking about. Sometimes I can't bear it. I want to get on my knees and worship them. Every day, I see one and wish I could spend all afternoon licking them. Just to hear one of them moan again, to plunge into one, Clive. God, I'd die happy. It's what it must be like for a junkie, surrounded by heroin and none of it on offer. It's been like this since I was fourteen."

"We used to joke about you, you know, saying that you should put it away and give it a rest. But I thought sex was a self-indulgent hobby, that you were just horny. This sounds like a compulsion, something you can't help."

"It is. I'm not claiming it absolves me. We are all responsible for the consequences of what we do. Even though free will seems like a necessary fiction—we just need it to hold society together, don't we? I don't feel there's much free-will about it."

"Well, the law certainly agrees with you. In some pleas of mental illness, for instance."

"Thanks, Clive. This sounds like stoned students doing late night philosophy." He looked at Clive and grinned. "Bit old for that, aren't we?"

Clive stared back patiently.

"Okay. I could say that women have free will, so end of problem. Who are you to judge? She slips into my bed. Is her desire subject to her will? Remember old Foucault—we're in France, may as well give that slippery bugger a nod—questioned whether free will was possible in the face of social construction. Good. So, if the women aren't free, willing, and able, then neither am I. It cuts both ways. *I couldn't help myself, your honour. I don't know what came over me. I've been programmed. I need to fuck. It's in the male genes. It's the culture.* Not guilty, on grounds of maleness.

"These are deep waters, Clive. Go and drown in them. I'll stick to political revolution, legislation, equality under the law. The right framework. Consciousness-raising, by all means. I've done my share. Even then, it will take generations. But personally, I don't have time to wait. I'm just going to fuck. Well, I would, if I could get any."

Over the years, Clive had wrestled with feminist theory, but had been too intimidated to question Celia, or anyone. He had never wanted to seem off message. The whole subject was a minefield. Fierce passions were aroused. He had always thought it wise to keep his head down, staying within the narrow lines of correctness. His problem was that, although he could see examples of patriarchy all around him, he could not ever recall personally experiencing male-domination. On the contrary, he felt he had been a lifelong victim of female domination, starting with his mother and ending with Celia. But it felt incorrect, even dangerous, to mention it to anyone.

They were out of the sun, sheltered under a tree, watching the men play. The clink of the pétanque balls and the exasperated sighs of the players made the conversation of these observing Englishmen seem incongruous. Clive thought the English should be playing this innocent game and the French should be discussing sexual obsession. Weren't the English meant to be repressed and the Latins sexually incontinent? Clearly, another empty conventional idea.

Clive said, "I've never felt anything like that for any woman. I've told you, they've always rather scared me, to be honest. Sex with them has felt like an end of term exam I've not done enough revision for." He gave Roger a warm apologetic smile. "There must have been times when there was no one; empty times. What did you do for sex then?"

"I always had a stand-by."

"A stand by?"

"I always tried to make sure that there was one ready whenever I needed it. She had to be crazy about me, of course, and if she was married, we had to be discreet. But it relaxed me to know that any afternoon, if I was horny and short, there was a woman waiting for the summons, aching to give it to me. That made me feel I could cope with life."

"And you found women like this?"

"Oh Clive, you are so naïve. Be mean to keep them keen. Some of the most militant in the women's movement, the assertive women; the ones you'd be scared of, Clive..."

He smiled and looked away at the sporting Frenchmen, as though he had noticed a good move.

Clive broke the pause. "You have someone in mind. Did I know her?"

Roger continued to stare. The pause became uncomfortable. Eventually he looked straight at Clive. "I may be a shit, but I am discreet. I'm prepared to talk about our sex lives, though you're pretty reticent about yours, I notice, but no names. Ever. Understood?"

"Sure, Roger, of course."

Roger relaxed. His face was looking inwards.

"There was one woman. Lasted for years. Married with a little girl, so the stage management of it was difficult. But what a fuck. She loved sex. I sometimes wondered whether I was available to satisfy her, her slave, you know, rather than the other way round. It didn't matter. She was my safety valve. Saved me from bursting. Lust is a terrible master, Clive."

"I'm sure it is."

With that, the two old men strolled back towards home. Anyone observing them could never have guessed the subject of their afternoon's conversation. Old men never think about sex, let alone talk about it. They had just been watching the pétanque.

Chapter 17

One bright morning, fortified by a large black coffee, Roger strolled to the bus station, and hopped on a bus down to the beach. He was determined to give himself a good talking to and thought the bracing sea air would help. He was going to analyse his situation, come up with a plan for his life, and snap out of this downward spiral of inertia.

I've got to be patient with Clive. He's conscientious and productive. There's just a lot to get through. Give him time and a book will emerge. My reputation will be saved. Don't panic. You've escaped death and pulled yourself back from physical decrepitude. You're in good shape. You know what the problem is. Solve it. It's not fucking; it's not about satisfying your cock. You're past all that now. Accept it. You're an old man. With a limp dick. Who no fit woman would fancy anyway.

He extracted this, experiencing it as a dull pain, but he knew it was necessary if he was to have any chance of a life in the actual present. Oddly, having said it all to himself, he achieved an emotional distance. Or at least through the space it afforded him, he could dimly see, for the first time, how remorselessly his physical needs had ridden him. His cock had been a greedy, indulged, spoilt child; peremptorily demanding satisfaction, insisting that everything else should be subordinated to the pursuit and conquest of anyone it fancied.

Yes, true, but I'd give years of the life I might have left, just to be like that again, just to feel a lovely young one melt and open up beneath me, to have the sensation of being inside her.

Well, dream on, that deal is not on the table.

So if I can't have all that, what the fuck do I want? No, what do I need? What's the need now? Be honest.

I'm lonely. It scares me. Not just the dull emptiness of it. I've experienced that, off and on. I'm scared of getting older and older, and dying on my own. I want warmth, a warm body next to me, I want intimacy, tenderness. I want someone to care that I'm bloody alive. It's not just a tidy house, and clean shirts and food on the table. I can buy all that. I want to be cared for, sure, but I want to be cared about. I want to be loved.

He had been loved and admired all his life. More women than he could count had loved him, not wisely but too well, and had broken their hearts on his cruel indifference. He had spent love carelessly because it was not his own. He had not understood it. Filtered through the narrow gauge of sex, it had lost its subtlety and depth. It had become something irrelevant and irritating. He saw that now.

He had walked all along the front, further than he had intended. The sand was giving way to a rocky section of beach, one to be climbed, with puddles to be leapt over. He knew his limitations. Looking back over how far he had walked, and how far he must walk back, he was surprised and pleased. He was not such an old man. Not yet.

The Mediterranean looked sprightly in the breeze and the elegant big white sails were out, catching the sun. He would stay down in Provence. It was healthier, warmer, and more congenial. He would only return to London when he could enter in triumph, vindicated, his head held high.

On the walk back, with the wind behind him, ruffling up what little hair he had left, the sand softly giving way to his weight, something lifted inside him. A half-acknowledged struggle was abandoned. He stopped fighting. He threw in the towel, and he felt lighter. He allowed all his feelings for Céline to pour in, and all the possibilities for the future to sneak in behind them, until his mind could not think of anything else.

Céline. Well, who'd have thought it? My cleaner. My solid, simple little cleaner, dumpy and plain, face it. Has it come to this?

He stopped abruptly, catching himself.

You ungrateful, stupid... social and intellectual snob. Wash your mouth out with soap and water. I hate you sometimes. She's warm and cuddlesome. She speaks ten times better English than your bloody French. She's tender... and fucking human in ways you'll never be. And she wouldn't have you—why would she? She looked after you like a baby, out of the kindness in her heart, that's all. Anyway, they want to be pleasured, they want a man to deliver, as a man. You're a dud.

He phoned for a taxi and sipped a coffee while he waited. Back in Hyères, he ate a couscous at the Arab restaurant near the bus terminal. He walked home and went to bed. He was exhausted. Life was a bitch.

When he woke, the first image in his head was one of Céline. He went downstairs, made some tea, and stood by the sink, sipping it.

She's actually rather attractive, in a homely way. She'd be a ripe handful. Breasts. A change from all those skinny types I used to have. Someone to cuddle. I think she wants a man to look after. She looks the type. Why not me? I'm going to win her. Maybe I'm not a busted flush, sexually. The hospital said come back, didn't they? Might end up making myself look like a prat, but sod it, I can't go on like this.

He bought some flowers in the town and knocked on her door, nervous for the first time since adolescence.

"Ah, Monsieur Roger, ca va?" Her eyes were on the flowers.

He bowed a little, or more accurately, leant forward, presenting the bouquet. "Céline, dear Céline, please, I will never be able to thank you enough for your kindness. Now I am well, I wonder if you would allow me to take you out to dinner. A small appreciation for all you have done for me."

Her eyes widened. She accepted the proffered bouquet. "Monsieur Roger, there is no need. I was happy to help. I am so glad you are well."

"Dinner, Céline?"

"Ah. Well. When?"

"This evening. Pourquoi pas?"

Her face broke into a smile, either at his urgency or his drift into French, but the awkwardness was broken. "That would be good. A quelle heure?"

"Shall I call for you at eight? Huit heures?"

"Yes. Thank you, monsieur." She smiled again, dipped her head a little, and disappeared.

He walked home feeling like a sixth former who had bagged that pretty one in the mall.

***

As he let himself in, he looked at his watch. Ten past five. Plenty of time. He went up to his bedroom and began a leisurely and meticulous toilet. It had been a long time since his last date—in fact, the word itself had not seemed appropriate for years. He could not explain why he felt so young, but it made him happy and excited.

He showered and shampooed what little hair was left. He shaved, carefully. He deodorised under his armpits and sprayed Lempicka au Masculin toilet water all over his abdomen. He dressed casually, but with a crisp white shirt, buttons open, showing some hair on his chest. After much deliberation, and trying on in front of the mirror, he selected a double breasted, navy blue blazer. It looked smartly British and partly disguised his paunch, which, despite his new regime, was stubbornly resistant to shrinkage. He was good to go, and although it was immodest, he thought he looked tasty, for his age. At least she would know that he had made an effort for her, and that must score some points.

She opened her door seconds after he rang the bell, ready and waiting. A good sign, he thought. Her hair was up. She wore dangly earrings, but seemingly no makeup. Roger knew that absence might merely signal subtlety. Her flowery, bright dress was cut daringly low on her generous bosom, supported by a firm, no nonsense bra. She was tightly belted.

"You look a picture, Céline."

She frowned. "A picture? Monsieur?"

"Yes. Like a painting. A beautiful painting. A work of art."

"Oh, monsieur, you make fun with me."

"No, Céline, on the contrary."

She blushed a little, smiled, and looked down, like the adolescent she was overjoyed to be that evening. Then she took his arm as they negotiated the steep hill to Marius. Her heels were high.

They sat on the square in the warm evening. He ordered champagne, which they drank with the oysters. Then there was a sweet Beaune with the chicken, in honour of her native Burgundy, a detail she acknowledged with a shy smile and a nod. They chatted and their adolescent awkwardness dissolved.

She told him that her husband's health had been delicate, so they sold their charcuterie in order to retire when he was sixty. Hyéres had a reputation for longevity and they had fallen in love with the Old Town. The hours had been long for both of them and they looked forward to a life of quiet leisure together. But he died suddenly one evening, of a heart attack, just three months after they had settled. She was alone in a new home, bereft. Their only son was a pâtissier in New York, doing very well, and was unlikely to return to France.

She recounted this quietly and unsentimentally. He was moved not by the facts—shit happens—but by her refusal to milk them.

Yes, it had seemed cruel, and it was difficult to adjust to. Yes, she was lonely, especially at night. She was proud of her son and wanted him to be successful. His place was not at her side. She was lucky to have made so many good friends here. She was well. Life was good.

This innocent show of simplicity made him feel shabby. Her perfume was affecting his senses. It was flowery and young, but had a dark, sensual undertow that was hauling him in. His eyes kept drifting to her bosom, as though to their default position. Constrained as her breasts were by their strict bra, he was excited by the possibilities if they could break their constraints.

Amazing. Must be late fifties, but I actually fancy her or would do if the equipment was in working order.

His own back-story was filtered through his internal Stasi and followed a purified party line. He spoke of a life of academic research, of his pastoral satisfaction tending generations of students and his lifelong activism on behalf of women's equality. He expressed his sadness at not having become a father, and his sense of loss that no love affair had become lifelong. He was sad to be alone.

"But we must play the cards dealt us by fate, Céline. I am thankful to be well again, and to have made such dear friends, such as you."

He smiled bravely, noting that this gloss on his life had seemed to go down well. She touched his hand sympathetically and said he looked so much better now, better than she had ever seen him.

He took immediate advantage and held her hand, squeezing it softly. "That is because I had a wonderful nurse, Céline. You should meet her one day. She is very kind and clever. She is the best cook in the world. And she is very beautiful. I was a lucky man, the luckiest man in the world."

She took her hand away and looked down at her plate. "You make fun with me. Again. You always make fun with me. I know you English."

"No, Céline, I tell the truth. Always. And I thank you from the bottom of my heart."

She looked up into his eyes and smiled sweetly. "It was a pleasure. You were a very good patient. No. At first, when you hurt all over, you were like a baby, a little boy. And naughty, like a little boy."

They grinned at each other. The evening was swimming along.

***

He escorted her home, resisting the temptation to kiss her at her door, thinking it too public a place. In a small town narrow street, there were always curious eyes, and he did not wish to spoil the magic by embarrassing her. Better to leave her hoping for a kiss. He squeezed her arm and watched her safely inside.

In his own kitchen he made tea, not because he craved tea, but because he craved cognac and cigarettes. The ritual would give him something to do. He was too high on the evening to be ready for sleep. He leant with his back to the sink, cup in hand and thought the difficult thoughts.

The problem is not her. She's perfect. Amazing I've only just clocked that. The problem is me. Whether I'm up for it. Literally. The problem is impotence. I never thought, in my wildest, most pessimistic fantasies, that it would be a problem. My cock has just been ready, wanting action, straining at the bloody leash, impatient to get in there, all my fucking life. Never occurred to me there'd be a problem. Impotence. What a word. I can hardly bring myself to say it. Shameful, somehow. Well, if I can't crack it, I'm fucked. Or not, as it were. The bloody tablets, they're not reliable.

He had experimented with them, using internet porn as stimuli. The brief films he clicked on were no substitute for the real thing. They were formulaic and cold. The male actors' cocks were incredibly big. They intimidated. But the girls were pretty and admirably hungry for sex. None of them got him very excited. Each time he tried, he would go off half-cocked, at best. This was not good enough to risk in real action. To fail when put to the ultimate test would be humiliating. It was time to go to London and take them up on their offer.

He courted Céline assiduously and with old-fashioned formality. He took her on outings around the Var, enjoying walks and leisurely lunches. They would take the ferry and spend the day on the island of Porquerolles. True, sitting side by side with her on the bus, he thought they were like Darby and Joan—embarrassingly similar to his Auntie Edith and Uncle Harry going on the bus over the moors after he had retired from the garage.

The poor chap was so bored; he used to think a trip to the Co-op was an adventure. Do we all revert to type on the last lap? Fight our way to being as different as possible for years. Then come back to the starting point, like elastic stretching and snapping you to position one. I even look like my old uncle now. It'll be bloody cricket next, if I'm not careful, or boring everybody on the bowling green. What do they say, you can take the lad out of Rochdale, but you... Fuck it, I'm in Provence, a retired Professor, not bloody Gracie Fields.

After three weeks of outings and little presents, handholding and sweet kisses goodnight, Céline invited him into her tiny house and cooked dinner. Just the two of them. He brought a bottle of Fleurie. She served dorade on a bed of thinly sliced fennel in a light cream sauce, followed by a green salad full of herbs that he did not recognise and a local goat cheese, light and not farmyardy. It was divine. She looked pretty and shy and a delicious handful. The evening was relaxed. She laughed at his jokes and flirted with him, playing that adolescent game of hard to get, so come, and get me. It took him back. He knew it was a good sign, possibly a green light. Timing is everything, he knew. Do not move too soon or they might run for it; do not wait too long or they might cool.

As the dinner wound down, emboldened by the wine, he kissed her, tenderly. Ardent, but not hot with lust, a kiss which, should retreat be necessary, could be passed off as thanks for a lovely dinner. She kissed him back hungrily. This was welcome, but it presented him with two dilemmas. As they snogged, he wondered how appropriate it would be to push ahead towards the finishing line. Should he go on, so that she would have both the satisfaction of stopping him, while proving to herself that he is keen? A woman wants to know she is wanted, even though she needs to be able to say no, or at least, not yet. But what if she did not stop him? What if she called his bluff? He judged that to be unlikely. She was, after all, a petit bourgeois, respectable widow in a Catholic country. But he was not certain. The prospect of failing to deliver on cue convinced him to quit while he was ahead.

There was a deeper reason. He was no longer the hungry

cocksmith, coolly weighing up a prospective conquest. He was not looking for temporary excitement, for sexual relief. He was a suitor, desperate for this woman to accept him and care for him. He wanted her love and devotion. So even a successful seduction, should it be possible, was not enough. Could he persuade her to live with him, permanently? A discreet affair was all she was likely to consider. She had to guard her reputation, and this was a small community. She surely would not consent to live with him outside marriage and even if she did, what would stop her leaving him when he finally descended into the senescence he dreaded? What would keep her? But if he could persuade her to marry him, that would secure her, for better or for worse, in sickness and in health. Marriage is a binding contract for a woman like this.

Fuck me. Marriage. I've railed against it most of my life. Would have taken bets on never doing it. Forgive me Engels, for I know exactly what I do, and why.

He lifted her chin and made her look up at him.

Now's the moment. Go for it. Seventy, and the first time. You're a virgin. Where's Mills and Boon when you need the fuckers? Okay, do it.

"Céline, I love you. I have fallen in love with you. Is it too much to hope that you would consider an old man who is devoted to you? Would you do me the honour of marrying me? Would you be my wife, Céline?"

She stared at him without expression.

Oh fuck, this is going pear-shaped. How do I slide out? I can't make a joke of it now.

"Marry you?"

"Please forgive me. Maybe you need time to think. I have surprised you. Forgive me."

Just get out of here.

"No, Roger. I do not need time to think. I am flattered, but no."

She smiled sweetly.

"Forgive me, Céline."

He held her to him gently, thanked her again for a beautiful dinner and left, kissing her hand chastely as he went.

Well done. You've fucked that up. You've been well told.

***

Céline stood for a moment behind her front door. Her consciousness separated from her physical existence. The latter ticked over like an automatic motor. It knew what to do. Her conscious self was preoccupied.

The cat purred round her feet with cupboard love. She poured milk into its bowl. She then filled a glass with water, put out the lights and prepared for bed. She took off her dress and hung it carefully. Eased off her earrings, one of which had been chafing her ear, and wiped away the invisible make up. She applied the night moisturiser, had a pee, removed her stockings and garter belt, the slip and the daring little knickers, and got into bed naked. She clicked off the light but knew she could not sleep. Too many thoughts were bouncing noisily around her head. There seemed no order in them and her will was unable to impose one. She allowed them to flow and became a passive spectator.

It was odd, she noted, considering what she urgently needed to think about, that her thoughts were back in England. She was seventeen. The place was a detached suburban house with a big garden in Kidderminster, where she had gone as an au pair, for her English and for adventure. There had been too much English, of every sort, and not much adventure, but the most indelible memory was of Dr. Rigby. She smiled now at the intensity of her adolescent infatuation. It had been so magical and had hurt so much, her first adventure of the heart. Totally one sided, because he had behaved impeccably, indeed only peripherally noticing her existence. This tall, handsome man, overworked and exhausted, distant and unattainable, had been Jean Belmondo and Lord Byron in one gorgeous package. When her two years were done, they thought her tears were for the two children she would be leaving. Fond of them as she had become, her tears were for the only man she would ever love, the noble Doctor. His reserve and proper manners had been like insurmountable obstacles, the difficulty of scaling them making him even more desirable.

She adjusted her pillows and sipped her water.

Ah, so long ago. I have not thought about those feelings for years. Why tonight? Roger is English, that is all. They are so different. Possibly I had the fantasy that Dr. Rigby would have made love to me like Roger did tonight. Silly girl. Marcel certainly never did that.

She smiled at the thought of dear, practical Marcel turning into the romantic lover. His proposal had been more down to earth, more practical, and business-like. Her parents had approved. He would be taking over his parents' charcuterie soon, after all, and was a steady lad from a good family. She had fitted into the adult life expected of her, leaving storybook fantasies to the storybooks. He had been a faithful husband. She missed him.

I have had a good life. And now this man has thrown me into turmoil and I don't know anything. I'm in such a tumble of feelings. I must calm down and be sensible.

So, first, you're right to have refused him, even though he has touched your heart and made you imagine you're a girl again. Well, you're not. He is the first man to court you and you are old enough to be a grandmother, which you would be if Patrice would take his head out of the flour and find a wife. Roger has given you a leading role in a romantic novel, with the flowers and the dinners and the talk of love. You know nothing about him. He has never married. Clive was too discreet to say anything, but you could tell he was worried. I am filled with desire and want more. I want his touch. But marry him? I like my independence now.

What could he see in me, this handsome Professeur? I am an old woman, uneducated, overweight. Does he just want someone to look after him, to clean and cook for him? But I do that anyway. He does not have to marry me for a clean floor or a coq au vin.

What is he up to? Could he possibly love you? Love? Me?

She lay still in the dark, looking at images of Roger in her head. His mocking smile. His earnestness when making a point. His shy sincerity when he asked for her hand. The deep, masculine timbre of his voice and its sexy Englishness. She felt again how deliciously possessed she had felt when enclosed in the arms of this big man. How she had fought back the urge to melt into him, offering herself in a most inappropriate, or at least premature, way. The memory now shocked her. Excited her.

She admitted that she was attracted to him. She did not feel rational. She did not want to be rational. It was not a time for rationality. She wanted him. She wanted to release herself from this weighing up the pros and cons, which sucked the life out of her euphoria. She was so lonely since Marcel had died. She so wanted a man; a man who would make her feel like a woman. Roger was a man clearly, a real man. He was mature, yes, but still handsome, and so charming. What a wonderful, unexpected gift at her time of life. God was good. And mysterious. She could be alive again. Again? Really alive, she thought, deep down, for the first time. Love was everything. It makes us feel alive.

She knew she would not sleep. She slipped on a dressing gown, went to the kitchen, and made some herb tea. The cat came to her.

"I should have put you out for the night, but I'm too soft, aren't I."

The cat kneaded her lap with his paws. It purring was louder now, as though an electric motor was driving it. She stroked his back and up his tail, smiling down at him.

***

Céline was on automatic pilot as she busied herself with the morning routine. Her conscious mind was in the past. It was early in the New Year and she was in the Rigby family Rover, on the way to Birmingham. The children were excited. It was difficult to calm them. Her own excitement was in danger of overflowing. They were all dressed up. The Doctor was like a boy as he teased the children. Layers of adult cares had lifted from him. He seemed closer to Céline's age today.

They took their seats in the handsome Alexandra Theatre and Cinderella began. Céline was confused to see an attractive young woman playing the male lead. Was this appropriate for an audience of children? Dr. Rigby was relaxed, explaining it away as *traditional*. She loved the slapstick and the audience participation, spending half the time watching the children's delighted faces. A strange experience, this English pantomime, but a magical afternoon.

Now, her best dress safely hidden away in the wardrobe and plain in her everyday work frock, she must go to clean Roger's house. She felt like Cinderella. Last night with the prince was last night. Midnight had chimed. This morning is this morning. She wondered how awkward it would be. His declaration last night had taken them over the line. The relationship was no longer employer and employee, where work and cash are exchanged. She was now about to go on stage, but did not know who to play, or what her lines were. She was nervous. She decided she must go as normal, pretending nothing had happened.

Roger had resisted the temptation to rush down to the Excelsior to avoid her. He knew that would just be putting off an inevitable embarrassing moment. When she let herself in with a "Monsieur?" he met her with a smile, but did not go over to her. They stood awkwardly. She looked down. The silence was too loud for comfort. It was up to him to repair the relationship.

"Céline, I have not slept."

Lie, but it sounds good. Always let them know your feelings for them are causing you suffering.

"I thought all night, not just of how much I love you, but of how much I respect you. I could not bear it if my behaviour yesterday caused you distress. If I went too far. The last thing I want is to put you in a difficult situation, to make you feel awkward. I meant every word I said, and I still do, a million times over, but it was presumptuous to assume that you want a man in your life now, least of all that I might be that man. I'm sure I'm not worthy. I ask you to forget what I said. We will, I hope, be able to carry on our relationship, dare I say friendship, as before."

You're laying it on with a trowel, but she'll love it.

Céline looked at his earnest face. She stepped over to him and smiled. She then kissed his cheek.

"Thank you, Roger. I hope so, too."

His relief was tempered by the lurking thought that he had lost the initiative.

***

When she had finished her work in Roger's house, she went

straight to Alain. She had so much to tell him and wanted to think aloud.

"I have something you will not believe, Alain. You will never guess."

"Nothing bad, I hope."

"Oh no. Monsieur Roger came to my house last evening, and he declared his love. He asked me to marry him. What do you think of that? A surprise, no? A surprise for me."

"And what did you say?"

"I could not believe it. I said no, of course. Though I would become his lover, Alain. If he wishes." Her grin was irrepressible. "But marriage? At my age? I have had one marriage. One is enough."

***

Roger was at the Excelsior. The first cognac had steadied him and he was now sipping the second with a coffee. He had felt astonishment, then humiliation when Céline wrong-footed him. He had now righted himself and decided to be *philosophical* about it, though what it had to do with philosophy, he had no idea. Only Céline and he knew of this business. The damage was limited.

You walked straight into that, though, didn't you? What exactly did she mean? Was she hinting she'd be up for an affair instead? Bloody hell.

The rejection had highlighted his loneliness. He was approaching old age, infirmity, and isolation, waiting to die. He ordered another cognac. To hell with the no booze resolution.

***

Céline, alone in her kitchen and relaxing into the familiar rhythm of cooking, allowed her mind to roam around this amazing turn in her life. She had certainly enjoyed Roger's attentions. The dates and adventures, the compliments and the flirtation had been delicious. She had felt a flutter of desire when he had kissed her, a desire long buried. She had even wondered if it would lead to a discreet affair, something she had not even fantasised about...

well, she *had* fantasised about, but not thought possible, at her age.

Then there came this proposal of marriage. Having already said no, she felt liberated, happy to think about it hypothetically. She certainly did not need to be married in order to enjoy an affair. Did he need marriage before he could enjoy sex, or did he think she would require it? He was difficult to read. An Englishman, a retired academic, a man of a certain age. It was possible.

So what if she did marry him? A wedding. Her wedding day. She smiled at the prospect of being at the centre of such a day. Her Marcel had died long enough ago for her remarriage to avoid comment. If she moved in with Roger she could let her house— rents were going up in the Old Town. She knew that two could not live as cheaply as one, but it would be more economical together than separate. She did not know how wealthy he was, although a generous pension from the University was certain. He spent money generously. Together, they would have a surplus for all sorts of treats, even trips abroad. She had longed to go to New York to see her son, and had been shopping for a cheap flight.

So what if she did marry him? Was it such a bad idea, now that she had weighed it up? How valuable was this independence, after all? Was it not just another word for loneliness?

She would think about it.

***

When Alain told Clive later, he was amazed. This was unpredictable, out of character even.

"I don't believe it. Are you sure? There must be some awful mistake, a misunderstanding. Roger has never been married, is ideologically opposed to marriage and all it represents, has written extensively on the subject, and would never even contemplate it."

"Well, according to Céline, he proposed to her."

"I am shocked, Alain."

"Why?"

"Roger is a shit, a twenty-four carat shit, where women are concerned. I can't understand what he's up to. He wants a cheap housekeeper, I suspect, now he's finally realised he's getting old. Céline is right to refuse him."

"Clive, love is a mysterious thing. You are obsessed with him in ways I do not understand. But your feelings about him are about you, not necessarily about him. Maybe he loves her."

"Loves her? He has never loved anyone. He doesn't know what love is."

"Well, maybe he will change. Or maybe she has enough love for both of them. It is overflowing in her, you can see. I wish she had said yes."

Clive snapped. He looked at Alain's tranquil expression and wanted to hit him.

"Just who do you think you are, Alain? What gives you the right to talk about other people's love? You know nothing about Roger. You should hear the horrible things he says about you. Then you wouldn't be auditioning for sainthood."

This bounced off Alain, barely touching him. He nodded at Clive and spoke even more slowly and clearly, as though explaining something complicated to a child. "If they are horrible, well, so? Those feelings are his. He must carry them and suffer. They are his problem, not mine."

"I'm not wasting any more time with this paper-back mystical bullshit. Think what you like."

Clive bounced out and went home. He sat quivering for a while and then made some tea. Alain was so irritating when he adopted this persona. Clive's liking for him had soured.

But then he felt ashamed. This hostility was not like him. Or was it? Maybe he was discovering new elements in himself. Maybe he was too immersed in Roger's past. That extraordinary diatribe about girls and older men had shaken him. But that was just Roger being outrageous. He was now an old man, alone in the world, seeking comfort and love. Maybe Alain was right, damn him.

***

Céline had cooked too much. She always cooked too much. She would put some in the fridge. It would keep. Then she thought of Roger and on impulse, decided to go to him. She looked in the mirror by the front door. Her hair was a mess and she was flushed from the cooking. "Oh, if he wants me as a wife, he will see worse than this."

As she reached his front door Roger appeared, on his way out. "Céline." He looked awkward.

"Oh, Roger, you're going out."

"Just to eat at Marius. Is there anything wrong?"

"No, Roger. Nothing wrong. I have dinner waiting. Please come and share it with me."

He stared at her, frantically struggling for the subtext. Maybe it was a peace offering, a *let's be friends* gesture. Whatever. One of Céline's dinners was tempting. He smiled and murmured his thanks.

She served blanquette de veau au vin blanc with rice. Roger ate one helping quickly and greedily, and another slowly, with a slight smile. It was delicious. He barely managed the cheese and refused the fruit.

She looked at him across the table, noting the results of her work.

"Roger, I must ask you to forgive me. What you said to me last night, and again this morning, threw me into confusion and I did not know what I was saying or doing. I am still, now, in turmoil. This does not happen to a woman of my... years."

She stopped and looked down. He did not know whether he should interrupt or allow her to own the pause. After a few seconds he spoke, almost in a whisper. "Céline, if anyone should apologise, it is me. I had no wish to upset you."

She looked at him. "Did you mean what you said. Do you still mean it?"

"With all my heart, Céline."

"Then I accept, Roger. I will be your wife, if that is what you wish. I could not believe you really wanted me."

It took a moment to penetrate. He then went to her. She stood up, close to him. He put his hands on her waist.

"So you believe now?"

"Yes."

He kissed her tenderly on the mouth, and she melted into him. This was a romantic movie and she was in it. Something she had longed for all her life, all the while telling herself not to be silly. Now an old woman, it was actually happening.

Their awkwardness disappeared, giving way to a shy intimacy, as they began to adjust. They kissed and smiled and then sat down side-by-side, holding hands.

"Céline, first, we should get someone else to help out. I can't have you do all the work, not now, and if left to me, the house would be a pig sty in short order."

"Roger, what do you say to me? Do you think I will allow another woman to look after you?"

They talked in such a practical way that Roger was shocked. This marriage business was turning actually into a business, not a romance. First, the date. At least, he had never been married before, which he assumed would earn him brownie points. They would have a wedding party, certainly, which she hoped her son would attend, but he might not be able to. They would live in Roger's house and she would let her little place. The rent would go into their joint housekeeping. All this hard-headed practicality came from a petit bourgeois mentality quite foreign to Roger. He reminded himself that she came from a background of small shopkeepers. At least she would keep an eye on the Euros and organise his comforts. What was there not to like? He would relax on it and leave it all to her.

He did not put his biggest worry on the table, ensuring her satisfaction in bed. Whether she wanted sex or not at her age, and, if so, how often, was difficult to guess. He had no experience of post-menopausal women. But he assumed he had to be ardently full of desire on the night, erect and ready for action, even if she demurred. She would want a real, fully functioning man at her side. Potency, not senility. He had time, between now and the wedding. She probably would refuse sex until God had sanctioned it. That would give him time to get to London and repair his deficiency. Modern technology was wonderful. He hoped.

***

Roger was thrown completely off centre when he left the house and faced the town. Marriage, he knew, was a public declaration, a matter for society, not just for the couple. But this was ridiculous. He did not know whether to bask in the attention, soaking up the congratulations like a gracious star, or lock his front door and hide. He had not considered that a private arrangement with Céline would be of such public interest.

He had mentioned it to no one. He did not have to be Poirot to guess how the news had spread, or who was the source... that little poof, Alain. He and Céline were close.

Wherever he went, people came up to him and shook his hand. They beamed at him. Strangers.

You'd think I'd won the Nobel Prize. Have they nothing else to do, the bloody French?

But he smiled, nodding his head modestly, accepting the congratulations with noblesse oblige, and rather enjoying his status. He certainly felt more accepted and approved of in this little world than he did in the wider one.

Just for making an honest woman of her. Not come very far, have we, after fifty years of feminism?

Céline felt, and started to look, younger. She wore brighter and more feminine clothes. She had her hair restyled. Respectable widowhood gave way to French chic. Her heels were higher and she swayed provocatively as she navigated the cobbled streets.

With Roger she was flirtatious, blushing, and smiling with adoration, like a girl. Her lowered neckline revealed more of her tantalising breasts. She would offer her face up to be kissed. Yet she remained a mother. The combination captivated Roger. She took care of him every day, leaving a salad of chevre and pine nuts or a thick tranche of rough pate and some crusty bread, covered in cling film, ready for his lunch. Most evenings the bell rang and there was Céline with a casserole dish. She would put it into the oven to warm through, sharing a glass of wine with him, laying the table, and making a side salad as they chatted. She would then place the casserole on the table, kiss him and leave him feeling lonelier than ever. Occasionally, she would join him or invite him over. When he tried, for forms sake, to make love to her, she would lower the *no entry* barrier after he had fondled her breasts, from the outside. Kissing was allowed, until it got too hot.

He thought it was just her conventional, old-fashioned modesty, keeping herself 'til the marriage night. He did not realise, and was never told, that she would have taken him as a lover; but now the prospective marriage was public, she was adopting the traditional means of securing it. Céline was practical in ways that, had he known, would have shocked him.

This is weird. This is back to when I started, trying to get into a girl at St. Marks bloody Youth Club.

He knew this was bravado. Her conventional modesty saved him from humiliation. His ardent advances were a promise he knew he could not keep. He had to make that appointment and book a flight to London. He left her to get on with the arrangements; hoping modern technology would not let him down.

Chapter 18

Roger had been waiting for fifty-five minutes past his appointed time. He looked at his watch again in an exaggerated way, like an actor looking at his watch, but there was no audience for his exasperation. No one caught his eye. There were no looks of complicity, no smouldering rebellion. Just seven men sitting either side of a narrow corridor in the hospital basement. Each had been patiently waiting all week, by the look of them. He wondered if they were all limp dick cases, but he said nothing. Breaking the funereal silence with a question like that might have caused a scene.

The large nurse appeared again and this time called Roger's name, looking round enquiringly.

"Yes."

"Please come this way."

Her manner was brightly cheerful. There was no apology for keeping him waiting. He wanted to smack her, at least verbally, but thought this unwise, considering she had his future potency in her hands. He smiled and followed her, feigning meekness. He failed, but she did not seem to notice. She asked him to sit, looked at him, and assumed he was nervous and apprehensive. She was used to that.

"I'll be with you in a moment, Mr. Burton."

She flicked through his notes. For years, the title *Professor* had been useful, and he had used it. Before, he had tried using *Doctor*, assuming it would open doors and elicit respect, but it had just been trouble. People assumed he was a medical doctor, and when he then had to explain that he was a Ph.D., he got tangled up trying to explain how a Doctor of Philosophy could be an Historian and know nothing about Philosophy. He stopped using it. Here, *Professor* was ignored, or not noticed, and he was called Mr.

So much for a lifetime's distinguished contribution to academia. Just another bloody Mr. to Nurse Collins. Probably just another dirty old man who shouldn't be thinking of sex at his age.

"So. We're having a little difficulty after our radical prostatectomy, and the tablets don't quite do the trick? Well, not to worry. Today, I will demonstrate the injection procedure. It is quite straightforward. You will soon get the hang of it. You can take one home with you. We have had very good results. I'm sure your married life will be back to normal, very soon."

He had never been shy when it came to showing his genitalia to a woman. He had always been proud of his cock. But there was something about Nurse Collins that made him feel awkward. It was not her looks. She was quite attractive, around mid-thirties, nicely built, if a bit large. Her face was actually handsome. You could imagine her out of that hospital coat, clothes off, and she would be interesting. Better, clothes off but in that hospital coat, and then taking it off, slowly. It was the circumstance and her matter of fact tone that drained all possible eroticism away, leaving an awkward void.

He had never been told by a woman to expose his penis. He had imagined it, in a sexual fantasy about a horny little number, desperate for it, but this request threw him.

He obeyed. The embarrassment disappeared as he looked up and saw that she was not watching. In her hand was a syringe-type device. She was drawing into it a liquid. At the end of the device was what looked like a needle. It was certainly sharp. She looked up at him and smiled. Her voice was clear and neutral. She could have been explaining how to refill a fountain pen. There was no retreat. He was pinned back against the chair, at her mercy. What she had been saying during this preparation had barely registered.

"What this does is increase blood flow to the penis. Increased blood flow to the genital region helps establish and maintain an erection. But it is important to administer the solution properly. I'll now demonstrate. You might feel a little prick."

The unintentional joke was lost on her and he was in no mood to giggle. She had said all this as though reading from a script. No doubt it was by now automatic. Roger watched as she took hold of his cock like a butcher handling a piece of pork loin. She swabbed near the base, picked up the needle, and plunged it into him. He cried out and screwed up his face. He had always hated injections, but he never in his maddest fears thought he would get one in his cock. It was very sensitive. She pressed a cotton ball at the injection site.

"Important you do this, it will prevent bruising."

They were quite close. He could smell her talcum powder. He could easily have put his arms round her. She was chatting away, as though this was a cookery class.

"You have two, what we call corpora cavernosa, each side of you penile shaft. You should alternate the left and the right side. Avoid the top and underside of your penis, won't you—not advisable. Also any visible veins, like that big one there. You should use the thumb and forefinger of your non-dominant hand, like I did, to hold your penile head and stretch the shaft. It's a good idea if the length of the penis is resting firmly on your inner thigh, like this."

She held it firmly in place and looked up into his eyes. He returned the look.

"It will keep it steady."

She continued with her instructions and said he would have a chance to try preparing the injection before he went.

"Then you can practice at home. You may like to teach your

wife to administer the procedure. Many men find it more intimate to share this preparatory stage."

He looked at his doleful cock. It was flaccid and dejected, clearly unimpressed, and sulking, which did not surprise him. But he felt it was letting him down in front of this woman and willed it to perk up. There was no response.

Always had a mind of its own. Come on, show willing.

She kept talking. Roger wondered if he would remember it all, and hoped there would be instructions with the kit.

He felt a small twitch down below, not much, but enough to give him hope. He looked at it. His hands were on the arms of the chair. All on its own, without any manual encouragement, his cock started to swell. It gradually woke up and thickened, as though it was being pumped up with air. The size increased and it unfolded until there it was, erect and hard, swaying a little as if it had cunt-seeking radar. Roger was proud and relieved. He covered his embarrassment with a joke. "We have lift off, Houston."

Nurse Collins was unimpressed. She was busy checking his bag of goodies for home use.

All in a day's work for her. Wonder if she'd get a buzz from turning water into wine. She turns men on for a living, all day. Make her horny? Is there a man at home waiting to get the benefit? Shit, she's so blasé. Mine's not worth more than a glance.

He was given more instructions, warnings about overuse, and told to call if there were any problems. He thanked her and left with his precious bag of kit. He made his way back to the Savile, with one of the best erections in his fucking career and nowhere to bestow it.

No one at the Savile, that's for sure.

Chapter 19

Roger's return to Hyères was rather like the guest appearance of a great opera star. The production of *The Wedding* was traditional and familiar. It had already been arranged, dressed, and rehearsed. Everyone looked forward to the show, waiting for the foreign artist, who was much loved. All Roger had to do was put on his costume. It was a dark suit, his only suit, and a tie, an outfit a little out of date and now rather baggy on him. It had seen service at funerals and formal University ceremonies. He always felt awkward in it, but he strode out, brightly buttonholed, to meet his bride and his public.

By default, Clive had become the producer, or Master of Ceremonies, assisted by Alain, but both knew they were under the strict eye of the co-star, Céline, who had firm views. It was her day and would be organised to please her.

Cars were inappropriate in those narrow streets and it was, as usual, a fine day. Céline, on Alain's arm, walked through the Old Town, past the shops, to the Town Hall. She wore a long, pale blue dress, matching her eyes. It was tight at the waist but high at the neck. It had been made especially by her friend Suzanne, and she looked beautiful—ripe but chaste, inviting but reserved. Her hat was navy blue and from it hung a discreet veil. She carried a bouquet of flowers. Her heels were too high for the steep hill, but Alain held her arm firmly and she managed without mishap, her head high, smiling and acknowledging the good wishes all around her.

Roger was already at the Town Hall, waiting with Clive, who had organised his morning to the minute, with military precision.

"Any regrets, Roger?"

"Not a single one. Amazed to find myself in this position, yes. Gobsmacked actually, since you ask, having avoided marriage all my life."

"And argued against it."

"Indeed. But I want Céline and if marrying her is the only way to get her, well, here we are. Just no photos for Private Eye."

Clive grinned. "Cameras are everywhere these days. We have them on our phones. We are all paparazzi. Sorry."

"Very funny. I will say that having moved abroad, I was merely respecting the local customs. How about that?"

"Thin."

The room was filling up with friends, all smartly dressed. Céline and Alain arrived to general appreciation. Roger conceded to himself that she did scrub up well, indeed.

They stood together and the ceremony began, conducted not by the mayor, alas, but a motherly woman, clearly in-charge. She was warm, making the formal occasion informal. Roger barely understood the proceedings, but had been coached well enough to play his part.

Céline looked at him adoringly, and he kissed her to general applause after they had been pronounced man and wife. They thanked the official, and after all the signatures, led the way out to more applause and smiles, with kisses for Céline and handshakes for Roger.

The party walked further up the hill where Christophe had prepared a large table at Marius. All the way, shoppers stopped to admire the group and some applauded. It was street theatre. What a palaver, Roger thought. But he loved it.

***

Clive was happy to propose a toast to the bride and groom. His ambivalence had evaporated. Roger's past life with women was not on today's agenda. The old heartbreaker looked happy today. He had been through difficult times—his public reputation and physical health had been reduced painfully. He was old. Who would begrudge him a little happiness now, on the last lap? Both he and Céline seemed serene. As Alain had said, the Roger that Clive knew was different from the Roger that Céline had decided to love. Maybe she needed Roger. She would be good for him; one hoped he would be good for her.

The lunch was winding down. The bottle of cognac was circulating over the coffee, though Roger abstained, Clive noticed. Tapping his glass with a spoon, Clive rose. The table came unevenly to a halt, everyone looking at him.

"Friends, may I apologise, my French is so pathetic that I will not spoil the occasion by making you suffer it."

Alain was translating in a low, clear voice. Clive watched him gratefully and paused to give him space.

"I have known Roger for over fifty years. He has, it must be said, known many attractive women, but has remained single 'til today. I never thought this permanent bachelor would ever marry. But then, I did not expect him to meet the most attractive woman of them all, our dear Céline. And I certainly did not expect her to be brave enough to take him on. You will have your hands full, Céline, but at least you won't be bored. He is a very lucky man. You have nursed him back to health, and magically, back to youth, by the look of him. So behave yourself, Roger. And Céline, be strict with him. We all wish you many happy years together. It has taken you, Céline, and Provence, to make this Englishman honest. I ask you to rise, ladies and gentlemen, and join me in a toast to the bride and groom."

They all stood and raised their glasses, looking pleased.

"The bride and groom."

There was applause. Alain smiled warmly at Clive and nodded. Clive felt pleased.

Roger rose and his voice silenced the conversation. "No speech from me." Cries of protest erupted from around the table, which was inebriated and raucous. Roger raised his hand. "No. I will just say this…"

He paused. There was silence. His voice was low. His face serious. He spoke slowly in English. Those who could translate for their neighbours did so in whispers.

"Clive was correct. I am a new man—because of this woman. I am well—because of this woman. I am young—because of this woman. Well. Younger."

Everyone smiled. She looked at him, not sure what he was going to say.

"I am happy—because of this woman. I am in love—because of this woman. I am married to this woman and I will never let her go. I thank you for breaking bread with Céline and me today. Now go home. I want to be alone with my bride."

As he sat down, there were *ooh la lahs* from around the table and Céline blushed happily. Everyone stood, shook Roger's hand, kissed Céline, and began to drift away slowly. Clive also kissed her and patted Roger's shoulder.

He walked thoughtfully up the hill with Alain, who put his arm round him.

"You spoke well, Clive. They were both happy. That was generous of you."

Clive looked gratefully at his friend. Alain stopped them and faced him.

"I have not apologised for upsetting you over this. I do now. Please forgive me. I know that I am… I am not sure, in English…"

"We say, holier than thou."

"Holier than… you?"

"Yes, and it's very irritating. Do you really think you are above us all; that you alone have no bad feelings?"

Alain was relieved to see he was smiling. "No, my dear friend. It is my way, only my way. I do not think that."

"Good. Because it is a pain in the arse. That is another of our sayings."

"Yes?"

"Yes."

"Pain in the… arse? Okay."

They continued their stroll, Alain's arm lightly round Clive's shoulder.

***

Most of the other tables at Marius were full, mainly with tourists enjoying the bonus of this free theatre. The locals stood, congratulated, and applauded as Céline and Roger slowly made their way through, attempting to escape. The waiters beamed as Roger thanked them for a fine lunch. He had never expected to be a bridegroom. In fact, he had publically vowed, when an undergraduate—never, ever to marry. At others' weddings, he had discovered that it made the guests horny, particularly the women. He had also noticed the same at funerals, oddly, and had taken full advantage of both. His wedding seemed no different from all the others, in that it provoked joy even in strangers. He could not figure why. He was not an anthropologist. Whatever the reason, he enjoyed the stardom, waving acknowledgement, like royalty, protectively leading Céline out of Marius, and up the hill, smiling graciously.

They reached his house. It was the middle of the afternoon. He had decided to take her straight to bed. She looked flushed and excited. Better now, with the alcohol working for them, rather than later, as its aftermath brought them down.

This is the moment of truth, lad. You've got it well rehearsed. Go for it.

As soon as they were inside, he took Céline in his arms and looked at her. She was like a fluttering bird, clearly enjoying playing the role. She had her own lines, mainly drawn from romantic fiction where men were dashing and commanding, and women were submissive and yielding. Roger knew this one well and he fitted into his role like an experienced nineteenth century actor, slotting into a well-known play.

"My darling Céline, I have you to myself at last. You look so beautiful. You make me so happy."

He kissed her deeply and held it, his hand caressing her breast. He disengaged and looked at her face. Her eyes were shut and her breathing heavy. He took her hand and led her upstairs.

In the bedroom, he murmured that he needed a pee and disappeared into the bathroom. He had two reasons. One, for her first time, he thought it considerate to allow her to undress and get into bed privately. There would be time in the future for him to watch her, indeed tell her what to wear and how to strip. He particularly liked stockings and garter belts, hating tights. But she needed time to relax with him before receiving instructions in his fetishist needs. Second, and crucially, he needed a minute's privacy in order to achieve the erection. She must not be allowed to see the backstage machinery or question the achievement—the final flourish should just appear, out of thin air, provoking a gasp of appreciation.

He did need a pee, which was easier now. He could stand up for it, like a man. Then he took out the device, loaded it with the precious fluid, and steeled himself for the injection.

No pain, no gain.

He winced at the sharp jab into his skin, but managed not to cry out loud. He was soon rewarded. His cock magically rose, standing to attention, ready for assignment.

This is no mock raid, my son, no more manoeuvres. This is real action. It's been a long time.

His nerve cracked. There must be no failure—falling at the first fence would be disastrous. He reached for the packet of little blue tablets and took one with a glass of water. The odd failure to perform might be waved aside down the road, his potency not in doubt, but it must go with a bang today. He would impress her with his manliness. He glanced again at the blue tablets and swallowed another.

He felt great. A fuck, after all this time. There was nothing in the world to beat the feeling of a hard cock and a waiting woman. Except the feel of it inside her.

He left his shorts on. Holding his stomach in, he entered the bedroom. She had closed the curtains, softening the harsh afternoon sun, and was lying demurely in bed, just her head and arms showing. He slipped in beside her and began caressing her tenderly. Keen as he was, with his induced erection, he made himself slow down. He would take time, build her slowly, and wait 'til she was begging for it, before he claimed her. He had read that it took post-menopausal women longer before they were ready. This was exclusively for her. A rave review would ensure a long run. His reward would simply be in getting and staying hard. What an accomplishment that would be. What a relief, after the barren years. His life could actually begin again, this very afternoon.

Although she had a stocky build, her breasts were pillowy and sexy. Her skin was like satin. She was looking at him adoringly, imploringly. Showtime. He slipped off his shorts and pulled the sheets off them. Her hand went to his cock and stroked it approvingly. He could not resist any longer. He raised himself on top of her, between her open thighs and felt the wonderful warmth of her vagina as he pushed into her. She was tight, and cried out, but he was in thrall to his cock. Nothing would stop it now. She accommodated him. He hoped he would not ruin it by coming too soon, and ordered himself to slow down, but as though on a bolting horse, he had lost control. He started to fuck her, faster and deeper, years of abstinence and impotence begging for absolution. Then the rising ecstasy reversed into disaster. The faster and deeper he went, the softer he became. The urgency had produced a limp and sullen refusal. He ordered, pleaded for resumption. There was no response. The disappointed question on Celine's face quickly turned into a sympathetic smile. She hugged him. He rolled off her and lay on his back—humiliated and angry. She cuddled him, murmuring that they should sleep. It had been a long and exciting day. He looked at her. She seemed on her way to a deep sleep already.

Well, at least she's not too upset. Maybe I'm just out of practice. It'll improve.

But it was a while before sleep came to him.

***

The next morning, the bright light fought its way through the closed curtains and woke Céline. She got up on one elbow and inspected Roger. He was in the same position, on his back, and snoring. She pecked his cheek and got up.

Downstairs she made tea, as she had learned to do when an au pair, and waited for it to be ready. She would take Roger his morning tea every day now. It would be an intimate treat for him, a reminder he had a loving wife.

She stood in the kitchen, turning over memories of yesterday. The wedding had been beautiful and she had basked in the compliments—her new dress had impressed everyone. The sex with Roger had promised more than it delivered. With Marcel, it had rarely been unpleasant but had felt like a wifely duty. It had lacked intensity. Roger had been confident and assertive. He had taken her as though he needed her. He had just been tired. He was no longer a young man.

She took the tray upstairs, looking forward to gently waking him and offering him his tea. They would chat as he became fully awake. Would he be grumpy at first? She expected he would.

At least he had stopped snoring. It had been a long time since she had lived with that noise. She would get used to it again.

She laid down the tray and sat on the edge of the bed. He looked so sweet. She saw the little boy buried inside the man battered with age. She caressed his face with her fingertips. "Roger, wake up, chéri, I've made you some tea."

She smiled. He would be a difficult one. He did not do anything by halves: his sleep was deep.

"Roger, some tea."

Unease spread through her like a dank tide. She shook him affectionately and then vigorously, in a gathering panic. He was lifeless. Her Roger was now a body.

No breath. No pulse.

She again drew her fingers down his lifeless face. She felt icy cold inside. She did not weep. She looked at her optimistic future, now disappeared.

After a few minutes she dressed and walked to Alain's house. He was making his morning coffee.

"Céline, ca va? Oh, Céline, que s'est-il passé?"

She fell into his arms and his warm concern melted her. She burst into sobs.

Alain took charge. He made phone calls and then told Clive. He poured Céline a cognac, for the shock.

Chapter 20

C live sat alone in his kitchen, nursing a cup of tea, staring at the wall. He was not in shock, but he was shocked.

Poor Roger. Just when he was looking and feeling better. Thought he had years ahead of him. What a terrible shock for poor Céline. On their wedding day. They both looked so happy. Awful. Awful. I should call Celia. Who else? I've no idea how to get in touch with his relatives. Don't think he's been in touch for years. Emma will be sorry. Her Uncle Roger. Always fond of him; he used to spoil her. Oh dear, what about the arrangements? I must be practical. The funeral? Alain will help. An announcement? The press? What about my book? All his papers? Who do they belong to? I doubt he has a will. Is Céline the next of kin? Oh dear.

He felt overwhelmed by too many questions. He felt inadequate. His own life had been turned upside down. He felt guilty about this feeling, with poor Roger in the morgue. He did not know what to do about it.

Get a grip. First, call Celia. She had been his friend, too. She will tell others.

He had not spoken to her for a while. The physical distance

between them had made him realise how apart they had been, even when in physical proximity, and how painful that had been for him. At this distance, he could see things clearer. He was on edge with her, perhaps even afraid, which was pathetic. He could never please her, could never be this elusive man she needed. He had realised that the fault perhaps was not in him. That it was in her. No one could satisfy her. She was in a permanent state of disaffection. He had not caused her irritability. He was merely the recipient of it, the whipping boy. He certainly felt better in Hyères.

I'm more myself, somehow. No, life here is more one of discovery, of a new outside world and a new me. Now it might be over. My reason for being here is dead.

He braced himself and called her.

"Yes?"

That was unmistakably Celia. That one word was really saying, "Who the hell are you, it had better be good, how dare you interrupt my busy day like this, come on, speak up, spit it out."

"Oh, hello, Celia, it's Clive."

"Clive. Thought you'd disappeared. How's the Cote d'Azur? Did you know that Somerset Maugham called it a sunny place for shady people? Met any shady people yet?"

"Yes, I did know the quote, Celia, and no, not that I know of. I don't think I would recognise one if I met one."

"You've not called to tell me you're coming back, have you? Still enjoying being Roger's amanuensis, or has he sacked you?"

"Well, Celia, it's about Roger, actually. I have some bad news, I'm afraid. He died, quite suddenly, this afternoon. I'm sorry to be the harbinger of bad news. As it were."

There was a long silence.

"Tell me what happened. What and why?"

"Well, he had just got married, and…"

"Married? Married? What the fuck? Roger? Married? Are you drunk, Clive, has the sun got to you? I can believe he is dead, I saw him recently. He looked like shit; an old man. But married? Roger?"

"Yes, unlikely as it sounds. A very nice local woman—his cleaner, actually. I was at his wedding reception. He looked fine, very happy, actually. They went home together, and Céline, that is her name, said he died in bed, just like that. There will have to be an inquest, I'm sure, but it sounds like a heart attack. That is all I know, at the moment. I thought you would like to be informed."

"Were they at it? Did she say?"

"Well, Celia, I don't think that is an appropriate enquiry. She is devastated, the poor woman."

"They were fucking. Had to be. In bed, just got married, heart attack. Obvious. Clive, if I did not know you better, I'd say you were making all this up. But you don't have the imagination. Or the sense of humour."

This hurt Clive. Even after decades of her tongue, she could still hurt him.

"I don't know what to say," she said.

"Not like you, Celia."

"I'll call Emma."

"Thanks. Is there anyone else we should call?"

"I don't know. I'll give it some thought. Give me your number down there again."

A moment after putting the phone down, she lifted it to call Maggs, who listened with her mouth open, so wonderful was this story.

"They were at it," was her immediate conclusion.

"That's what I thought. Unconfirmed by Clive though."

"Had to be. The question is this. Did it hit him before he came, or after?"

"Or during?"

"Indeed. Or, did he die of disappointment because he couldn't get it up? At his age, that's a possibility. Even with Roger."

"Well, possible. That humiliation would kill him. He wouldn't want to go on living anyway. I fuck, therefore I am. I'm impotent, therefore I die."

"Who said that?"

"Some famous philosopher. Forgotten the name. Sexist wanker."

They both collapsed in hoots of laughter, like two schoolgirls sharing a private joke.

"Celia, you've made my day. Roger dead on the job. What a way to go."

***

Celia called Emma and talked in a more neutral way, repeating Clive's information.

"I thought you ought to know."

"Thanks Mum. Poor Roger. How cruel, just as he seems to have found some happiness. And you'd nursed him back to health, Mum. What an awful thing. Will he be buried down there?"

"I've no idea."

"I think I'd like to go. Will you let me know?"

"Really? Well, of course. Clive will call, I'm sure."

"Thanks. Yes. If I can. It will close the book on him, somehow, being there."

"Okay, Em, I know you loved him. Sorry to bring you the news."

They chatted a little about their lives, and the grandchildren. Celia felt empty after she put the phone down. She felt lower and lower as the day wore on and could not settle to anything.

In bed later, she let her upset come to the surface and that relieved the pressure. It was no longer funny that he had died so appropriately, nor shocking that he had married. He was dead. It was a nail in her coffin every time she read a contemporary's obituary. Each day, she would cast her eyes over the Guardian obits to see who was there and notice their date of birth. But Roger was special. Would the Guardian run one on him? Who would they get to write it? Not that bitch Anna, she hoped.

The fire of her feelings for him had died down, but she remembered her desire, her anger, and her desperate physical need of him. She remembered their bodies together. She remembered him inside her. She cried. Life was running out; its passing was punctuated by days like today.

***

Céline was sitting at Alain's kitchen table, where she now spent much of her time. Alain refused to allow her to mope on her own in her flat. She looked composed. She had recovered at least the outward semblance of normality. It was as though her skin had thickened enough to cope with the world, buying time for her inside self to do its work of mourning. She was sturdy. Both her parents had died, and both her husbands had died. But her son was alive, thank God, as she said to Alain. He replied that death was a fact of life. They sat together, discussing the practicalities of the funeral. She wanted a proper, public event with a meal and speeches after the burial. She wanted her husband to be acknowledged, for everyone to say goodbye to him in style. She would welcome friends from England. This was her second funeral in Hyères. She was a widow once more. Marcel's funeral had been modest and very sad. They had just begun their new life there, and they knew only a few people. This funeral would be different, a celebration of the life of the famous Englishman. Clive had amplified what she had learned from Roger himself, and she was proud of how important Roger had been. She would be a sad widow, but a proud woman standing before everyone at the funeral.

Clive came by and sat with them in his quiet and unobtrusive way. There was something he needed to ask Céline. Even though it might be an insensitively wrong moment, he plunged in.

"Céline, please tell me if what I am going to ask is premature, something for another day... as you know, Roger had asked me to write his biography, a professional biography, about his work. To that end, he gave me access to his accumulated papers, and I have been going through them. What are your wishes now?"

"I wish you to continue. But if you do not wish..."

"Oh, I do, more than ever really, but only with your permission. Thank you."

"You have a key. The house, whatever you need there, is yours."

He nodded. They continued to talk about the funeral. The expense was not a constraint. Alain would ask Marius to cater a buffet lunch. She asked Clive if he, as Roger's old friend, would make a speech at his grave. She felt she could not speak. The reception would be a celebration, a party he would have enjoyed. He would be there in spirit, after all, said Alain. He was used to being the star, and would be even in death, said Clive. They all smiled.

***

Clive was surprised that both Celia and Emma had chosen to come all the way from England for Roger's funeral. Celia, he could understand—they had both been close friends of the old rogue for decades. Despite her tart comment over the phone that she was coming down just to make sure the old bastard was really dead, he knew this was Celia being Celia. But Emma, with two children at school and a job, to come all the way from Canterbury was a big event. Her husband was a good chap, of course, and he would take care of the children. Clive realised he had forgotten quite how big an impression a grown up can have on a child. He remembered her beautiful little face lighting up in gleeful anticipation when told that Uncle Roger was coming for dinner. She would flirt with him, delighting in his generous and rather inappropriate gifts, and be impossible to settle down at bedtime. It would be closure for her, he thought, rather disdaining his use of an ugly modern term.

It felt creepy, standing alone in Roger's empty house, looking round at the paraphernalia of his life. But he knew it was not helpful to be morbid. Céline had invited him to use the house. He went upstairs. There were two bedrooms. The smaller one had a single bed, which was made up and ready for a guest. He had slept there on his arrival in Hyères, and it was comfortable. The bigger one, Roger's room, was a more delicate proposition. First, it was Roger's bedroom, and somehow, whatever one's attempts at rationality, was still possessed by him, his spirit. Clive shook this primitive thought off, and decided to clear the wardrobe and drawers and bathroom of everything that reminded him of Roger, and put them in the documents room. He had the key to that room. All of Roger would be locked inside. The police had taken away what they thought necessary. The second problem was delicate. If he put Celia here, she would know that the bed was the bed Roger was in with his bride, the bed where he actually died. What would she think of that?

Well, what is the alternative? I could book them into a hotel, but that seems mean. It would be expensive. My flat is very small. I could fix a camp bed up there, I suppose. But I don't want to.

She could easily have joined him, slept beside him. Why not? They had slept together for nearly forty years, they were common law man and wife. Yet, something in him said no. He did not wish to sleep with her ever again. This separation, this stay in Provence, this… he did not know the cause, but he was over Celia. She was part of his past. They were no longer a couple. He had ruefully thought for years that maybe she longed to be on her own, free of him. Now he knew that he felt the same. Looking back on his many years with Celia, he wondered, why her? Originally, dazzled by her beauty, he had thought that must be the reason. In later moments of self-analysis, he had speculated whether he had been drawn to her by succeeding the legendary lover Roger, as though some of his magical masculine charm would rub off. He certainly had never aspired to be at her side. He was not in her league. She had made all the moves, while he looked on adoringly, not believing his luck. He now thought it was her domineering, bossy nature that had enthralled him. He feared her disapproval. Was this to do with his mother? He had certainly been afraid of her and had always tried to please her. This was dismissed as too paperback Freudian, a facile habit of thought he despised in others.

He would invite her to stay in Roger's house and see how she felt. His guess was that she would think nothing of it, or be amused. Sentimentality was not one of her weaknesses.

Clive looked round the documents room, now orderly, the piles of papers in chronological discipline, patiently waiting to be used. There were two unopened boxes that he had casually inspected. At first glance, they seemed to be full of miscellaneous junk, but he knew he must go through them. He was ready to begin a first draft of the book. Going through all this raw data, some of it detritus, some of it illuminating, had reminded him—over the months of digging and sifting—just how close the historian comes to being an archaeologist. The two disciplines joined hands.

It was strange to stand before this material, in Roger's house, now that he was dead. That irreversible jump from one state to another altered one's perception of everything. It would take some getting used to. Roger was not having a lie in. He would not bang noisily down the stairs, taking it over with his bulk and deep voice. He is a mere memory now. All those decades and then, in a moment, nothing.

Céline had told him to keep his key, to use the house and in particular to do whatever he thought best with Roger's papers.

"You were his great friend, Clive. I knew him for so little time. You were dear friends all your life. He would wish you to continue. He trusted you, I know."

Clive thought all this was a generous gloss on the truth, but he did not argue. Whatever Roger's agreement with his publisher, he took Céline's word as a green light. He would write a book—his book—and it would crown his career. Retirement had suddenly become a time of opportunity. He had mixed feelings about Roger and his death. He knew that lurking behind his consciousness was the stuff he wanted to keep there. Alain had already gently hinted, in his penetrating way, that Clive had never acknowledged his love or his hatred, his envy or his resentment of Roger.

Well, no doubt it will all come out as I write, or some of it. I'll not allow a fear of it to inhibit me.

The funeral was in two days. Alain was helping Céline with the arrangements. Celia and Emma would fly in tomorrow and he would meet them. Morbid as it seemed, he saw no reason to delay. He would continue his work. But he noted his reaction to the silence—how primitive, he thought, is our reaction to death. He died upstairs only hours ago and my knowledge of that seems to throw a morbid cast over the place. He smiled at this superstitious nonsense, determined to carry on as normal.

He looked at the neat piles, now all waiting further orders. The sight pleased him. He was ready to deal with each in turn and begin a rough draft, in note form at least, of Roger's life. It would gradually take on a coherent shape. He remembered something his dad used to say. "Let the dog see the rabbit." His dad had been a tidy and methodical man. He glanced at the remaining boxes. Although having relegated them as of no importance, he looked at them again with irritation. He knew his tidy mind would be uneasy if he did not deal with them before he began the next stage, even if it meant dismissing them as irrelevant. He lifted the lid of one and poured the contents onto the table. His first glance was confirmed. It was a miscellaneous mix of papers, letters, postcards, menus, wine catalogues, lapel badges, newspaper cuttings, flyers of public meetings that advertised Roger as the main speaker, agendas of Trades Union meetings, an assortment of photos, some from his childhood.

I suppose some of this will be useful, though. Provide colour. Human detail. Maybe into his private life. In so far as I want to enter it, that is.

His eye went to some envelopes, all the same light blue, scattered through the mess of stuff. He recognised Celia's handwriting.

Why would she be writing to him? Probably from her student days, when they had that brief affair. No use for the book.

The affair had not hurt him and did not hurt him now. It was an historical fact and had occurred before he and Celia had come together. He remembered having envied Roger at the time, but he had envied him often, as he moved from one delicious girl to another, girls beyond Clive's aspiration.

I was too scared of her at the time to even say hello, let alone ask her out. Me and most men. Could kill you with a look. Mind you, nothing much changed over the years, did it? She still scares everybody.

He smiled with what he liked to think of as rueful fortitude.

I'll glance through them. See if there's anything useful. Take me back to student days, at least. This whole bloody book is not so much scholarship as a trip down memory lane.

He sat down, picked the letters out of the mix, and stacked them. There were eight, varying in length, but roughly falling into two groups. The first was filled with bitter, angry rants about Roger neither calling nor returning her calls, about how he was using her. The agony was raw and the depth of hatred was ugly and painful to read. The second were joyous verbal descriptions of how he made her feel, how she was only alive when in his arms, how insatiable she was for sex with him. Some of this was explicit and for Clive rather distasteful, but he continued to read. There were professional reasons to go through all the material, and the fact that one of the protagonists was his wife was irrelevant. That would have been the answer if he had been asked the question. The truth was that he could not take his eyes away. None of this material would be used in his book, but he was transfixed. She described the depths of her feelings in detail. She even analysed the different sensations he provoked as she submitted to his will. This last celebration went too far for Clive.

It's pornography. She was only a student, as well. Did she get off on writing this stuff? Did she think it would turn him on? Probably would, knowing Roger. This was not the Celia I spent all those years with, certainly. I wonder if she was afraid of losing his interest—he had a reputation as a womaniser—and she thought this would keep him. How humiliating. When he chucked her, it was probably the best thing to happen to her. When he left for America, she could pull herself together. Poor Celia, the horny bastard clearly caused her a lot of emotional pain.

After six letters, he gave up. Reading pornography written by his wife made him queasy in complicated ways he did not fully understand, but he knew he did not want to prolong the discomfort. Then he noticed the date at the top of one letter. He quickly inspected them all. On five of them, it simply said *Thursday afternoon* or *Saturday night, late.* But the other three had numbers. They showed dates only weeks apart. But Clive was looking at the years. Two years, in the seventies. He assumed that Celia's hurried writing had confused him. But however long he looked, the information was the same. It was impossible. Their fling was in the sixties, when she was doing her Ph.D. By the seventies, she was with Clive and Emma was growing up. They were a family.

He sat, completely still, staring at the letters. No acceptable meaning was acceptable—the cognitive dissonance fighting inside him demanded that something had to give. It was not going to be the pitiless fact. Just the foundations of his life. It would be sometime before the new dispensation settled, before he could find a way of inhabiting it, but he had to go on the ride. Suddenly, Roger's contradictory life as the sexual adventurer became personal. Until this revelation, Clive had prided himself on his maturity, his non-judgemental ability to make the separation between Roger the academic and polemicist, and Roger the naughty boy.

Now the betrayal, in all its rutting, smelly furtiveness, cut into him. For how many years had this been going on? She must have given herself to him shamelessly and then come back home to share the marital bed. She combined being wife, mother, and respected academic, with this secret life of mistress, at his beck and call, apparently. These were times when he was often round at their house, sharing their meals, playing with Emma, pretending to be Clive's close friend. They were living a secret life right under his nose. He had always thought *cuckold* was a peculiar word, one from an opera or an Elizabethan play. It was suddenly contemporary and it was his.

Roger's house and personal effects were now anathema. He needed to escape. He slammed the front door behind him, glad to leave it but knowing that the truth would live on, quietly eating him.

Clive sat in his kitchen, staring at the wall. He saw nothing. He was numb. Throughout his life, his default position had been passivity. His mind was heavy, yet empty. He remained like that for hours, as though with this stillness, the pain would pass him by. He was lying low, refusing to feel.

His phone rang. He had never been able to ignore its summons. In slow motion he answered, whispering hello.

"Clive... c'est toi?" There was a pause, which puzzled Alain. He thought the connection was faulty. "Clive, it is Alain, are you there?"

"Hi, Alain."

"What is the matter? You are not well?"

"I'm okay. How's Céline?"

"I give her alcohol and send her to bed. She will sleep, I hope. I worry about you, so I call. You must be upset, the death of your friend. You sound sad. It is normal. Come to me for a drink. Do not be alone, Clive."

***

Alain's warmth and a glass of wine thawed Clive. He had not intended to mention his discovery of the letters—it was too humiliating. But Alain had a sympathetic ear and it was a relief, once he began, to share the weight of it. Giving the facts to him had broken the seal on his feelings and Clive began to weep, quietly and bitterly. Alain moved to sit next to him and put his arms round his shoulders, drawing him into an embrace. They sat like that for some minutes, saying nothing, just Clive's little shudders punctuating the tears. Finally Clive pulled away and reached for a handkerchief, murmuring, "Oh dear," and "So sorry, I'll be okay, really," and "How embarrassing, a grown man." Then, when he had recomposed himself, Alain held his hand and looked at him. Clive could not return the look. He gazed down at his other hand, clenching the handkerchief.

"You are wounded by this sharp truth, my friend. It will hurt you, why not? Think of it like that. It will hurt you, yes, for a long time, but not for always. You will have an ugly scar, but no more pain. You must live with it. There is no other way. The fact is there. But the meaning will take time."

"The meaning? I know what it means. It means she lived a lie. She made a mockery of our lives together, our commitment, our family. I want to expose her to the world as the two faced, cold bitch she is. I don't even blame Roger, not really, I knew what he was. I doubt he could help it. But Celia... you know what I want to do? I want to expose her. I want to kill her, actually. I'm almost out of control, the more it sinks in. This went on for... well, I don't know how long, but it was not some brief lapse, it was an affair. Oh, I know what it means, Alain, I know what it means."

He was shaking now. It was out of character to feel so

murderously angry. It frightened him. He breathed deeply and sighed.

"Do you? Did you know something was wrong between you and Celia? Something you refused to tell yourself? How was sex with her? Did you want her or did you pretend to want her? Had she always wanted him? Did you offer her to him?"

"Alain, I know you are trying to help, but this is silly, amateur Freudian…" Clive felt irritation welling up into anger and paused to contain it. "It is not helpful."

Alain smiled and nodded, which irritated Clive further. He looked away in the hope of terminating the speculation.

Alain said, "I don't think you ever decided whether you wanted to be him, or whether you wanted to be her. I think that what terrified you was the wish to give yourself to him, as she had done. The facts are of her betrayal. And of his. But the truth is more difficult, which is why you fight it, you have been fighting it most of your life. Your true nature."

"My true nature? This is all too French for me, I'm afraid."

"Ah, you joke. You English, you meet unwelcome… you English make a joke and it disappears."

"Something like that, Alain. It is our island genius."

Clive smiled. Alain was still holding his hand in both of his, which he liked, but thought it had probably gone on for too long. Not wishing to offend, he did not withdraw it. Alain squeezed, as though in punctuation, and started a new chapter.

"Well, in a way this is something for you and Celia, and no one else. It is not your daughter's business, is it? Why should she be hurt by this discovery? Celia has kept it secret from her, so should you, no?"

"Yes, Emma saw a different Roger, has a different Roger in her head. She loved him, especially as a child, her Uncle Roger. He was an important person. It would be cruel to burden her with this. Unnecessary."

"And Céline. She clings on to a romantic view of him. For her, Roger was a fine English gentleman. She is in mourning. She has suffered a terrible trauma. Do you intend to disillusion her, on the occasion of his funeral, in front of the whole town?"

Clive shook his head.

"And you. Do you want everyone to point you out as the man who... well, many would be amused; people are cruel. It is not how you wish to be described."

They sat while all this sank in. Clive nodded. He was sad. Realism had returned. He must plan his stance towards the world and it must be business as usual. After all, he was the only one, apart from Alain, with this information. Plus Celia, who thought she was the only one. That gave him room to manoeuvre.

"You are wise, Alain. I thank you. Yes. Quite right. Despite your ridiculous French theories. I bet you French have a theory about... sausages. And no one can understand it."

"Ah, several, in fact. And they are contradictory."

Clive managed a grin. Alain hugged him again. He went home. The effort to suppress his rage and hurt was a lead weight inside him, but he felt lighter on the outside. He knew he could handle the world.

Chapter 21

Emma's mood was buoyant, which amused her, considering she was on her way to a funeral. But it meant a break from the children, from chasing the day, fitting in paid work around the myriad pulls of domestic routines. Not so much a funeral as a holiday. She felt like a schoolgirl playing truant, half-expecting to be found out. It had also seemed right to attend, in a way that she could not explain. Roger had been an important person in her childhood and another in her student life. Yet she was not particularly sad that he was dead. The fact did not upset her. He was old, after all, and the last time she saw him he looked terrible, almost unrecognisable. With the insouciance of youth, she shrugged—old people tend to die.

She was in the window seat and enjoyed looking at the coast. It was her first visit to Provence.

Thanks, Roj, for dying down here. Most considerate.

It would mean a couple of days in this town her father had raved about. She looked at the sea below and thought of the children.

You are weird. Missing them already. Well, don't let that ruin your time.

Her mother's signals were still on red. She had been like that all morning. Emma had arrived at Stanstead airport, and was eagerly looking forward to some time with her mother. They saw each other so seldom and Emma felt a little guilty about neglecting her, especially now that she was retired and probably lonely. But Celia had put up a *do not disturb* sign and Emma knew her head would be bitten off if she did not keep her distance. Her mother had always been moody and fierce.

Celia's depression had not lifted since Clive's call. She felt out of sorts, ill tempered, cheated in an unaccountable way. She noted contemptuously that the bastard still controlled her moods, even though he was dead. But it was largely self-contempt. She did not know if she had loved him or if her feelings had been a sick obsession. Perhaps love, that kind of love, was a sick obsession. Well, it had run its course. She could not get interested in the current stage of her life. Who wants to be an old woman? She was fit, had a comfortable pension, grandchildren and friends. She could write, take a course in something or other, relax, garden, travel—there was a long and varied list of opportunities. But they were all vanilla. She regarded them with indifference, or worse, distaste. She could not explain it. Roger had rejected her years before. Was it the tender rapprochement during his illness that had wrenched her feelings back? She had loved caring for him. She had loved his dependency even more. Now, suddenly, he was dead. It was over; irrevocably over. She was waiting to die. And it sucked.

As they walked through the airport terminal, trailing bags on wheels as though they were obedient dogs, Clive was waiting to meet them. He smiled and kissed Emma's cheek, saying it was good to see her, but he looked strained. The atmosphere between him and Celia was cordial, in that repressed English way, but Emma sensed a tension. She guessed that the death of their old friend had hit them both deeply and she was sorry.

The taxi took them into the Old Town and they walked up the narrow streets, past the shops, to Roger's house. Emma could see what Clive had meant. It was enchanting. The bright colours of the local fruit and vegetables, and the smells from the rotisserie, made her hungry. If her dad was really going to settle here, maybe she could bring her family down for a holiday. The sea was near.

At the house, Clive led them upstairs, showed Emma the small room, which she said she loved, and took Celia into the main room. He had decided to just allocate them and not go in for any explanations or apologies. If Celia objected, she could book a hotel. He knew she was too mean to enjoy that option.

"Is this your house, Clive? Where will you sleep?"

It was clear she did not intend sharing the bed with him.

"I have a little flat three streets away. This was Roger's house. His widow has made it available."

"Very generous."

Celia was tart. She looked at the bed.

"So this must be where his final scene was played out, his climax, as it were."

"If that is a problem, there are hotels not too far…"

"On the contrary, Clive, it is hilarious. The sheets have been changed?"

"Of course."

"Well, I hope the noisy bugger isn't a ghost already. I shall want a good night's sleep, without him. Right. Put the kettle on. A nice cup of tea would be welcome."

She opened her bag and started to make herself at home. Clive left her. He would put the kettle on and they could all have some tea. It was going to be a trying time. He hoped his self-control would last until they were on the plane again.

***

The funeral was set for ten thirty in the morning. Clive, Celia, and Emma, Céline, Alain, and three of Céline's women friends attended. There were others who Clive vaguely recognised, but had not met. The dress code was relaxed. Céline and her friends looked dramatic and chic. Céline's black dress was long, the heels of her shiny black shoes were high. Her hat was black, her lipstick was bright red, her face's whiteness emphasised by cosmetics in a way beyond Clive's comprehension. She was the star and looked every inch a star. Emma had made an effort, having brought a black business suit, a tight skirt, and jacket. How to dress for the occasion clearly had not entered Celia's mind: she wore grey trousers and a dark blue Marks and Spencer's cashmere jumper. Clive had put on his suit and he had bought a black tie. The others had not put on a costume. They were there just to pay their respects. No other friends of Roger. He did not have friends, and acquaintances do not attend your funeral. No relatives. They were in Rochdale, ignorant of his death. There were some flowers from the Excelsior and from the staff at Marius. Céline had talked to her son on the eve of her wedding, and again after Roger's death. He was too committed in New York to be with her. She understood.

Clive's speech crowned the occasion for Céline. It cost him. He was both proud to have helped her, and despised himself for his hypocrisy. If he had said half of what had been in his heart, the day would have been truly shattered. When he saw Alain's approving smile and nod, he was grateful. He knew that he had so much wanted to please him. In fact, Alain's warm approval seemed to penetrate his whole body. It made him feel happy, despite recent events.

He spoke quietly, looking often at Céline, not even glancing at Celia. What he said was meant as a balm for Céline and thorns for Celia. Alain translated, phrase by phrase.

"I first met Roger when we were new students, more than fifty years ago. Over the years, he grew in status, becoming a distinguished academic, a brilliant public speaker, and a brave advocate of feminism and socialism, which he thought were indivisible. He was also a wit, a raconteur, a bon vivant and a ladies' man. That is to say, the ladies loved him—fell at his feet— but he did not love them. Until he met Céline. She was everything he craved for and needed. She was—is—beautiful, caring, loyal, charming, and a cook of such skill it needed a palate of Roger's sophistication to appreciate her efforts."

A murmured chuckle rippled through the mourners. Clive was encouraged by this, but thought it was probably the result of Alain's felicitous translation. He noticed with inner satisfaction that Celia's face was ugly with bitter fury.

"Roger did, however, suffer from an innate capacity for

creating high drama. Nothing about his life was low key. He lived it on the edge, which would have seemed exaggerated in the rest of us, but in him just fitted his larger than life personality. It is Céline's tragedy that his death was no exception. He was taken from her, cruelly, at the very moment their lives together should have begun. In thinking today of what might-have-been, we offer her our deep condolence and love. She deserved to be happy with him for many years. He was snatched away from her. She will, I know, respond with her usual grace and dignity. We hope our love for her will help.

Let us spend a moment remembering the Roger we knew."

He then lowered his head, looking into the grave, and the others followed his example. They all stood like that for a minute. After the ceremony was over, they gradually, in ones and twos, drifted away. Clive with Alain, who touched his arm in thanks; Céline with her friends; and Celia with Emma.

They gathered in the upstairs room at Marius, where a buffet had been arranged and wine was poured. People stayed briefly, to offer their respects and support to Céline, then drifted away. Emma introduced herself to Céline and chatted sympathetically for a moment. Emma's French was halting and ungrammatical, but she made herself understood. Céline was moved that she had come all the way from London, and said she hoped Emma would return to Hyères. Celia remained aloof, looking imperious, but feeling isolated and wretched. Alain tried to chat with her, but his questions were met with monosyllabic discouragement. After about an hour, Céline came over to thank Clive again for his words. She kissed him and assured everyone she was fine, but would like to go home. She left with her friends and everyone drifted away. Alain asked Clive to come to his place for some coffee, but Clive said he would see him later. There was some time before the afternoon plane to London, and Clive thought he should spend it with Celia and Emma, although Celia was making it all heavy going. He would be glad to watch the plane take off, but was determined to see it through in a civilised and calm manner.

Just another hour or so.

***

The three of them gathered in Clive's kitchen and living room. It was small. They were close and this physical intimacy fought the emotional distance, threatening to rupture the politely formal surface. The women were packed and ready to leave. The time hung in the air.

"Cosy."

Celia accepted a glass of wine and stood by the window, looking out into the street, absenting herself.

Emma and Clive sat at the kitchen table. Emma raised her eyes and pursed her lips, looking back from Celia to Clive, like a parent wondering how to make a difficult child behave. Clive smiled at her with a look that said, "I know, what can one do?"

Emma went over to her mother and put her arm round her.

"I know you're hurting, Mum, and I'm sorry."

Celia turned and looked at her coldly.

"Don't deny it. It's okay. He was a friend, shit, since ever. I know how you feel."

Celia looked away in dismissal, glaring into the street. "No, you don't. So stop pretending you do. You have no idea. You were fond of him. I loved him. When you grow up, you will know the difference."

This irritated Emma. She resented her mother treating her like a child. "It was a long time ago, Mom, you were students. There's been a whole life since."

Celia turned to Emma and smiled, giving a little snort, a quick breath out of her nose, as much as to say, "That's what you think. Well, think it."

Clive snapped. As he opened his mouth he was silently instructing himself to stop, but the gap in his knowledge was too difficult to deal with. It was eating away at him. He needed to know the worst. He had to know the extent of the betrayal, have it confirmed. Here was Celia practically admitting it, shamelessly.

"But it wasn't quite so long ago, was it Celia? It was much more recent. For how long? How long did it go on? That's the question."

Celia turned to him. "What on earth are you gibbering about, Clive? What fantasy is eating you now?"

"Don't deny it. It's patronising, and I won't be patronised, not any more. I've read your letters, disgusting, demeaning letters. You were his lover, in his bed, at his beck and call, while we were together, while Emma was at school. Just tell me, how long? Months? Years?"

It was as though the pause button had been hit. They were still and silent—Celia and Clive's eyes locked, Emma looking at Celia.

"You betrayed me; you lived a double life. I just want to know the truth, now that it's over. Think of it as my professional interest. I want to establish the historical record."

Clive was shaking. Celia was incapable of even attempting to limit the damage. Her unhappiness and disappointment in life, in the prospect of a barren retirement, of death, triggered by Roger's death, made her want to lash out with her bitterness. Clive's funeral speech could not have been more wrong. Or demeaning. Now he had made the open wound public.

"Years, Clive, years of passion and snatched love-making. He was everything to me. He kept me alive, wanting to stay alive. And I was everything to him. You were wrong. He did not love that house cleaner. He just needed someone to look after him in his old age. That's all. I was the one he loved. Satisfied?"

"No. How long? When did it end?"

"Late nineties. When he went off with that bitch who shat on him in the Guardian. Served him right."

Clive nodded. Now he knew. It had gone on under his trusting nose for much of their life together.

Emma looked puzzled. Something was not right here. Afterwards, when she was telling Jon all about this amazing stuff, she laughed at how, in the middle of the most intimate and hurtful sexual revelations, they could be having a disagreement about dates.

"I know Dad's an historian, Jon, but I mean…"

At that moment all she could think of was that none of it made sense. She also thought it was not her business. It was really for the two of them, but she was cross because she knew Celia was wrong. Why was she lying? She was protective of her father and was used to her mother saying mean, caustic things to him, hurting him. But this was unnecessary cruelty, however upset she might be at Roger's death. There was no need to take it out on her poor father.

"I don't know what you're up to, Mum, why you're trying to hurt Dad, and it's really none of my business, I know. But you and Roger could not have been having an... been together, not then for sure, so why are you making it up? Just don't believe her, Dad."

"And what would you know, you little madam? Don't like the idea I was his lover, your favourite Uncle Roger? You know nothing, so stay out of it."

Emma looked steadily at Celia.

"I know, because for some of that time—I was an undergraduate—he was having an affair with me. I was round at his place, in his bed, three or four times a week. It went on for months. So you're a liar. I don't know why you're a liar."

Celia and Clive stared at Emma, who looked down, thinking she had gone too far.

"I ended it when I got pregnant. It was his, although I didn't tell him." She looked at Celia. "You helped me with the abortion. I've always been grateful for that."

Celia stared at her daughter. She had one thought, an idea she needed to be true. She spoke quietly and with cold precision. She felt her life depended on Emma giving the right answer. "Well, dear, I know—we all know—that Roger was a powerful personality, affected us all deeply, you especially, perhaps. As a child you were enchanted by him, were rather in love with him in that innocent childish way. No doubt his death has affected you, too. But inventing a love affair, which is a grown-up matter, is an odd reaction. It seems mentally unbalanced, which is not like you. So please pull yourself together, acknowledge your grief, and stop this nonsense. My relationship with him must be a shock to you, as it is to your father, but I didn't make it up. No one was hurt by it—no one would have been hurt, if your father hadn't decided to become the self-righteous detective and make us all miserable. So enough, let it be, we'll put it down to the upset we're all feeling. You're hysterical."

Celia's rational manner was a mask. Her attempt to tame unacceptable facts was desperate. Emma refused to allow it. She was not a child. She would not be talked down to. "I didn't start this, but it's out now and maybe that's all to the good, or will be, in the end. Maybe we can all be honest with each other. Looks like it's about time. I had every right to take Roger as a lover. He was unmarried. So was I." She looked at Celia and her meaning was clear. Celia was not the only one with a piercing tongue. "Who was I betraying?"

Celia turned away and stared bleakly out of the window.

"What do you want? Shall I tell you little things about him only a lover would know? About his body, sexual things, details of his bedroom? I will, if you still refuse to believe me."

"Stop this." Clive had raised his voice. This was rare for him. Emma looked at him. "Enough, Emma. I have heard enough from both of you for one day. More than enough. Your mother will make of it what she will. I think we should stop this conversation now."

Celia turned into the room. "Hmm. Trust you Clive, to start something and then stop it just when it gets interesting. You got more than you bargained for, didn't you? Serves you right. Not only a cuckold. Your own daughter, too. Well, old Roger has been true to form. He fucked all three of us. And none of us knew." Her smile was bitter. She held herself together. She put down her glass. "I need something stronger. Alone. I will make my own way to the airport."

She turned to Emma. "Do not try to sit with me. I will not want a heart to heart, a *let's make up* journey home." She took her bag and left without looking back.

***

Celia walked down through the Old Town, upright and staring ahead, holding her bitter self together. She saw a café, the Excelsior, and sat at an outside table. Marie came to her.

"Cognac. Grand."

It disappeared in two scorching gulps. She ordered another, sipped and waited for the warm anaesthesia to kick in. She and Roger had drunk Cognac together, lounging in bed after sex. He would give her an orgasm, leaving her limp and content and pour large glasses of Courvoisier. This would make her feel languorously decadent. She never wanted to leave him.

But she had a home to go to. She had no illusions about her place in Roger's life—he was a lover, not a husband. She would return to the bed she shared with Clive. He always assumed she had been on a girls' night out with Maggs, and smiled tolerantly at the signs of alcohol. He did not do boys' nights out.

Her pain dulled by the alcohol, she considered Emma. Dirty little bitch. She did not blame Roger. He had always been weak, faced with sexual temptation. Emma had adored him through childhood, so no wonder she had to prove herself by actually seducing him in adolescence. Poor chap had not stood a chance. Probably only happened once or twice, after drink. She had exaggerated it into some grand affair, possibly even believing it.

She knew that Roger had enjoyed many women, and many women had enjoyed Roger. But she, Celia, was his true love. She and Roger had shared a deep need for each other. It had extended over many years. For the others he had merely felt a passing desire.

The old man she had nursed was not her Roger. He was an echo. Now she had even seen him buried. It really was all over. She must get used to it.

***

Emma sat silently. Clive was looking at the floor. After a while she spoke. "Sorry, Dad."

"I think you should leave, too."

She went over to him and kissed his forehead, touching his arm. "I'm truly sorry. I love you."

She left. He did not watch her go. Alone with his wine glass, he refilled it and drank. He filled it again. He had never been a drinker. Alcohol did not agree with him, so he had only ever drunk socially and moderately. But he wanted to drink now and not think of how his stomach would feel later. He did and was grateful for the effect it had.

He considered his situation. The past was in debris. He had tried to be a good husband, according to the rigid new rules; to be a good father; to be a good friend. He had failed, clearly. Or should that be others had failed him? No matter. It had all failed. Celia's contempt for him cut deeply, but in truth it was an old wound. He had felt inadequate in her eyes for decades, but however much he had tried; he had never won her over. What he had just learned merely confirmed it, fitted detailed facts around the truth. It was like the knife re-entering the cut to make sure it was deep enough really to wound.

Emma's confession—no, not a confession, that assumed what she had done was wrong, or she thought it wrong—her statement, had shaken him. He was shocked that he should be so shaken. She had been over eighteen, in her majority, an adult, perfectly free to have sex with anyone she chose. Roger, he knew, was cock-driven and shameless, so why should he be so shocked? Now he thought about it, why was it even a surprise? Was it just an old-fashioned father's pain, knowing that his daughter had given herself sexually to another man? If so, how backward of him. It would be admitting his wish to own a woman. He reminded himself that Emma's marriage was marked by a pared-down civil ceremony—he had not been asked to give her away.

His shock was not at Emma. He could rationalise and excuse his way round her behaviour—she was young and impressionable and Roger must have been at his most seductive. Despite knowing him better than anyone, Roger was the source of his shock. How could his best friend betray him so totally? In a marathon of deception, he had cuckolded him and all the time, evening after evening round the family dinner table, he had been good old Roger, academic colleague and political brother and intimate friend. Had he looked at Celia over the dessert, anticipating fucking her tomorrow? Had he flirted with Emma, watching her grow up, deciding when he would have her?

It was torture to think about, yet he could not stop. This same man had then used him as the biographer who would rescue his public reputation, a reputation that had run aground because of his very deceptions and sexual incontinence.

When the wine bottle was empty Clive considered opening another, but concluded that it had done its job, and enough was enough. If he could get upstairs and into bed he would sleep. Tomorrow would be another day, an inane truism, he thought, but vaguely comforting to say. He had been a fool. His life had been a lie. The truth was now out. That was cleansing. He would go to Alain. He would tell him everything. Alain would be wise. A cuddle would be nice.

You're drunk. Up the wooden hill. Hmm. Our dad used to say that when I was little. Up the wooden hill. Backs at night, faces in the morning. Yes .Oops. Careful. What else? Ah. Little boys should be seen and not heard. Dad. He never had to put up with this... shit. Life was simpler in his day.

The muttering in his head faded as he lay down. The alcohol did its duty. He slept.

***

He woke feeling wretched, as he knew he would. His head ached. His mouth was dry and foul. His body felt heavy, as though it had been poisoned, which, as he reminded himself, it had. He went downstairs, drank glass after glass of water, made some tea, and sipped it.

He thought of the events that had reached their climax the previous afternoon and wondered how they had affected Celia and Emma. He knew that for him, yesterday was the end. All he had was hope that today might be a beginning. At that moment he was not sanguine.

I don't care about Celia. I don't ever even want to see her again. I've had more than a lifetime of trying to cope with Celia.

He knew this was uncharitable, that he ought to be ashamed, that such vicious rejection was unworthy, but it felt good expressing these feelings. He had only recently been aware of this poison in him and he revelled, guiltily, in spitting it out.

He worried about Emma. They had not been in touch much after she married and moved away. Since he had gone to Hyères they had barely spoken. He knew that to break the bond with her finally would be difficult to bear. He resolved to repair it. He was not going to give his daughter and his grandchildren to Celia without a fight.

I hope she was not too upset. None of it was her fault. She had done nothing wrong. It was Celia and Roger. What a shock it must have been. I was too selfishly inside my own hurt to realise.

He would write to her when he felt up to it, very carefully, and try to re-connect. He could then build on that.

She must be hurting terribly, poor lamb.

He went upstairs and stood for a long time under the shower, rather extravagantly, he thought, and allowed his imagination to wander. He became a hard-boiled Los Angeles private eye who, after a savage beating, drank a fifth of Bourbon and then took a long reviving shower before going out finally to solve the case. He had no idea what a fifth of Bourbon might be, but he smiled at this conceit—a meek, retired academic pretending to be a wise cracking tough guy.

I used to like those books... what were they, not Dashiell Hammett... the other chap. Blast. Am I having a senior moment?

As he rubbed himself vigorously dry, he felt his energy return and noted he had just smiled.

Well, that's an improvement. Yesterday, I thought I would never smile again. I will call Alain. Coffee with Alain is what any good doctor would prescribe.

He shaved carefully and dressed in jeans and deck shoes and his pale blue Marks and Spencer shirt, the one Alain had said he liked.

***

Clive's imaginary doctor had been right. Alain's coffee was excellent, strong, and black, accompanied by a delicious home-baked madeleine. He came to sit close to Clive at his kitchen table. Basking in the warm, sympathetic smile and listening to the beautifully accented English, Clive knew there was a future, here in Hyères among friends, with his friend. He simply loved this man, with no undertow of anxiety, of wondering if he was doing it right. He basked in Alain's pleasure, only marvelling that he could be the source of it.

"So, now you know you have lived a lie. You think it was not your lie. But it was. You knew, but denied that you knew. That was your lie. You have spent your life pretending to be someone you are not, and refusing to see others as they are. Living a lie is not living a life. Maybe now you can be you, discover you. The burden you have been carrying... what is your word? There is a word in English."

"You slough off a burden."

"Slough. Yes? Is that the word?"

Clive grinned at him. Alain looked back warily. "You think I am a... pain in the... arse?"

"Yes, arse. No, I don't, Alain. I don't at all. But how did you get so bloody clever, huh? Know all this stuff?"

"I am not clever, Clive. I only know this... stuff, as you say, because I too lived a lie. I would not accept myself, truly, when I was young. Then I learned that if we try to be who we think the world wants, we pay a big price. I paid that price."

"Tell me about it. You've never said nearly enough about your life. I'm interested."

"I will. Someday. But we talk about you, now. What will you do?"

"Well, I will not write the book. Céline can do what she wants with his papers. Burn them if she wants. I shouldn't say that, should I? I am, was, an historian."

"You could help her find a home for them, some University, perhaps. I meant you. Will you stay? You now think it is time to go back to London, perhaps?"

They looked at each other. Alain's tone and expression seemed neutral.

Clive's nerve drained away. He knew that his answer depended on Alain's answer to another question, one he dreaded asking. "Would you like me to stay?"

He spoke in a whisper, looking down. "Very much, Clive. Very much."

He squeezed Clive's hand. Clive looked up at him. He was smiling, almost imploring. Clive returned the squeeze.

"Then I will stay. To be with you, my friend."

Their hands intertwined, they continued to look at each other, smiling with relief and happiness.

Chapter 22

Emma had been shaken by her mother's behaviour. She could hardly believe what had been revealed, but there seemed no denying it. She could not wait to tell Jon all about her experiences in Hyères. He was amazed. They started to laugh, in shocked admiration at the antics of their parents' generation, although Emma felt sad for Clive. His smacked face as she left still haunted her.

"This is the wrong way round, isn't it? Shouldn't they be conventional and boring and respectable? Shouldn't they be shocked by the stuff we get up to?"

Emma had been hurt at first, to learn of Roger sharing her, but then the French farce enormity of him juggling mother and daughter in and out of his apartment set them off again. Just to imagine it was an entertainment, though Emma did say that she would have drawn the line if he had suggested a threesome.

"Mind you, I wouldn't have put it past the dirty bugger, if he thought he could get away with it."

"But you have to admire the sheer fucking energy of the man, to keep it up like that."

They fell about again at the double entendres that seemed to ambush any attempt to discuss Roger's lifestyle.

She recalled the moment when she discovered her pregnancy, when the game became serious and her life darkened. The memory of her mother's support, organising the safe abortion, holding her hand and not being judgemental took on a deeper meaning now. Then she had been glad that Celia had showed no curiosity about the identity of the father. Now she was doubly grateful and moved—her mother had been her mother, not just Roger's lover, not a competitor. For all her tart manner, she had been a brick when it counted. She recalled other turning points when Celia had been there for her, memories from childhood that she had forgotten.

The whole thing settled in her memory after a while. It did not trouble her. It was an odd, slightly scandalous adventure she was now quite fond of, just an exotic episode in her youth. Her life was too busy juggling children, work, and marriage. It was full and satisfying and solid and exhausting. Well, satisfying some of the time and exhausting most of the time. Her life had daily incident but was uneventful. This occasionally made her feel short-changed by the ordinariness of it all. Was she too ordinary? Were others living on a higher level of experience? But most of the time she felt confident and secure.

***

Celia did not see the funny side. For her, there was no funny side, although, as Maggs pointed out, she was short of the humour gene, or it had atrophied through lack of use. Celia forgave her this insensitive remark because she was a little tipsy at the time. They both were.

Life continued normally. It was over, of course, with Clive, but as she told Maggs, it had been over for a long time. That is, if it had ever really begun. She continued to go regularly to the British Library, and it continued to be no more than a way to structure the day. She had run out of intellectual curiosity and of ambition. Her friends were a balm, especially Maggs. But she knew she was swimming against the tide. There was nothing to live for, at least, nothing that could convince her. There was nothing in her inner life. There were no fantasies, or warm memories, or fondness when remembering her own youth, to lift her. It had all died a bitter death. She had long known Roger to be a shit. But she had always believed that he loved her, and only her. That he was her shit, treating her brutally, using her and objectifying her, but needing her. That she had satisfied him. He had merely fucked other women. He had loved her. She knew it in the intensity of his lovemaking, in the child-like urgency of his demands, and in her deep satisfaction in satisfying him. He truly loved her and only her.

But believing that now was a stretch. Had she just been one of a crowd? He had juggled her with another, cynically, stage-managing the process deftly, and that other had been her own daughter. The ultimate humiliation. Had he compared Emma's young tight teenage body with her middle-aged imperfections? Had he delighted in teaching Emma, in introducing sexual pleasures to her?

She spent months writhing in these agonies until they were spent. They eventually disappeared from exhaustion and repetition. They became upsetting aftershocks. The memories that had lifted her up were now dead. They had turned out to be false memories. She was becoming a bore. She bored herself. The basis of her self-belief, the element that had defined her emotionally, which had justified her being alive, was now in doubt and turning into dust. Her astringency, which her friends had enjoyed, had soured into bitterness and negativity. It was now more than a welcome hint of lemon against cloying sentimentality. It no longer amused.

Life went on. She watched herself get older, with a detached indifference. None of it mattered any more. Her grandchildren were the only balm. Seeing them infrequently meant she could treasure every moment in their company and never become irritated. They loved her openly and generously, which brought out her own warmth, blinking suspiciously and gratefully into their world. Life with Emma was complicated, although as her friends reminded her, the relationship between mothers and daughters is always a weird, chancy business. Roger was never mentioned.

Then, one morning, her fatalistic depression lifted. She had so got used to being one of the living dead, as she categorised herself, that she could not remember feeling anything else.

"I am alive just enough to experience what it is like to be dead".

She was rather proud of this, thinking that she really could write something good, if only she could be bothered, but Maggs just told her not to be so morbid.

Her intention had been to make her regular, redundant visit to the British Library; but instead she was drawn elsewhere. Curiosity took her to a sweaty, crowded lecture theatre in University College. It was the long vacation, but the whole campus was alive. She was surrounded by the buzz of young women, a sprinkling of earnest men, and a few middle-aged campaigners with Trades Union badges. Innocence and optimism were in the air, sentiments Celia had long ago discarded.

Innocence could never be reclaimed, but this optimism was infectious. Her black mood lightened. She had seen the prospectus for the Marxism 2011 conference by chance, and noticed a session on Engels' *The Origins of the Family*. This was a surprise. Was there really an interest now in Faithful Fred? The British Library could wait. She had to find out. Just sitting in the body of a lecture hall, rather than lecturing to a lecture hall, made her feel young again.

Well, younger, darling. Don't get carried away. The lecture might be revisionist crap.

It was not.

Engels was given his proper historical place and contemporary relevance. At the centre of Marxist analysis was the family, the role of women, private property, and the State.

"Abolish class society and you can abolish the oppression of women."

She looked round at the serious, absorbed faces, drinking this in. Some swots were even taking notes.

The historical story was unfolded—the gradual, incremental submission of women and their *world historical defeat*.

She then heard the lecturer say, "A women's lib which is not a socialist women's lib is false."

It was not this familiar mantra that made her want to weep. It was the context. It was the anger and enthusiasm and determination of speaker after speaker, who shyly and haltingly came to the microphone. Why now, so suddenly?

Maybe a generation was responding to the unfolding economic crisis with a hunger to understand. Could the scales really be falling away? Would a class-based feminism be revived? Could it be? Celia was buoyed up by these children—they all looked like children to her—and she felt the sap rising in her. She had spent decades working in the Union and the Labour Party, making tiny incremental improvements, fighting the reactionaries and the opportunists and becoming exhausted and demoralised. She had watched the world around her change, not in the direction she had naively thought inevitable, but in reverse. Over the last thirty years, she had been a horrified witness to the erosion of the gains of her youth, leaving her clinging to an ideology that seemed daily more redundant. Observing these earnest young people was like seeing the embers come to life. Maybe her beliefs were not anachronistic, after all. Maybe they had just needed a change in the objective situation to bring them to life again. Maybe, by extension, she was not an anachronism, either. Could her own involvement be resuscitated? Was she, after all, still alive?

Ah. The "objective situation." A phrase from the past. Don't get carried away. You're too old and tired now. You don't have the bloody energy. Do you?

Asking the question was an act of optimism. Looking at the purity of purpose around her, she felt a baton being handed on and firmly grasped.

Maybe her life, for all its mistakes and disappointments, had not been in vain. Maybe she could even get involved again, among these earnest young women, and be borne up by their energy. At their age, anything is possible.

Maybe there was hope.

Chapter 23

Clive stood in the cool marble arrivals hall. He saw them first and waved as the family came through. Emma noticed him and grinned. Jon was herding the children, who were taking their role as travellers seriously. Charlie's rucksack was nonchalantly over one shoulder, signalling the cool of a very grown-up seven-year-old. Little Polly's was shaped in the guise of a pink furry animal and was almost as big as her. She saw Clive and rushed to him, the animal bouncing up and down on her back. He lifted her up and hugged her. She was chattering so breathlessly, needing to convey so much vital information. The others had to wait for their greeting until the grave Clive had listened, and finally said, "You must tell me all about that, Poll." He then shook hands with Charlie and rubbed his head, which the boy did not care for, but it was the sort of thing male relatives do, so his attitude was just to live with it.

"We saw the sea, Granddad. The plane went over it, like, showed us, and flew back here. We bent right over, like this." He put his arms out wide, like wings, and did a tight turn.

"We'll go to the beach tomorrow, Charlie. The sea will be freezing, mind."

Jon shook Clive's hand and Emma kissed and hugged him.

***

Céline had lent them Roger's house, which she still had not sold. They were all to eat with her that first night. For lunch, they went to Alain, where he had made bruschetta and stuffed little courgettes and tomatoes the Provençal way. He cut slices from a chocolate cake. The children loved the food and liked Alain. He said he would teach them some French.

Clive had been wondering how they would feel about him and Alain. When the German couple had returned, Alain had invited Clive to move in with him. They were happy together, cooking and visiting the region's restaurants, mushrooming and finding new wineries. Céline cooked for them, and they cooked for Céline. Clive was included in Alain's circle of friends. He even shyly tried to improve his French, and did not mind when they laughed at his mistakes.

He felt loved.

But he need not have worried. The children did not even think about it and Emma was happy to see him so relaxed. She had never known her father to smile so much, to be so full of fun. Jon just nodded. It was cool with him. What's the problem?

They had a fine two weeks together, going on expeditions, even on the boat over to the island of Porquerolles. They ate fresh fish. They spent hours in the sun at the beach and got brown. They explored the Old Town, especially the patisseries.

The children hugged Clive and asked when they were going to come back.

"Soon. I hope. Come back soon. Anytime."

Life was sweet.

Printed in August 2021
by Rotomail Italia S.p.A., Vignate (MI) - Italy